Bluebirds

A Battle of Britain novel

Melvyn Fickling

The Book Conspiracy

Table of Contents

Dedicated to Adrian Francis Laws DFM

Acknowledgements

Above all, thanks to Adrienne Chinn for her editing advice. Thanks to Kenneth L. Weber for information and encouragement concerning the American connections at the very beginning of this project. Thanks to Su Baccino for her support for my telling of a story that impacted her more than most. Thanks to the contemporary pilots who wrote memoirs or spoke on film about their experiences. That my combat narratives have any realism at all is entirely down to them.

PART 1

EVOLUTIO

CHAPTER 1

Innocentia

1st May, 1920

Samuel Drew hosed the last of the blood from the concrete floor. In the next room the thwack of meat cleavers parting vertebrae echoed from the walls as the men butchered the recently-killed carcasses. Samuel shut off the tap and looped the hose over its hook. He grabbed his jacket from the locker and, without a word to his fellow workers, strode across the yard to the gates.

The sun hung low above the dark slopes of the moors and fingers of shadow lengthened along Whitby's lanes. Children skipped home from the beach, their faces reddened by the spring sunshine and salt breeze.

Samuel's step quickened as The Jolly Sailor came into view. He crossed the road and shouldered his way through the pub doors. The smell of yesterday's brown ale mixed with the resinous scent from the log-fire, freshly lit against the evening's chill.

'All right, Samuel?' The landlord polished a pint pot in expectation.

'Yes please, Vic.' Samuel nodded towards the hand-pull. 'Bitter.'

The landlord pulled at the beer engine and the dark liquid gushed into the dimpled glass.

'How was your day?' Victor placed the pint on the bar.

Samuel dropped a coin onto the stained wood and took a deep draught of ale. 'We did bullocks today. Twelve of the bastards. Bloody hard work.'

'Well, Samuel,' Victor leant forward, resting his elbows on the bar, 'I could always use a big strong lad like you in my cellar. I'm getting too old to lug barrels around. So if you ever want to give up the slaughterh—'

'Give up the slaughterhouse?' Samuel leant his big frame on the bar, bringing his face close to Victor's. 'I love it there.' Samuel drained his pint. 'Same again, Victor, and give me a rum chaser. Large one.'

Victor poured the drinks and picked up the coins. 'Has your missus delivered yet?'

'That's woman's work.' Samuel's sidelong look of warning into Victor's eyes set the barman to glass polishing in silence.

The Jolly Sailor's door swung open and two trawlermen strode to the bar in their heavy sea boots. Before the door closed, a chill breeze flowed across the floor.

****

No cooling breeze reached Eileen Drew's bedroom as she sweated her way into the seventh hour of labour. Worried Eileen was fading; the midwife worked hard to help her patient cope.

'Come on, Mrs Drew. Let's have another bash at getting the little bugger born.'

The pregnant woman's slight frame and slim hips exaggerated her bulging belly. The midwife sensed the approaching wave of the next contraction and bent to examine her patient.

'All right, Eileen. Everything's ready down here. It's up to you now. Push.'

Eileen's face contorted as the contraction dragged her into a maelstrom of inescapable agony. Clenching her teeth and gasping out her breaths, her spine curved forward in the spasm's grip, pressing her chin against her chest and colouring her head to crimson.

'The baby's coming, Eileen. Keep it up. You can't stop now.'

Eileen whimpered in despair and her head lolled backwards onto the pillow. Her whine mutated into a deep growl and she thrust her head forwards again, staring in defiance at the lump on her torso.

'Get out! Get out!' Her cries broke up into a ragged wail as a bolt of pure agony pierced her world of pain. Slumping backwards in a wave of cleansing ecstasy she descended into quiet racking sobs, not knowing and past caring.

The midwife busied herself with something on the wet bed. Then the disconsolate wail of the baby cut short Eileen's tears.

'It's a boy, Mrs Drew. It's a lovely, healthy little boy.'

The midwife wrapped the child in a white towel and handed him to his mother. Eileen attempted to hitch herself up the bed, but the other woman's restraining hand stopped her.

'Try not to move too much, Mrs Drew. The baby has torn you quite badly. I'll clean you up as best I can tonight and the doctor will come tomorrow. He'll sew you up then, dear.'

3rd July, 1922

The two boys cycled in silence up the hill. The hedgerows stifled the thin summer breeze and the high sun jabbed its heat between the branches. They pedalled the last mile along the narrow road, sustained by the prospect of the corned beef sandwiches and barley water they carried in their saddlebags.

Andrew Francis, the eldest by a month, pulled away in front. Perspiration plastered his black hair across his forehead, forming a bar over his intense brown eyes. Standing in the pedals, he zig-zagged up the road to kill the gradient.

Peter Ellis trailed behind, his front wheel wobbling from side to side. He carried too much weight and his close-cropped ginger hair glistened with sweat from his exertion.

Andrew stopped at the top of the rise. A wide farm gate cut a break in the dense hedge. Beyond it the flat agricultural face of Norfolk stretched to the horizon.

Peter shuffled to his side, pushing his bicycle. 'I hate that hill. My bum hurts.'

Andrew climbed onto the farm gate to survey the pasture beyond. A tall wire fence bounded the bottom end of the field. Beyond the fence lay a wide grass track circling Bircham Newton airfield, their final destination.

Over to their right a small flock of sheep grazed the rough grass, raising their heads to monitor the boys with blank eyes. Andrew jumped into the paddock. Keeping a watchful eye on the sheep, he opened the gate while Peter ferried the bicycles through. Leaning their bikes against the hedge, the boys collected their picnics and set off towards the distant fence.

A faint drone intruded overhead. Both boys stopped, shading their eyes and scanning the sky.

'Look,' Andrew pointed, 'DH-5s.'

Peter peered at the tiny shapes in the vast blue vault. 'Sopwith Camels.'

Andrew sucked in his breath and shook his head. 'DH-5s.'

'Nah, Sopwith Camels.'

'DH-5s. Definitely'

High above, two biplanes reeled in a mock dogfight. Side-slipping and barrelling, the pilots' battle spiralled earthwards. As they descended, the aircraft became clearly visible, the strange stepped-back top wing marking them out as DH-5s.

'See,' Andrew said, 'I told you.'

The machines' dull olive outlines stood stark against the crystal blue sky. The wide roundels on their wings stared like the eyes of swooping owls. The pilots, engrossed in their game, were locked into each other's moves like dancers.

Rooted to the spot, entranced by the roar of rotary engines, the boys stared. Sheep blundered past them in a panic-stricken stampede to nowhere, splitting around them like a river around a rock. The sun blazed and still the planes dropped from the sky.

'Stop!' Andrew's hand flew to his mouth. 'Stop, it's too low!'

One of the protagonists pulled up with throttle wide open. His engine note rose to a squeal as his aircraft levelled out, climbing away from the paddock.

Already committed to a barrel-roll, the other machine lost more height before coming right-way-up. The engine screamed in protest as the pilot slammed open the throttle and pulled hard on the stick. The plane swooped through the air in front of the boys, larger and noisier than they could ever have imagined. Clawing at the last few feet of altitude the machine levelled out, its fixed undercarriage striking the grass with a jolt, bouncing it back into the air. The plane skimmed the fence and climbed away over the airfield with thick black fumes trailing from the straining engine.

Andrew's pulse pounded in his temples and his knees twitched with the need to run. His stomach lurched as he imagined the plane ploughing into the earth yards from where he stood. He watched the machine join its circling companion. He breathed deeply, the tension draining from his clenched muscles. Despite the sun, the sweat on his brow was cold.

'Did you see that, Andy?'

Andrew blinked at Peter. He tried to answer but only a croak escaped his lips.

Peter slapped him on the shoulder and took off across the paddock towards the fence. 'C'mon, I'll race you.'

Andrew shook himself out of his daze and sprinted across the grass, too late to overtake his friend.

'Ha, ha. I beat you.'

Andrew uncorked his bottle of barley water, gulping a draught down his parched throat. 'You cheated.'

Peter opened his mouth to speak but the biplanes roaring in to land drowned his words.

The boys clung to the fence cheering and waving as the first plane swivelled off the runway and taxied along the perimeter track. Moments later the second machine bounced in to land and followed it on to the perimeter. The pilot leaned out from the open cockpit and gunned the engine in short bursts, steering with the rudder. Andrew whooped in salute as he taxied past. The airman glanced over, his face wet with tears.

****

The two boys cycled down the hill side by side, the whirr of their free-wheeling bikes set a backdrop to Peter's constant chatter. Andrew remained quiet, distracted by what they'd witnessed, still shaken by the sheer brutal proximity of the lumbering biplane so close to destruction.

'...exciting if it crashed!' Peter's words dragged Andrew back from his musing.

'What? Crashed? It would have killed the pilot.'

Peter flushed under Andrew's angry gaze. 'I hadn't thought of it, Andy. I just didn't think...'

They cycled on in silence.

Wells-on-Sea lay motionless under the sun's drumbeat. The inshore trawlers lined the stone-walled quay in rows. Their crews sat fixing nets in the sunshine; no catch would be made with the weather so high. Nearing home, Andrew and Peter picked up their pace, the sea breeze ruffling their hair as they pedalled along the coast road.

The bakery at the edge of town sat squat beneath the sultry summer sun. Men dressed in white moved about in the gloom, firing the ovens for the evening's bread-making. Open windows belched more heat into the afternoon's simmering haze. Andrew lived close by the bakery, so both boys skittered to a halt and Andrew dismounted.

'I'm sorry, Peter. I didn't mean to shout at you back there.'

'That's all right Andy, I know you're serious about aeroplanes and everything. I'm sorry too.'

Andrew smiled. 'See you tomorrow? How about gilly-crabbing?'

Peter beamed. 'All right, call for you at ten. I'll get some fish-heads on the way. See you then.'

Peter cycled off and Andrew pushed his bike up the lane. Swifts wheeled and flashed overhead in fleet mockery.

4th July, 1922

Peter arrived on time with a hessian sack dripping fish-blood onto the doorstep. When Andrew answered his knock, he held open the bag in triumph.

'Wotcha'. I got six plaice heads and one cod.'

'Well done, Peter. Let me get my stuff.' Andrew emerged a few minutes later with his crab-line under his arm, fastening his sheath knife to his belt. 'Come on, let's go.'

They walked the few hundred yards along the road to the harbour. Arriving at the quayside, they knelt by the edge and bent to prepare their lines.

'They gave me the plaice but I nicked the cod,' Peter said, laying out the glistening heads on the rough hessian.

'So you should get the honour of chopping it into bits.' Andrew passed over his knife and watched Peter set about his slippery work. 'Be careful, mate. It's sharp.'

Peter grunted acknowledgement and continued to hack at the fish head.

Andrew stared down at the water. 'I want to be a pilot.'

Peter didn't pause in his butchery. 'I knew you did,' he said without looking up, 'yesterday just put the tin lid on the whole thing. You should've seen your face on the way home, you looked like a love-sick sissy.

'I want to be a train driver myself.' Pausing his dissection he looked into Andrew's eyes. 'Did you know the train leaving here on a Friday goes as far as London?' Genuine awe coloured Peter's voice. 'My Dad took that train when he left for France.'

Peter held Andrew's gaze for a moment longer, then dropped his head to his task. Peter rarely mentioned his father.

'I'm not sure he'd take a train anywhere if he knew you were driving it,' Andrew joked.

13

Peter smiled, waggling a slimy finger in Andrew's face. 'You'll see. One day I'll take everyone to London.'

19th July, 1924

The blue dome of the Minnesota sky rolled from horizon to horizon, unsullied by a single cloud. Gerry Donaldson and his father stood at the edge of the meadow's rough grass next to the sacks of insecticide.

The pneumonic rattle of an aeroplane engine scarred the silence, swelling in garish volume. The crop-sprayer's biplane circled the farm once and swooped in to land, the engine note dropping as the pilot cut the revs and taxied in a long arc, coming to rest in front of the pair.

The pilot cut the engine. 'Hey, Mr Donaldson,' he called. 'My crew are trucking in with the petrol tank an' all, but they shouldn't be long. Do you wanna make a start loading the hopper?'

'Call me Bob.' Gerry's father stepped forward, reaching up to the cockpit to shake the pilot's hand. 'Do you have time for coffee and a cookie before we get to work?'

The pilot's smile cracked open his grimy face. He unhooked the straps and eased himself out of his seat. 'I sure do, Bob. I sure do.'

Gerry watched the two men walk towards the farmhouse and turned back to regard the strange machine before him. This had to be better than cookies.

Gerry reached out a hand to touch the closest wing-tip, revelling at the smoothness of the tight, shiny fabric under his fingers. Rubbing away the grime of engine oil and pulverised insects revealed the fading yellow paint beneath. He walked his fingers across the wing's surface to the smooth profile of a rounded wooden strut, one of six attaching the lower wing to the upper. With his other hand he plucked at the diagonal bracing wires. Bobbing down, he wondered at the concave underside of the wing with its hinged panel on the rear edge. Still on one knee, he gazed up at the nose of the plane, admiring the half-exposed engine with its sinuous exhaust and the twisted sweep of the laminated propeller.

The pilot's laugh in the distance alerted Gerry to his father's return. He sauntered away from the aircraft as the two men approached, swigging coffee from tin mugs. Throwing out the dregs on the grass, they both tied cloths over their face and each hefted a sack onto his shoulder.

'Move away, Gerry,' his father warned. 'Stand up-wind, son, this stuff's not for breathing.'

The men boosted the sacks up to the edge of the rear cockpit, emptying them into the makeshift hopper bolted there. The pilot pulled a lever by the front cockpit and some of the powder ran from beneath the fuselage. Nodding in satisfaction, he shut off the flow and went to get another sack. Four more sacks followed before he judged the load sufficient. As the airman lashed a tarpaulin over the hopper his three-man crew pulled up in their truck, tooting the horn in greeting.

Bob Donaldson gave directions to the two flagmen about the fields which required treatment. The third man unhooked the fuel tank, retrieved the hose from the truck and walked over to check the plane.

Gerry breathed in the twin scents of oil and aviation fuel with a short thrill of excitement.

The pilot climbed into the cockpit, jiggling the controls to make the hinged panels on the wings and tail waggle up and down; the mechanic trotted around the machine checking their movement. Walking back to the nose, the mechanic grabbed the tip of a propeller blade and braced himself, waiting.

'Let's go!' The shout came from the cockpit.

The mechanic flipped the propeller down and around, spinning his body away from the plane. The engine coughed, kicked and roared into life.

The pilot pulled his goggles over his eyes and gunned the engine while the buffeting slipstream lashed his hair into a swirling mess. Wheels rolled into motion and he swung the plane around, accelerating across the meadow.

Gerry squinted his eyes against the momentary fury of the backwash tugging at his shirt. Then he sprinted after the plane. For a few moments flying machine and boy careened through space in unequal harmony until the crop-duster left the ground. Gerry stumbled to a halt, captivated by the sway of the plane as it settled into its cushion of air. Standing alone in the centre of the paddock, open-mouthed, he watched this man-made bird claw its impossible way into the sky.

CHAPTER 2

Signi

7th June, 1930

Bob and Mary Donaldson sat on the porch overlooking the yard. Outside the barn Gerry worked hard stripping down the tractor for the third time, searching for whatever caused the machine to keep stalling. The family had not long finished supper but Gerry refused to rest; he was determined to find the fault. His parents sat with their arms around each other, watching their son work on the vehicle.

'It's his 18th birthday soon,' said his mother in a low voice. 'He deserves something special.'

'What can we give him that's special?' No reproach coloured her husband's reply; he stated a simple fact. 'We don't have the money for a car or a motorbike. What we can afford he most likely wouldn't want.' Bob shook his head. 'Sure, he should have a special gift, but I just don't know what we can do about it.'

'He'd love an aeroplane,' she said, watching Bob's profile with amusement, waiting for his reaction.

He continued to stare across the yard. At length he spoke. 'For better or worse, Mary, I promised you that before God. But I have to tell you, I struck a private deal with the padre; I can send you back as soon as you go mad.' He turned on the bench to face her. 'Unless you've got a stack of money you've forgotten to tell me about?'

'Listen to me' – she turned to match his posture, taking his hands in hers – 'an aeroplane costs an awful lot of money.'

'Uh-huh.' He smiled at the game.

'And we only have a little.'

'Amen.'

'So' – she paused, looking at her husband with mock concern – 'this is the math: instead of spending a lot of money on a whole aeroplane, we spend the money we have on a piece of an aeroplane.'

Bob's face dropped into genuine confusion. 'You mean, like, a wheel?'

'No, I mean a seat.'

Gerry raised his head from the tractor's bowels to watch his father drive their pick-up truck out through the yard gate and down the dirt road, a wisp of brown dust spiralling in his wake. He stood staring for a moment, then turned to look at his mother on the porch. She flashed a broad smile and waved at him. He raised a grimy hand in response. His eyes dropped once more to the stripped carburettor and in moments he became engrossed in his work.

28th June, 1930

Gerry's birthday fell on a Saturday. He woke early and dressed in his overalls. Padding to the breakfast table he walked in to a lusty rendition of 'Happy Birthday to You' and a plate of ham and pancakes. His mother placed a small jug on the table.

'What's that?' Gerry asked.

'Maple syrup.'

'Wow, really?'

'It's a special day, Gerry.'

Once he'd emptied his plate and coaxed the last drop of syrup from the jug, Gerry walked to the bench by the door and pulled on his work boots.

'No work today, Tiger,' his father called across. 'Go and change out of those overalls, we're taking the day off to do something special.'

'Special, sir?'

'Yes, Gerry,' his mother announced, 'we're going on a picnic down by the river.'

Minutes later the family emerged into the summer sunshine, loading the picnic basket into the truck. Bob fired up the engine and pulled out through the yard gate, accelerating along the hard dirt road.

Approaching the entrance of their neighbour's farm, Gerry spotted three trucks standing in the drive. He recognised their neighbour and two other families from across the valley. He craned his neck round to see them pull out behind and follow. He turned back as they passed another farm entrance in time to see two more vehicles. The occupants waved as the Donaldsons passed and pulled out to join the procession. So it went over the next few miles. Each farm added one or two vehicles to the convoy, friends and neighbours all heading north.

When they drove past the turn-off to the river, Gerry looked at his mother in confusion. She just smiled and shook her head. His father, whistling at the wheel, simply winked.

****

Max Anderson watched the dust cloud rise into the clear sky as 20 or more vehicles snaked their way towards his airfield and pulled in to the gateway.

Gerry's jaw sagged open when he caught sight of the aeroplanes lined up by the runway, colours clashing under the bright sunshine.

'We've come to watch the planes taking off,' Gerry muttered under his breath. He turned to his mother. 'We've come to watch the planes?'

'More than that,' his mother said.

'More?'

'Everyone helped us to buy you a special present. All of our friends have contributed.' Her voice wavered. 'Happy birthday, Gerry.'

The trucks and cars spilled out their occupants around the Donaldson's vehicle. The air filled with shouts of 'Happy birthday', 'Many happy returns' and 'Happy landings'. Gerry climbed out of the truck into a throng of people slapping his back, shaking his hand and saying things into his face he didn't hear or understand. One face replaced the next as hand after calloused hand pumped his arm.

The coughing blast of an engine blew all other sounds from the air. Gerry's heart leapt. He squirmed through the crowd to look at the aeroplane. The biplane's wings sloped backwards on the fat body. Its red and white paint scheme flashed in the sun as the machine vibrated in sympathy with the idling engine. In the rear cockpit sat an engineer in blue overalls, checking the flight controls. Another engineer stood at one wingtip, eyeing the motion of the flaps and ailerons.

Next to the plane stood a man who could only be the pilot. He wore oil-smudged red overalls and his worn leather helmet shone with a smooth patina, disrupted by a dark sweat stain across the forehead. Despite the warm day he wore heavy boots laced high up his calf. From under a bushy white moustache, stained yellow from tobacco smoke, Gerry received his first dazzling smile from Max Anderson.

'Hello, boy,' Max shouted, his booming voice shredded by the engine's roar. 'We'll take her up as soon as my mechanic tells me it's safe.'

Gerry looked beyond the pilot to the plane. His eyes roamed the lines and curves of the machine, committing the moment to memory.

The engine note dropped as the engineer throttled back and the motor slackened to an easy tick-over. The thick wooden propeller became visible as a blur at the nose of the craft.

Max stooped over and talked directly into Gerry's ear. 'We'll take off into the wind and climb away from the airfield until we have the height we need. Then I'll do some gentle turns and bring us back over the field. When we get where your friends can see us again, I'll do a loop and we'll land.

'If you get nervous at any point and don't want me to do the loop just clasp your hands on top of your head and I'll bring her down as quickly and steadily as possible. You're sitting in the front cockpit but there's no way we can talk, so remember the signal, hands on top of your head.' Max slapped him on the back, propelling him the first few steps towards the aircraft.

Gerry felt like a giant crossing the field at Max's side. He glanced back over his shoulder at the people who'd made this possible as they spread out their picnic blankets like an audience at some vast open-air theatre waiting for the show. He grinned, blowing a kiss to his mother.

By the time they reached the aeroplane the engineer had left the rear cockpit and taken up his position standing by the free wingtip. Max showed Gerry the places on the wing strong enough to support his step and, as Gerry settled into the cockpit, leaned over him to pull the straps tight. He tapped Gerry on the shoulder to get his attention.

This close to the engine Max resorted to shouting. 'If you need to get out in a hurry, pull the release pin from the buckle. On the floor you'll find a leather helmet, goggles and gloves. Put them on and keep them on until we've landed and the engine is switched off.'

Gerry pulled on the helmet and gloves while Max climbed into the cockpit behind him.

At a signal from Max the chocks bounced away and the craft bumped across the grass. It lacked the solidity of purpose a truck might have, moving instead like a man wearing outsize trousers, waddling from side to side as first one wheel and then the other found a depression in the grass. With each bump the wings waggled with aftershock and Gerry could sense through his buttocks the creaking of the airframe. He had an urge to clasp his hands over his head and stop the whole dangerous adventure immediately. He glanced out at the engineer walking by the starboard wingtip. The man caught his eye and winked. Gerry smiled back and felt a little better.

They reached the end of the grass runway. The men at the wingtips pushed and pulled to line up the aircraft with the prevailing breeze. The two engineers stepped clear, waving their hands over their heads. Max gunned the engine and the machine rolled forward.

Deafening noise interlaced the blast of wind from the propeller. Gerry bunched his stomach muscles and leant forward into the acceleration. The plane surged ahead and the wheels bounced and lurched.

The tail bit the wind and lifted, the engine dipped and the horizon appeared. The fuselage yawed to accommodate the air and the bumping lessened as one wheel left the grass. Almost too softly to notice, the machine rediscovered its soul; the second wheel came away from the ground and the bumping stopped. The whole structure of the craft dangled in space as the wings swung into harmony with the airflow.

Gerry craned his neck over the side, awed by the rushing panorama speeding away beneath them. A fence flashed by, then a stand of trees, reaching up as if to claw them from the air. Fear gripped his throat. It wasn't unreasoned terror, more a calculation of the odds: if something went wrong he could expect little help from straps, goggles or gloves.

As the aircraft battled for the open sky, the clattering propeller took on an infernal undertone. Gerry eyed the dangerous ground until the rushing slowed and individual features shrank to become part of the landscape, too small to hold any menace in themselves. His fear receded along with the earth.

The plane levelled out, its precocious escape from gravity complete. Gerry gazed up at the sky's blue bubble and then back to the cockpit. The aircraft felt frail as it bobbed in the wind, dependant on the tenuous cushion of air to keep it high above the hard ground.

Learning to trust the machine, Gerry relaxed. Looking away to the horizon, he thought he could see a perceptible curve. God's great globe had revealed its humble dimensions to him; the revelation came with an exultant flash. Gerry threw his head back, laughing into the void. Twisting his neck against the straps he looked back at Max, treating him to a fierce grin and an emphatic thumbs-up.

Max grinned back and threw the plane into a steep climbing turn. Most of his first-time flyers sat rigid with faces fixed forward like a passenger in a car's front seat. But Gerry leant towards the dropped starboard wing, looking in the direction the plane would go if it side-slipped. Max obliged, sliding away to starboard. Gerry's head bobbed across his vision, the boy moved to anticipate a climb. Max pulled into a shallow climb, a smile creasing his face.

Judging he'd gained sufficient height, Max banked around to line up with the airfield, now a few miles distant. He throttled back, settling the plane into the drag. Gerry remembered the loop and fingered his straps. Surprised at his nervousness, he resolved to sit on his hands.

Approaching the airfield Max increased the throttle while he dropped the nose to gain speed. Gerry stared straight ahead over the cowling and through the propeller. Their shallow dive took them towards the picnicking group at the edge of the field. He watched in fascination as anonymous shapes resolved themselves into the people he knew. All faces turned up towards the plane; the children jumped up and down waving their arms. For a split second he recognised his mother's face amongst them, her hand over her mouth in apprehension.

Max threw the craft into the loop. The engine roared in response to the wide-open throttle. Gerry's mother, the picnic baskets and the waving children dropped from view as the plane lurched into a steep climb. The Hand of God pushed Gerry down into his seat, his neck muscles compressing under the unexpected pressure of unseen forces.

Max backed off the throttle and the engine note dropped. The pressure on Gerry's shoulders lifted and he hung against his straps. He gasped as the horizon appeared upside down in front of him. Gerry and the Earth hung in unnatural juxtaposition for a long moment before the plane dived into the second half of the loop.

Now Gerry's vision filled with the flat, broad landscape and his stomach lurched as the plane dropped towards it. The horizon swung down as Max pulled out of the dive and the ground dropped away below the nose, returning heaven and earth to their rightful positions.

Gerry released his held breath and gasped in a great sob of air as the plane roared over the cheering crowd and banked into the wind to land.

The ground rose up below the plane and teased at the wheels. Max flattened out and dropped to stalling speed, the aircraft sinking the last yard onto the grass. The rumbling and shaking returned as the lumbering beast of the air became once more an ensnared prisoner of the ground.

Max brought the plane close to the picnicking crowd. With the engine spluttering to a halt, he applied the parking brakes and the aeroplane became lifeless.

Max pulled off his helmet and goggles and climbed out onto the wing. Gerry made no move. The cooling engine ticked and clanked and still the boy sat rigid in the cockpit. Max put his hand onto Gerry's shoulder and jumped as the boy convulsed under his touch. Gerry screwed his head round. Seeing the big pilot standing next to him he returned from his trance.

'Can we do that again?'

5th July, 1930

Bob Donaldson returned from his trip to the store, throwing the mail onto the kitchen table before busying himself with grocery sorting. Mary leafed through the pile. In amongst the regular bills she found a small brown envelope bearing meticulous handwriting, addressed to her by name and marked 'Private'. Opening the envelope, she tipped the letter towards the window to get more light and read the tiny script with care.

With the groceries stacked in the larder, Bob pulled on his work clothes. He heard his wife gasp and looked up from tying his bootlaces.

'What is it, honey? Who's the letter from?'

Mary beckoned him to the table. 'Come and sit. I'll read it for you.'

Bob crossed the kitchen, his half-laced boots flapping around his ankles.

Mary looked at him over the top of the letter, eyes sparkling. 'Ready?' she asked.

'Yes, I'm ready. Come on, honey, I should be working.'

'Dear Mrs Donaldson, I hope you don't mind me writing you this letter. I am writing to test out an idea. A week ago I gave your son a birthday joy-ride. The boy impressed me very much. He has a natural interest in the planes and the airfield. In short, Mrs Donaldson, I know your boy is needed on the farm for harvest, but I have a job here that could be his if he wanted it at the end of September. It's just general duties and I couldn't pay very much at all, but we will feed the boy and' – Mary looked over the letter at

Bob. Without looking back down she finished the sentence – 'I will teach him to fly.'

The couple looked at each other for long moments.

Bob broke the silence. 'Who's gonna' tell him?'

12th July, 1930

Andrew carried a box of ginger beer into the shop. Placing his load onto the scrubbed wooden floor he took out a bottle, wiping it with a cloth. He didn't check the bottle for dust; Mr Frost's rules stated all bottles and tins were to be wiped before they went on the shelves. The face of the shopkeeper loomed into his mind's eye and Andrew mimicked his shrill tone under his breath:

'The International Stores must be seen to be on the forefront of cleanliness and good service in order to maintain our pre-eminent position in the race to retail groceries, tinned and fancy goods to the populace at large.'

Andrew placed another gleaming bottle on the shelf and wished the 'race to retail groceries' could be a tad more exciting.

Mr Frost came down the back stairs from the office, paused on the bottom tread and, from this elevated position, surveyed his domain. In the last four years Andrew had seen him do this a thousand times. Every time genuine pleasure shone from the old man's face. Mr Frost caught Andrew's eye and strode across, smiling.

'Andrew, my boy,' he said placing a hand on Andrew's shoulder and inspecting the shelf for neatness, 'well done, good job.' He paused, sucking his breath over his teeth as if in the throes of making a difficult decision. 'You know, I think you're nearly ready to take on the meat counter.'

The hand squeezed Andrew's shoulder in gentle reassurance before Mr Frost strode off, running a finger along the shelf, checking for dust.

The tinkling shop-bell announced a customer.

'Good morning, Mr Frost. I must say the tide is high today.'

Mr Frost beamed from behind the till. 'It is indeed Mrs Burns, exceptionally high, I'd say.'

While shopkeeper and customer regarded the harbour from the shop window, Andrew finished stacking the ginger beer as quickly as he could and escaped to the warehouse to pack the orders for delivery.

3rd September, 1931

Anthony Francis and his son stood in the garden as the sun westered on the late summer day, their bodies settled into the same discomfited posture. The unseasonably warm day beaded sweat on their temples and the stickiness under their suits did nothing to ease the tension.

'Why does it have to be the RAF, Andrew? Why can't you be happy where you are?'

The young man remained silent, looking at his father.

'There's no money in it, you know,' the older man said, 'And no security either. They're making cuts all over the place, not interested in armies and things these days, what with... with the Great War and everything...' He trailed off sensing his argument's weakness.

'Your mother will miss you, boy.' He looked into his son's face again. 'You're all she has.'

'I'm not all she has,' Andrew countered, 'she's got you too.'

'But I'm not about to mangle myself in one of the government's blasted new-fangled flying machines.' His father's voice didn't rise, but it hardened.

'Nor am I, Dad. There's nothing to say they'll let me near a plane at all. There's nothing to say they'll even let me polish one in my spare time. So don't worry about me. They'll give me food and provide my clothes. So what if there's no money in it, there's nothing to spend the money on.'

His father opened his mouth to speak but Andrew spoke over him: 'Whatever happens it's better than what's likely to happen here.'

The pregnant criticism hung in the air.

'What I mean is' – Andrew paused – 'you went to France, Dad. You saw something of the world. You met people who didn't live on the same street and didn't go to the same school as you.' He sighed: 'What I mean is... I want more than the meat counter.'

His father's eyes narrowed. Turning away he took out his pipe and filled the bowl from a worn leather tobacco pouch.

'Yes, I met those people. Most of them were your age. Most of them went to France with the people who lived in the same street, or the pals they had at school. And I saw an awful lot of them get broken into pieces.' He put away the pouch and hung his head. 'I'll not consent' – he turned back to face his son – 'for your mother's sake.'

Creeping hostility dangled between them in the evening air before Andrew turned and stalked away.

Anthony watched him go and lit his pipe, the flame leaping in the gathering gloom. Suddenly choked by smoke he heaved into a wracking cough. After a few moments the coughing subsided, but the tears continued to flow.

CHAPTER 3

Semino

24th September, 1931

Gerry finished packing his things. Everything fitted into a small attaché case except his plimsolls, which he tied to the handle by their laces. Clutching the case he went out onto the porch to sit with his parents in the early morning sunlight. Max Anderson would be here soon.

The family sat huddled together, all watching the road for dust clouds. Promising clouds appeared, but each time the vehicle creating them drove past the turn-off to the farm.

Mary opened her mouth to speak but a flash of light in the sky stopped her short. She shaded her eyes with her hand and the light came again. The sun, still low in the sky, glinted on some shiny surface.

'What's that?' she murmured, 'In the sky... there.'

A distant droning teased the air.

Gerry stood, also shading his eyes. 'It's a plane,' he said. 'It's a red and white plane. He's picking me up in his plane!'

The aircraft dipped and bobbed as it lost altitude.

'You've got good eyesight, son,' his father said.

'You have to look *at* the sky rather than *for* the plane,' he answered.

The biplane roared over their heads, 50ft above the ground. Colourful streamers flapped and writhed from the wing struts. Passing over the Donaldsons, Max pulled the plane up into a shallow climb, the wash from his propeller swirling dust and leaves around the yard.

The engine's roar subsided into a grumble as Max lined up to land in the hayfield beyond the farmyard, setting down with a perfect three-point landing. The machine rolled to a stop and the idling engine dropped to a bubbling chuckle, the streamers twitching behind the wings.

Gerry and his parents walked across the yard to the hayfield.

'Goodbye, sir.' Gerry shook his father's hand.

'Work hard and be respectful to Mr Anderson, son. We'll see you for Christmas.'

Gerry turned to his mother who stooped to kiss his forehead.

'Write to me about the things you're doing, Gerry,' she said.

Gerry nodded, unable to speak past the lump in his throat.

His father handed him his case, caught his eye and winked.

Gerry swung through the gate into the hayfield and walked to the plane. He remembered the places on the wing strong enough to bear his weight. Placing his luggage on the cockpit floor, he swung his legs in afterwards and settled into the seat. He pulled on the helmet and gloves he found there and secured the straps.

The engine noise rose to a crescendo, Max waved to the Donaldsons and kicked the rudder to turn the plane into the wind. As they sped across the field Gerry looked back at his mother.

Soft tears ran on Mary's cheeks as she watched the biplane drag its way into the sky. Her breast filled with conflicting emotions. Her pride burned through her sadness, but both mixed with fear.

Bob's hand squeezed her shoulder as he turned towards the house. She heard him walk across the yard behind her, but didn't move to follow. Instead she watched the aircraft recede and vanish, her vision blurred by quiet tears. Even then she stood for long minutes alone before wiping her cheeks with her handkerchief and turning from the hayfield.

25th September, 1931

Gerry's eyes snapped open. The first rays of sunlight sliced through the cavernous space above his head. Confused, he stared at the tiny motes of dust drifting across the sunbeams until the events of the previous day rushed back and he recognised the dark, shallow-vaulted roof high above him as an aircraft hangar. He pulled himself up onto one elbow to look around.

His straw-stuffed mattress lay on a wooden pallet at the back corner of the building, diagonally opposite the fuel pumps that stood next to the huge doors. From where he reclined he could see all six planes. Beyond them, one of the doors stood open. The other door inched along its rails. Through the gaps between wings and struts he could see Max straining against the weight of the structure.

A few yards from Gerry's cot a door led to a small washroom. He climbed out of his bed and went to wash his face and torso in the cold water from the single tap. As he emerged Max finished his struggle with the door and threaded his way through the parked aircraft. He dawdled, distracted as he filled and lit his pipe. Satisfied with the burn, he looked up to see Gerry pulling on his shirt.

'Hallooo!' he called, the reverberations of the metal building lending his big voice a sonorous timbre. 'It's a beautiful day. Indian summer, I think.' Max waited as Gerry tidied his cot and pulled on his boots.

'Good morning, Mr Anderson. What do you want me to do?'

Max grinned. 'From now on I want you to open the hangar in the morning. Damn doors are getting heavier.' He walked back towards the entrance. 'You'll be in charge of the gas pumps too. It's important to keep good records' – he paused to look back at Gerry – 'are you good at math?'

Gerry nodded.

Max smiled in satisfaction and continued his journey across the hangar. 'The important thing to remember about gas pumping…'

Gerry stroked his fingertips over wings and craned to peep into cockpits as he trailed behind Max.

'… otherwise there'll likely be an explosion!' Max turned on his heel to face the boy by means of punctuating his sentence.

'An explosion!' repeated Gerry, his mind racing to dredge the rest of the instructions from behind his daydreaming.

'But not to worry, I'll supervise the first two or three fills to make sure you don't damage my beautiful aeroplanes,' Max concluded.

Gerry exhaled in relief. 'And when there's no gas pumping to do?' he asked, anxious to look keen.

Max shrugged. 'Whatever Floyd and Winston need you to do.'

Two men strode through the hangar entrance. They both wore begrimed overalls and carried steel toolboxes.

'Floyd and Winston,' Max said by way of greeting the new arrivals. 'Gerry.'

'I'm Floyd,' the first man introduced himself, pumping Gerry's hand once. 'D'you know how an engine works?'

'Yes, sir, I do—' Gerry began, but before he had time to add qualification to his answer the other man took up his hand.

'And I'm Winston. I hope you slept okay. It'll be a bit different from what you're used to I expect. Still I'm sure we'll all be getting along fine.' All the time Winston spoke he held Gerry's right hand in his, squeezing to emphasise his sentiments. The rough dryness of his skin, desiccated by the ravages of aviation fuel and engine oil, chafed Gerry's palm.

****

Learning filled the rest of Gerry's day: safety procedures, emergency routines, runway and perimeter track etiquette, fuel capacities, aircraft types, record keeping, security requirements and mealtimes. It was late afternoon before Max called a halt and led Gerry across the field to the canteen door.

Inside Winston stirred a large pot of baked beans on the stove-top while Floyd toasted thick slices of bread on a fork in front of the open stove door. A wooden table with six rough chairs stood next to the stove at the room's centre. Old armchairs lined the walls and a bookshelf held a collection of tatty books – technical journals jumbled in amongst trashy fiction and comics. A long black stovepipe reached up to the ceiling. The warm atmosphere made the space convivial, a feeling magnified by the spicy aroma of the beans.

Winston lifted the pot from the stove, serving the beans onto four plates. Floyd added the fresh piece of toast to the pile in the middle of the table and bent to close the stove door. The four men sat down to supper. Gerry wondered if the engineers approved of the extra mouth at the table.

Self-conscious, he broke the silence. 'These are good beans,' he announced to the room in general.

Floyd looked up from his plate and smiled. 'They're good beans,' he agreed, 'They're not your mommy's beans. But when you're hungry, they're damn fine beans.'

'Amen.' Winston reached over and ruffled Gerry hair.

Silence dropped again onto the group. Feeling at home, Gerry reached out for another piece of toast.

****

Max finished his meal, pushed away his plate and filled the bowl of his pipe with fragrant tobacco.

'How's the Brougham running, Floyd?'

Floyd paused from mopping the bean juice off his plate. 'Perfect, Boss. She's just been tuned and re-greased.'

Max grunted his satisfaction through the first plumes of blue smoke from his fresh pipe. 'Good. Tomorrow afternoon Gerry starts his lessons.'

29

26th September, 1931

Max rolled the Brougham out through the hangar doors with short bursts of throttle. Floyd and Winston walked at his wingtips, ensuring safe passage through the other planes. Gerry walked backwards in front of the aircraft, waving Max on and out through the doors.

Clear of all obstructions, Max waved Floyd and Winston away and turned off the engine. The engineers made their way back to the hangar. Gerry stood still, confused.

Max, climbing out of the plane, sensed Gerry's disappointment and smiled. 'Oh, no, young man. There's more than enough to learn here on the ground before we venture up there.' His eyebrows waggled skywards. 'Come over here and we'll make a start.'

The Brougham had a wide, boxy fuselage with an enclosed cabin behind the engine. The single wing ran across the top of the cabin. Struts sloped up from the undercarriage to support the wings. The fuselage narrowed aft of the cabin and tapered to the tail. After the streamer-bedecked bi-plane, it looked like a combine harvester. Gerry joined Max beside the aeroplane.

Max pointed at the hinged flap on the back edge of the wing. 'This is called an aileron…'

For the next hour the man and the boy worked their way around the aircraft. From time to time Max ducked back into the cabin to move the control column or rudder bar to illustrate how this altered the control surfaces on the wings and tail. Gerry ran his hands across the surfaces as they moved, envisioning the flow of air and struggling to conceive the differing forces coming to bear on the plane in flight. Max used his hands to demonstrate angles and enlivened the lesson with anecdotes.

When they'd finished the tour of the machine Gerry took a step back, regarding the whole aeroplane once more. It was more pigeon than eagle, but nonetheless a flying machine, and now he understood how it performed its magic.

'Put some chocks under those wheels, Gerry. We'll leave her out tonight' – Max studied the sky – 'the weather is set fair'.

'We've finished?' Gerry blurted the question in his surprise.

'Me,' Max said, 'I've finished.' His smile broadened. 'You' – he jabbed Gerry in the chest – 'you have to wash the plane.'

30th October, 1931

Gerry looked at the sky in hope but the clouds hung far too low. Winter stalked the late autumnal skies and despite the overcast; a morning frost sparkled on the grass. The season's first snow was not far distant.

Gerry was buoyant. He glowed with achievement from his first solo flight, snatched the previous day during a break in the heavy weather. Now he needed to log as many hours as possible before the spring and his licence application.

He retreated to a chair just inside the hangar, keeping the door ajar to maintain his weather-watch. Pulling a notebook and pencil from his pocket he started a letter to his mother. He'd barely written a paragraph before a movement across the field distracted him.

A girl walked along on the grass, her faded red dungarees reflecting the red of her hair, tousled in the growing breeze. Despite the cool weather, she'd rolled up her trouser legs and walked barefoot. She carried her pumps in her right hand, her left arm looped through the handle of a large basket.

Gerry caught himself staring, and bent back to his letter. But he could only resist for a second before his eyes darted back to the girl. Standing, he dropped the notebook onto the chair. He took a deep breath and strode out of the hangar door, hoping he looked like someone on his way to somewhere else.

The girl did not notice him. He drew closer but she remained lost in her daydream. Gerry swallowed hard and jumped at his last chance to speak before they passed.

'What are you doing?' He meant to speak with a confident air of authority but his nervousness made his words abrupt.

The girl jumped at the sound of his voice. 'Feeling.' She yelped the word in surprise. The two looked at each other with mounting embarrassment.

The girl regained her composure first. 'Feeling the grass between my toes,' she explained. 'It's like paddling in the ocean, only softer. Have you ever seen the ocean?'

Gerry groped for a reply, 'Yes... no... I mean only in books.'

'I haven't seen the real ocean either,' she went on. 'It's just the way I imagine it.'

The early frost had melted to heavy dew and the droplets covered the girl's feet, emphasising the smooth white of her skin. Gerry felt himself staring again.

'Anyway…' he said, desperate to regain momentum, scrambling for something to say. The girl waited for him to finish his sentence.

'I came to warn you,' he stumbled on. 'It's very dangerous around here, with the aeroplanes and all.'

The girl glanced past Gerry at the closed hangar doors and the empty quadrangle.

'Hmm, I know,' she smiled, 'but if they're likely to hurt you they're generally making a lot of noise.'

Gerry's cheeks reddened. The girl saw his discomfort and offered her hand in rescue.

'My name is Devline. Devline Charwood. I deliver the bread.' She nodded at her basket.

Gerry took her outstretched hand. 'I'm Gerry Donaldson. I…' a smile broke across his face, '…I fly the planes.'

Devline bent to brush the water from her feet and replace her shoes. Tottering on one foot, she put out her hand to grab Gerry's overalls for balance. Gerry reached out and caught her shoulder. She glanced up and smiled.

'I'm on my way to the gate. If you believe I'd be safer with an escort you could walk with me.' She pulled on her shoes and stood up straight.

'I'd be happy to.' His voice sounded normal for the first time since leaving the hangar.

Gerry took her basket and they ambled along the track. As they walked they talked about themselves. Gerry described his birthday flight and the day Max collected him. Devline talked about her mother's recent illness which had prevented her from delivering the bread she baked.

As she spoke Gerry watched Devline's lips move and her eyes flash. Even the lank autumnal light picked out the myriad of colour tones in her red hair.

They reached the airfield gates where Devline's bicycle leant against the fence. Gerry's cheeks coloured again.

'Will I see you again?' he asked.

Devline smiled. 'Tomorrow' – she reached for her basket – 'when I bring the bread. And the day after that and the day after that. Until you get fed up with seeing me or fed up with bread.' Smiling in farewell she mounted her bike and cycled off.

Gerry watched until she was out of sight.

12th November, 1931

Eileen Drew bustled around her room getting ready to leave the house. Pinning back her hair, she hummed a tune to herself. The after-hours job cleaning local offices suited her temperament and she valued the time away from her house, away from Samuel. She trotted down the landing to get hand-cream from the bathroom. On the way back she stuck her head into Vincent's room.

'It's nearly six, Vincent, I'll be off soon.'

The boy lay on his bed staring up at the ceiling. 'I know,' he replied in a flat voice.

'Stop it, Vincent. You're a big boy now. And your dad will be back in another hour or so. Let's not go through this again.' His mother's padding footsteps hardened as she pulled on her flat shoes. She clacked down the stairs, pausing at the bottom to pull on a raincoat.

'Goodnight, sweetheart,' she called up the narrow stairs. 'God, bless.'

Vincent remained silent, listening to her lift the latch and close the door.

Sometimes it felt like minutes before his father opened the same door. The silence of waiting throbbed in his ears with dark foreboding. His mouth dried with fearful anticipation and the air he sucked over his tongue tasted of brass. Sometimes he cried, but most evenings the hopeless inevitability kept his eyes dry.

There… the click of the latch and some shuffling in the dark as a coat is shrugged off wide shoulders. Then the footsteps on the creaking stairs.

13th November, 1931

Watery early autumn sunshine flooded through the window as Eileen walked into the kitchen. She sighed. The brown paper package on the kitchen table contained Samuel's lunch; he'd left for work without it.

'Vincent,' she called over her shoulder, 'Vincent, love, come in here a moment will you?'

The boy sat on the yard wall watching the neighbour release his pigeons for their morning exercise. The flock exploded into the air with a clatter of stiff-feathered wings and wheeled around the chimneys. Vincent followed their jostling flight as they circled the neighbourhood, wondering at the way they tilted and arched their wings in the air as they swooped to land on the roof ridge opposite.

'What for?' Vincent called back, his eyes still fixed on the birds.

'Just come here will you?'

Vincent swung his legs over the wall, dropped to the yard and sauntered inside.

'What?'

'First, get your hands out of your pockets' – his mother advanced on him and grabbed his jaw in her left hand – 'and then' – she moistened the corner of her apron with saliva and wiped a grubby smudge from Vincent's forehead – 'take your father's lunch to the slaughterhouse on your way to school.'

Vincent froze at her words. The daytime belonged to him. When his father left the house the man ceased to exist until the evening. This wasn't fair.

'Yes, mother,' he croaked.

She handed him the package and guided him out the door.

Vincent walked down the alley behind the houses. The pigeons burst from their roost into another crazy, milling circle. Vincent passed beneath, his eyes fixed straight ahead. He dragged onto the main road and down the hill past The Jolly Sailors, along the edge of the graveyard and down the lane to the slaughterhouse gates.

Built without the need for beauty, the large brick building sat squat and forbidding, its high-set frosted windows hiding its daily machinations. Vincent fought to control his breathing.

Red wooden gates breached the tall wall surrounding the abattoir yard. One gate held a low door for access. Vincent ducked through the door.

Scattered dung soiled the cobbles and across the yard the top section of the slaughterhouse stable door stood open. Vincent fell forward into his first step and lurched towards the door. His nostrils flared at a strange, cloying odour that clung to the hairs in his nose. He reached the opening and stopped.

A narrow doorway with a spring-loaded gate connected a small stable to the slaughterhouse. His father stood at the gate with bloodied hands fumbling to reload his bolt-gun. Securing the new charge in the breech, he reached over to open the gate. Through the gap Vincent could see young pigs in a huddled mass, their eyes flashing with fear. One of the beasts took the bait and bolted for freedom. The big man reacted, jammed the creature against the door-jamb with his knee and pushed the bolt-gun against the back of the pig's skull. The crack of the cartridge cut short the animal's squealing. In one smooth movement Samuel took up the spike dangling by a cord from his belt and plunged it through the creature's throat.

Samuel stepped back, bending to reload the gun. The pig dropped onto its side and the gate slammed shut to squeals of alarm from the corralled swine. The stunned animal thrashed as a fountain of blood hosed from the hole in its neck. The pig's legs kicked in a parody of flight and the body slipped across the blood-lubricated floor. The first slow, sliding motion evolved into a languorous spin. Vincent looked across the chamber to his father's previous two victims. They rotated still, intermittent spurts of blood pulsing from their dying hearts. Vincent looked back to his father as he reached out again for the gate. His face bore an expression Vincent recognised. Dropping the brown paper package Vincent ran for the gate.

15th November, 1931

Andrew reached the top of the hill and looked out towards the perimeter track. The cycle ride felt longer. Perhaps he missed Peter's company, or maybe the weight of guilt dragged him back.

Nothing moved across the airfield, but the small boy who still lived inside Andrew demanded he pause and look. Andrew breathed in the earthy silence of the autumn fields, turned and pedalled off down the road. No barley water at the perimeter fence today; this morning he'd go through the main gate.

The barbed-wire fence marched across the countryside dividing the airfield's rough grass from the cultivated soil of the surrounding fields. The fence cut a diagonal towards Andrew and for the next half-mile it ran along parallel to the road's edge. Buildings became visible in the distance, some made of brick with window frames painted green, and beyond them, in the middle distance, far larger buildings without windows. Andrew's heart quickened at the thought of what those hangars contained and, by the time the fence gave way to a gate, all traces of guilt had evaporated.

The guard stepped forward from his hut as Andrew approached. 'Yes son, what can I do for you?'

'I've come to join the RAF.'

CHAPTER 4

Portentum

7th March, 1934

Vincent fell from his seat and crumpled onto the floor. He huddled into a ball, his limbs twisting against his body. His eyes rolled back into his head and a line of drool strung from his mouth to the floorboards. The whole class sat in silence, mesmerised by the display.

'You, boy' – the teacher broke the spell – 'sit on him and hold his arms still so he doesn't hurt himself. Hurry up!'

The teacher grabbed the wooden ruler from Vincent's desk. Kneeling beside the stricken boy, he helped bring Vincent's flailing limbs under control and pushed the ruler between Vincent's grinding teeth. Unsure what to do, the teacher supported Vincent's head to protect him against the jerking spasms lashing up through his neck.

'What's wrong with him, sir?' asked the frightened voice of a girl in the next row of desks.

'He's fainted, that's all.'

'That's funny 'fainted" – a different voice, this time a boy – 'my auntie's always fainting and she don't dance around like a monkey.'

'Be quiet and open a window, boy.'

As suddenly as it began, the seizure passed. Vincent's quaking limbs stilled and the ruler dropped from his mouth.

'All right son, you can leave go now.'

As his reluctant helper scrambled to get off Vincent, the teacher glanced at his watch. 'Class dismissed, early lunch everybody, we'll continue this afterwards.' The room erupted into cacophony as 35 children closed their books, slammed their desks and scraped their chair legs on the floor in their hurry to leave. As the last pupil trailed out of the door Vincent regained consciousness.

'Are you all right, Drew?' the teacher bent to help Vincent sit up.

For a moment Vincent remained suspended in his daze, then snapped to attention as he remembered where he was. 'I'm not mad, sir.' Desperation scraped Vincent's voice.

'Of course you're not mad, Vincent. Get up off the floor, boy. I'll call the doctor.'

'No, sir.'

'But Vincent, you need—'

'No. Please don't tell anyone, sir. It won't happen again. I'll make sure it doesn't happen again.'

Vincent burned with defenceless shame and fear. He couldn't go to a doctor. He couldn't face the questions.

'I'm fine, sir. Thank you, sir.' Vincent stood and wobbled towards the door.

His teacher watched him go.

The fresh air revived Vincent and the slick of sweat on his forehead grew cold and evaporated. His classmates stood talking in small groups, and as he emerged they turned to stare. An uneasy quiet fell across the playground. One voice broke the silence.

'Vincent is a looney, Vincent is a looney…'

Others joined in and the chorus grew in volume.

'Vincent is a looney, Vincent is a looney…'

The litany droned on in its own pointless spiral and with the security of their growing number the children's chanting rose in volume.

'Vincent is a looney, Vincent is a looney…'

Vincent stood with his head hung down like a human sacrifice before the altar, helpless against the sheer weight of his classmates' derision. On it went until the strident clatter of the dinner bell cut across its rhythm and his tormentors broke into a run for the dining hall.

Vincent stood alone, staring at the ground.

****

Eileen walked into the kitchen and peeped out the window. He was there, perched on the wall like some shabby little vulture. Vincent, the best thing she'd ever done. She closed her eyes and enjoyed an up-swell of pride.

The light from the setting sun faded, draping layers of gloom over the back yard. Vincent sat hunched on the wall, his back to the kitchen door. The pigeons had roosted, so instead he tracked the gulls trailing through the darkening sky on their way back to the sea. Great V-shaped formations of a hundred birds or more straggled and jostled in their procession towards the coast.

As he stared skywards Vincent's vision blurred with tears. His head throbbed from the episode in the classroom.

'Oh, mother,' he murmured into his own misery.

9th March, 1934

Bob and Mary Donaldson sat on the porch, keeping an eye on the road. The yard had seen few changes in the two and a half years since Max had whisked away their son. They'd relished his visits each Christmas, but this time he was back for a whole month.

They had no idea which vehicle would deliver their hitch-hiking son. They let the sparse traffic flow past until one truck stopped by their gate. A familiar figure stepped out and closed the door, they stood and walked up the drive to greet him.

'How's my Gerry?' His mother pulled him into a hug. 'And how's Devline?'

'I'm fine, she's fine, Max is fine. How are you?'

Gerry kissed his mother and turned to shake his father's hand. 'Sir.'

'Son.' His father returned Gerry's handshake and reached to take his bag. 'What's new?'

Gerry put one arm around his father's shoulders and the other around his mother's waist and together they walked back up the drive towards the house.

'Good news. Max is expanding the business and making me the airfield manager.'

'Do I hear bells?' his mother asked at once.

Gerry smiled; there'd be a whole month of wedding hints. 'No, not yet Ma. And it's not because I wouldn't. It's just with Devline's mother being sick and needing her help, well, it just wouldn't be fair. We'll just have to wait a while.'

They continued swapping news over lunch, and as Mary cleared away the plates Gerry mentioned the newspapers he'd read at the airfield and the stories about the 'new age' of European politics.

His father sighed and swirled his coffee dregs. 'There's no benefit in getting mixed up in Europe again,' Bob said. 'We left far too many good men there last time, and where did it get us?'

Gerry nodded but looked his father in the eye.

'I think it needs to be watched, Dad. That's all.'

'Watching it is fine, son. God knows, we should've carried on watching in 1917.'

****

As the days passed Mary found herself drawn to Gerry's side. This month was an unexpected bonus and she wanted to make the most of it. She talked with him as he worked, occasionally holding something steady while he sawed or hammered. She soaked up every tale he told about his life on the airfield, particularly the stories about Floyd and Winston.

Two weeks into his visit Mary found herself drinking coffee with Gerry on the porch during a break from his work. The small talk lapsed and Mary gave voice to a vague concern nibbling at her conscience.

'You will be fair with Devline, won't you, Gerry?' Her question was vague enough to avoid embarrassment if its meaning was missed.

'I love her too much to cause her any trouble, Mom.' Gerry avoided his mother's gaze, preferring to study the depths of his half empty mug.

Mary nodded but did not relent. 'It's been over two years now.' Again her phrasing took the sting out of the unasked question.

Gerry paused before he answered. 'We've kissed and cuddled, sure. But I do know the right order of things, Mom.' Embarrassment crept into Gerry's voice.

'Do you need to speak with your father?'

Gerry burst out laughing. He cupped his mother's face with his hands and shook his head in mock disapproval.

'Have you not listened to a word I've said about Floyd and Winston?'

15th July, 1934

Floyd and Winston sat huddled over a grimy newspaper. They looked up as Gerry entered the canteen. Winston's permanent smile was missing.

'What's up, fellas'?'

'Damned Germans have started killing each other,' Floyd muttered. 'Listen to this: 'Reports are reaching this news office of an incident, or series of incidents, involving German military and political figures which has left a number of them dead and many more in prison. Many political dissidents are also reported as imprisoned or missing. Adolf Hitler has proclaimed: "There won't be another revolution in Germany for the next thousand years".'

Floyd shook his head in the heavy silence. 'What the hell is going on over there, Gerry? What kind of way is that to run a country?'

'Maybe Congress will do something about it.' Gerry leaned over the paper.

Floyd narrowed his eyes. 'They sucked us in back in 1917.' Floyd stabbed the paper with his finger. 'If they go again, they'll go without us.' His voice held an edge.

Winston fidgeted, unable to offer an opinion to change the balance of the conversation and uncomfortable about staying silent.

Gerry spoke up on impulse. 'If it's worth the fight, Floyd, there'll always be people willing to go.'

For a moment the silence hardened, then Floyd broke the spell with a rare grin, 'Maybe, boy. But I'm too old to get involved in any more fighting. And I've got flat feet. That's why I'm in the air force.'

Winston loosed a bark of laughter and the two men stood to leave.

'The air force.' Winston chuckled as he passed Gerry on his way to the door. 'Can you believe it, Gerry? The air force.'

Winston's chuckling faded as the door swung closed behind him. Gerry sat down and picked up the newspaper. He scanned the article Floyd had read out, pausing over the unfamiliar German names and wondering how a government could spend a night murdering people and carry on the next day as normal.

16th July, 1934

The Avro Tutor rolled to a halt and Andrew launched into the shutdown procedure. A tap on his flying helmet interrupted him. He craned his head over his shoulder and looked at the instructor in the rear cockpit.

'Let me get clear' – the man shouted above the noise. He pointed to himself and then to the ground – 'then take the circuit.'

Andrew nodded and turned to face the front. His mouth dried out. Here it was, the chance to write 'first solo' in his logbook.

The instructor scuttled away from the aircraft, pulled off his helmet and waved him away. Andrew released the brakes and taxied to the end of the runway.

Reaching the downwind end of the field he kicked the rudder and turned the nose crosswind. Breathing deeply to steady his nerves Andrew went through the final cockpit checks.

Routine actions took on a new significance. His eyes flitted over the petrol gauge and oil pressure gauge; he revved the engine and listened to its tone. Finally he gave a sharp tug on each side of his safety harness. Satisfied, he scanned the sky to his left for anything coming in to land. The clear summer sky held nothing but a few wispy clouds.

Andrew kicked the rudder and opened the throttle and in one smooth motion the bi-plane turned into the wind and rolled forward. He picked a tree beyond the airfield's perimeter as his marker. As the plane accelerated across the grass he touched the rudder to keep it travelling straight towards the tree.

Judging his speed sufficient, he nudged the control column very slightly forward. The tail lifted in response. Andrew concentrated on the distant tree, pushing and pulling with his feet on the rudder to maintain his course.

The suggestion of buoyancy crept into the aircraft. He eased the control column back and the wheels left the ground. The Trainer yawed as it settled into the wind and climbed away from the field.

21st August, 1934

Vincent strode past his old school's gates on his way to the bakery. He didn't glance into the playground; schooldays were over, today he was on his way to get a job.

Vincent had spotted the notice on the bakery gate that morning and ran home to wash his face and clean his shoes. Now as he hurried down the hill into town he marvelled at his own implacable determination to get the job.

The notice was still in place on the bakery gate. He sighed in relief, tore it from the drawing pins, pushed open the gate and entered the yard. Crossing to the bakery, he glanced through windows almost wholly obscured by flour dust. At this time of day the bakery was not busy, but Vincent could make out one shadowy figure moving about inside.

He steeled himself and knocked. The door swung inwards, exhaling a breath of warm air, piquant with the sweetly sour fragrance of bread yeast.

The baker's face, framed with grey hair, sported streaks of flour but, despite the heat, no sweat disturbed the dust on his visage.

'Yes?'

Vincent handed him the notice.

The baker looked down at the paper, looked back at Vincent and beckoned the boy into the building.

Vincent followed, closing the door. For a long moment the transition from bright August sunshine to the bakery's gloomy twilight defeated his vision. Gradually the details of the room resolved around the white-overalled bulk of the baker.

'It's hard work, lad, and at this time of year the heat gets something terrible.' An undercurrent of sadness ran through the man's voice. 'And you'll be starting at 10 o'clock of an evening and working through to 9 o'clock in the morning.'

'I'll take the job,' said Vincent, his voice steady and confident. 'When do I start?'

'Well, come back tonight and we'll give you a try for the rest of the week. How does that sound?'

'Thank you, sir. That's just perfect.'

Vincent opened the door and the blaze of brilliant sunshine embraced him like a re-birth. Dazzled by the light he stumbled towards the gate. The baker's voice followed him across the yard.

'Get home now and get some sleep. Be here by ten sharp. What's your name boy?'

'Vincent,' he called back over his shoulder, 'Vincent Drew.' It rang out like a war-cry.

28th September, 1934

The cooling ovens clicked and popped, a backdrop to the bakers' final clear-up. The last of the loaves were racked for cooling and Vincent mopped the floor. He worked quickly despite a long night of mixing and kneading dough. Finishing with a flourish, he returned the mop and bucket to the cleaning cupboard. With arms folded across his chest he waited to catch his boss's eye.

The old man looked up from packing deliveries, glanced at the floor, smiled broadly and nodded towards the door. Vincent treated the baker to a mock salute, hung his apron on the back of the door and trotted out into the gloomy morning.

The shift had gone well and Vincent had finished over an hour early. The darkness clinging to the lampposts should've warned him; the emptiness of the street ought to have given a clue. But Vincent remained unaware and hurried on towards his breakfast.

Vincent skipped around the corner into his deserted street. The two rows of solid terraced houses faced each other across a road uncluttered by front gardens. Each door opened straight onto the pavement with only the angled front doorsteps defeating the gradient. He'd made it halfway along before he saw his father closing their front door.

Their eyes met and Vincent stopped dead in confusion. He lurched backwards a step and steadied himself against the dizzying sickness clutching his guts. Trapped, he started forwards again, prepared to fly at the first hint of violence.

Samuel walked up the road to meet the boy. They stopped a yard apart and Vincent looked up into his father's face, his jaw clenched tight against the fear rising in his chest. Samuel placed a hand on the boy's shoulder.

'Hello, son.'

The bile rose in Vincent's throat. He swallowed hard against his revulsion and squirmed his shoulder away from his father's touch.

'It's been a hard shift. I need to get home.'

With a quick ferocity his father's grip tightened on Vincent. A hand used to guiding strong beasts to violent death closed like a clamp on the boy's bony shoulder and the man's eyes drifted out of focus.

A nearby door opened and a neighbour bent to put out milk bottles. The noise distracted Samuel and his eyes refocused. He looked back into Vincent's face for a moment and his fingertips squeezed deeper into the boy's flesh. Then Samuel flung him aside and strode off along the road. The neighbour watched him pass.

'Good morning, Mr Drew,' she said, pleased to witness his discomfiture. Receiving no answer she turned to Vincent.

'Good morning, Vincent.' She pressed her intrusion with forced normality.

Vincent regained his feet and rubbed his shoulder gingerly. He nodded at the woman, not trusting himself to speak. He lurched the few remaining yards to his front door, opened it and slipped inside.

A faint sobbing drifted down into the hallway. Vincent moved through the gloom and walked up the stairs. The noise came from his mother's room. Something in the timbre of the sound conveyed the deepest of misery. His mother's door stood open.

Eileen lay on the bed in her underwear. Her long white petticoat was ripped and something discoloured her thighs. A long moment passed before Vincent recognised it as blood. His mother turned to him with eyes that welled tears. Even through the pain her face softened for him.

'Oh, Vincent. My baby. I'm sorry.'

Vincent's vision swam and an intense buzz gripped his temples. He staggered to his bedroom. Closing the door behind him he sank onto the bed as the first explosions sparked in his brain and his muscles clenched, arching his back in the paroxysm of seizure.

CHAPTER 5

Expecto

10th December, 1935

The house lights dropped and the screen flickered into life. Devline snuggled closer to Gerry and put her head on his shoulder. A *March of Time* newsreel preceded the main feature. Devline only half-listened as ranks of earnest politicians in suits took turns to speak. Abruptly the film cut to a dead child, it's head covered in crawling flies.

'...*bombing Abyssinian tribesmen and their families with anti-personnel shrapnel bombs.*'

Devline gasped at the sight and felt Gerry's muscles stiffen.

The camera swept over a pile of contorted bodies. Men with cloths tied around their faces struggled to extricate the human knots tied by terror and death.

The narrator's voice ground on: '...*for these villagers. It seems they fell victim to gas shells fired by artillery or dropped from aeroplanes. The League of Nations has reaffirmed its determination to impose sanctions on Italy to prevent movement of the goods required to wage war. That means oil. Benito Mussolini, the Italian dictator, has said he considers such sanctions acts of aggression and they will be met by acts of war. Already apparently guilty of atrocities against Abyssinian civilians, it is for the world to wait and see what might be Mussolini's next move.*'

The images changed to smiling cheerleaders as the newsreel moved to a report on the recent Red Jackets' football game.

The couple left the cinema at the end of the feature and walked to their borrowed pick-up. A hard-edged cold charged the air and froze the piles of snow in place like banks of ground glass.

Gerry unlocked the doors and they climbed in. The engine laboured into life and Gerry let it run to heat the cab. The shock of the cold after the over-heated movie theatre had thrown them into paroxysms of shivering. Panting their condensing breath into the cab they regained control of their quaking muscles.

Devline broke the silence: 'It's a long way away, Gerry. It is terrible, yes, but there's nothing we can do about it here in Minnesota.'

Gerry's head dropped to his chest and he heaved a heavy sigh. The truck's heater blasted warm air into the cab and he dragged the woollen cap from his scalp.

'Mussolini is bombing the Africans and Hitler is stringing up his own people. Something will have to be done. It will be the French and British who start it, and when they've taken it as far as they can it will be us that'll go and finish it.'

'No, Gerry.' She spoke softly but an edge hovered in her voice. 'It will settle down soon. They're all too scared to go too far. They can't possibly want to go through that again.'

Gerry put his arm around Devline and kissed her on the forehead. His voice softened to match hers. 'Don't you think if America had lost we'd want to fight again and again until we won? That's the way the Germans are looking at it.'

'Why does it have to happen this way?' She pulled away from him and twisted in her seat to look him straight in the eye. 'Is it some secret boys' game? Someone has to lose, Gerry. Someone has to get beaten and stay beaten or the whole sorry mess just spirals on forever. We should be thinking about Christmas. Peace on Earth and goodwill towards men. You and me, together. Except now one stupid boy has killed a village full of people so another bunch of boys have to go and kill him. And even if they win it doesn't matter, because whoever loses is going to start the fight again somewhere down the line.'

Overwhelmed with frustration, Devline's eyes welled with tears and she turned her head to hide them.

'Anyway,' she continued, 'you'll be 24 next year. By the time they get to calling you up it will be finished one way or the other.'

Gerry released the hand brake and put the truck into gear. Sure, he'd be third choice for the infantry if the draft came. But the people in the newsreel had been killed from the air, and over and above all other things Gerry was a pilot.

11th December, 1935

The azure sky above Andrew's head formed a perfect dome of blue tranquility. Despite his altitude the wind buffeting his head held no chill.

The squadron of Demons climbed west into another routine patrol. Glancing to his left Andrew could see Cairo's streets laid out below like a model cast from sand. To his right the flat triangle of the Nile Delta faded into the haze, the river splitting into spidery fingers that groped for liberty in the Mediterranean Sea. Three feet behind him the gunner sat facing the tail, hands restraining the machine-gun in the slipstream's swirl. Around them the other planes bobbed up and down.

Squadron Leader Malcolm Fenton levelled out, taking the formation into a bank to port, heading south. Cruising over the Egyptian landscape, the ragged group had nothing to do except scan the sky and hold formation. For 30 minutes they continued on course before Fenton waved his hand above his head, turning them back for home.

A tail-wind hastened the return journey and they stacked up over their airfield at Heliopolis 25 minutes later.

Andrew circled with the others, watching his comrades landing one by one on the dusty airstrip. His turn came and he side-slipped towards the runway. Andrew recognised Brian Hale landing before him.

Andrew swooped towards the runway and flattened out his approach. Dropping the flaps and throttling back, he brought the Demon down to 3ft above the hard sand. He cut the throttle and kept the machine flying straight. With the engine coughing at idle, the bi-plane stalled, lost buoyancy and sank to a perfect landing.

Andrew braked to taxiing speed and followed Bryan out onto the perimeter track. Behind him came the roar and bump of the next Demon down.

The squadron taxied away from the runway, parking their planes in line abreast.

Bryan completed his shutdown as Andrew pulled up. Gunners unbolted machine-guns and handed them down to ground crew. Then gunners and pilots strolled to the operations tent for debriefing. Andrew climbed out of the cockpit, jumped to the ground and saw Bryan waiting for him. They walked off towards the ops tent together.

'When do you think they'll ship us down to Somaliland so we can get a crack at the Eyeties?' Bryan raised his voice against the engine noise as the squadron's stragglers came in to park, gunning their engines to swing their aircraft into position.

'No one's declared a war yet, Bryan. We're not going to get a crack at anything until the politicians make it legal.'

'But they're bombing the poor bloody peasants down there, Andrew. How long can it be before they put us in to bat? I heard the top brass has offered to bomb northern Italy from bases in France. And we're stuck in bloody Egypt, thousands of miles from anything.'

'The League of Nations—'

Bryan's derisive snort cut Andrew short.

'Bugger them! Bugger them in general and bugger Anthony Eden in particular!' Bryan turned on his heel in mid-stride and stood, arms outstretched, looking back at the fighters.

'All I want is to take one of those lovely silver floozies into the sky and shoot the arse off something Italian.'

Andrew gazed past Bryan's outstretched arms to the aircraft shimmering in the haze, waiting to become sabres or coffins.

Bryan's arms fell and he rested his hands on his hips. Silence hung over the field and the last aircrew trailed past them to the debriefing. Bryan's head dropped and he turned back towards the tents.

'Oh, and Mussolini,' he said as they walked away from the planes, 'bugger him too.'

12th December, 1935

Andrew glanced from face to face, each one illuminated by the stark light of the North African sun.

Bryan Hale flipped through a magazine, his eyes darting from picture to picture. His blond hair plastered across his forehead with the heat, he gave vent to exasperation with an occasional tut or sigh.

Next to him sat Alan Gold, snoozing sweetly as small beads of perspiration sparkled on his prematurely bald head.

Third in the ragged circle sat George Anders. His dark hair flopped over his hazel eyes as he picked the sand from under his fingernails.

'Bugger it!' Bryan threw down his magazine. 'Has it started yet, for Christ's sake?' He stood and walked off towards the line of aircraft along the runway's edge, scrubbing his hair with his knuckles.

His sudden movement stirred Alan from his slumber. Clicking his tongue against his thirst, he stood and made towards the canteen trailer to get water.

Andrew watched the two men walking away.

'Are you scared, Andrew?' George asked.

Andrew took a moment to consider the question. With a swell of emotion that pricked gently at his eyes he found his answer: 'I want to live long enough to get married and have a child.'

'Boy or a girl?'

'A girl first. For her mother's sake. In case one day I don't come back.'

'And her mother?' George prompted.

'I don't know. Pretty, of course, but strong. Someone able to look after herself when I'm away. Someone who's not afraid to laugh. Someone who can cope.'

'Cope with what?' asked Alan, slumping into his deckchair and slurping lukewarm water from his tin mug.

'With suppressed psychopaths like Hale over there.' It was George who answered.

They looked over to where Bryan stood, leaning against a wing, scanning the southern skies in the vain search for an adversary.

Alan sighed into the silence. 'When it starts it will be soon enough for everyone.' A congenial smile reinforced the wisdom in his words.

'If it ever does start,' George murmured. 'We've got the force, we've got the equipment and we've got the targets. Why are we sitting about like pensioners on a pier?'

'It's better for the politicians to talk it through, George.' Andrew dabbed sweat from his top lip with a handkerchief. 'I'm as fed up as anyone, but it must be better for them to talk it out before we start shooting.'

'It's like dogs and children.' Again Alan smiled as punctuation.

The other two looked at him, nonplussed.

'What is?' asked George.

'Well...' Alan leant forward to explain.

Bryan ambled back towards the group, hands in pockets, shoulders slumped. Andrew watched the desolate figure approach as Alan spoke.

'...if you let dogs or children get away with too much at the beginning, they get used to it and expect the same kind of treatment all the time. So, later when you try to rein them in, they fight it. If the League of Nations lets these bullies get away with all this today, in a few years' time we'll be left holding the leash on a mad dog' – he leaned back in his chair, this time without a smile – 'or two.'

Bryan shuffled back into the group and sat down heavily.

'Bugger it,' he said to no one in particular.

CHAPTER 6

Terra

12th February, 1936

The flat Anglian landscape rolled past the window. Despite the prospect of a week's leave, Andrew's deflated mood worsened as the train chugged on. The dark earth sucked the watery sunlight from the blue-grey sky. Leaden fields stretched unbroken to the level horizon, impaled in places by a solitary pump-house or a huddle of squat farm buildings.

Andrew mused about the people who lived in those remote houses – how they might have celebrated the Christmas just past; whether they had known about their government's military expedition in Africa.

The train pulled out of Ely, the squat megalith of the cathedral sliding away through the steam clouds from the engine. Then the monotone fields reasserted their dun dominance, slashed by an occasional watercourse, the smooth, reflective water running along the top of its own elevated bank.

Half an hour later the train pulled into King's Lynn. Nearly all the passengers alighted here and Andrew watched as a young sailor searched for, found and embraced his girlfriend. The guard's whistle pierced the air and the train clanked along the platform. Andrew's window drew level with the young couple as they broke their clinch. The girl caught Andrew's eye, beaming him a smile. The sailor bent to kiss her again and the train moved them out of sight. Andrew sat alone in the carriage.

The engine swung east and clattered through the port. As it broke free of the docks and warehouses, Andrew got a clear view of the North Sea. It seethed with hostile grey waves. Together with the washed-out blue of the late afternoon sky, it created a flat two-tone backdrop to a chill world.

A spiteful wind plucked at anything that moved. Gulls and terns careened through the turbulent airflow. One tiny tern bobbed in the wind currents, suddenly rolling over onto its side and tucking its wings against its body. Transformed from bird to bullet, it rocketed towards the water, hitting just behind the surf-line and emerging a second later with a thin, silver fish in its beak.

The surf curled a mint-green whiteness from the grey depth of the sea and crashed it onto the shingle beach. The purples and greys of the flint pebbles glistened in the foam like the entrails of a million tiny animals. The swoop of another tern pulled Andrew's eyes back to the cold sky, made more ominous by the mountainous, rolling clouds of an approaching weather front.

Andrew glanced back into the carriage as a khaki-clad figure pushed up the aisle towards the engine. Something about the soldier's demeanour caused a thrill of recognition. A few minutes later the heavily-built soldier lumbered back, his forage cap sitting askew on top of closely cropped ginger hair.

Andrew smiled and called out: 'Private Peter Ellis.'

'Yes, sir?' Peter's response came automatically and it was a moment before he spotted Andrew sitting near the window.

'Andrew Francis! It's been years,' Peter moved to sit opposite Andrew and admired his friend's uniform. He reached out and touched the wings on Andrew's tunic.

'I knew you'd joined the RAF, but I thought you'd be a fitter or something. When did they let you play with an aeroplane?'

'It took about three years to convince them. Now they let me fly one all the time.'

'So your dream came true. That's fantastic.' Peter lowered his voice, 'Don't tell the C.O. but I still want to be a train driver.'

Andrew smiled: 'So when did you become a pongo?'

'I joined early last year when it looked like there might be quite a stink with the Italians,' Peter explained.

'There was a stink for an awful lot of people,' Andrew said, 'but they didn't consider it a big enough stink for us to join in. My squadron just got back from three months of doing nothing in Egypt.'

'Cor! Egypt? We've just finished training for overseas service in bloody Wales.'

The two men laughed.

Peter pulled himself together for a moment and put on a Welsh accent: 'Now I reckon we're ready to invade Italy, all right?'

Their laughter died away and Andrew framed a serious question: 'How does your father feel about this?'

53

'He wasn't happy. But, after a little bit of shouting, he sat me down and told me things he'd never talked about before; he told me everything he could remember about the War. Most of it wasn't very pretty. But at the end he admitted he'd enjoyed it all.'

'Even the killing?'

'Especially the killing. When he'd finished, he stood up and said if I still wanted to join after what I'd just found out, then I had his full blessing. Then he went out and got drunk.'

'And you joined up.'

'The very next week.'

The train slowed as it pulled into the outskirts of Wells-on-Sea. The tracks took it through a series of cuttings, swinging around the back of the town into the small station.

Peter returned to his carriage to retrieve his bag. Andrew stayed in his seat until the train jolted to a halt. The chance meeting with Peter had dissolved his earlier melancholy. Outside his father would be waiting, and now that wasn't such a bad prospect.

Andrew stood, straightened his uniform, picked up his bag and stepped from the carriage. Peter was engaged in earnest conversation with the engine driver at the front of the train. Steam billowed around the pair, partially obscuring them from view. Andrew walked through the station building and onto the pavement beyond.

Anthony Francis stood bolt upright in his Sunday best suit. His shoes, although worn, were polished and his tie held a starched collar in place. He stepped forward, extending his hand.

'Hello, son. Welcome home, it's good to see you back in one piece. You're looking well.'

Andrew smiled and shook his father's hand. 'It's the suntan I think, Dad.'

Anthony took his son's bag and they started up the hill towards the town. At the top of the hill they turned down the main street.

Despite the chill wind blowing in from the sea, most shop doors stood open and in them gathered the shop owners and their staff. The engine's whistle had alerted the whole town and the curious had turned out to watch. Andrew's father chose a line directly down the centre of the narrow road and Andrew fell in behind him.

As Anthony neared the first shop he dipped his head and said: 'Good day.'

'Good day, Mr Francis,' followed by 'Good show, Andrew.'

The procession continued from shop to shop. Eventually they reached the end of the street where the International Stores stood with its commanding view over the harbour. Here the buildings funnelled the sea gales south through the town. The approaching weather front hung less than a mile north of the bay and the stiffening wind flapped and pulled at Andrew's uniform.

Mr Frost stood outside the International Stores, the remnants of his grey hair whipped around his head like candy-floss in the high wind.

'Hello, Andrew my boy,' he said, placing a hand on Andrew's shoulder and surveying the airman's uniform. 'Well done. Good job. I always said my loss would be the King's gain. Come inside.'

The three men pushed through the plate-glass door that swung shut behind them. Occasionally the heavy door lost its battle with the rising gale and opened a crack, allowing fingers of wind to derange the green tops of the carrots displayed near the entrance. They moved deeper into the shop and Mr Frost bustled behind his counter.

'I've just brewed,' he said. 'You'll have one?' He poured the tea without waiting for an answer.

Andrew browsed around the shop. In the four years since he'd left nothing had changed. He walked up and down the aisles. Everything was in the same place, in the same order. He stopped and gazed at the ginger beer for a moment.

Andrew became aware of someone looking at him. He turned to meet the gaze of a young man standing behind the meat counter. His greasy hair was badly cut, framing a sallow and spotty complexion.

'Hello, sir.'

The young man's voice alerted Mr Frost to his omission. 'I'm sorry, everybody,' the shopkeeper said, 'this is Jennings. He took over after you left, Andrew. He's a good lad, keeps the meat counter spotless.'

The young man blushed with pride at the accolade.

'Four years.' Andrew mused as he walked over.

'Hello, Jennings. Could I have a pound of your best sausages, please?'

Jennings leapt into action: 'Pork or beef, sir?'

'I think, Pork.'

While the sausages were weighed and wrapped, Andrew tried to catch his father's eye, but the old man avoided his gaze and chatted with Mr Frost about the price of coal.

Andrew and his father finished their tea and pushed out through the door into the teeth of the wind. Mr Frost thanked them for their custom and manhandled the door closed behind them.

They turned west towards the bakery and crossed to the road's northern side to gain the shelter of the terraced houses. Andrew pulled his collar up against the first drops of rain. 'It's good to see Mr Frost looking so well.'

'He's a successful man, Andrew,' his father replied. 'We don't all have to travel the world to make that claim.'

Andrew let it pass and they covered the last few hundred yards in silence, hurrying against the strengthening storm.

The two men bustled into the back porch of the cottage just as the front arrived over the town to unload its rain. Big drops of water lashed themselves onto the paving stones in the back yard, lifting a low, hazy mist from the debris of their destruction. Andrew grimaced at his father and both men smiled at their narrow escape.

From the porch they went through the small kitchen to the living room. The cottage was dark with low ceilings, and a faint smell of stale sherry hung in the air. The living space was crowded and untidy. Two large armchairs sat under the window with a double-leaf dining table and six chairs cluttering the rest of the space.

'Your mother's in the front room, waiting.' Anthony motioned his son through.

Andrew knocked and entered. A sweeter scent of fresh sherry mingled with the warm smell of the oil lamp lit against the afternoon's deepening gloom. Margaret Francis sat in an armchair like a small, dishevelled heap of second-hand clothes. Her wan complexion emphasised her gaunt frame.

'Hello, mother,' Andrew said and sat down in the armchair opposite. 'How have you been?'

His mother made no attempt to answer, she just looked at him with a thin smile.

'Anyone for a drink?' Anthony's entrance distracted Margaret.

'Sherry for Mother,' he murmured and handed Margaret the glass.

She accepted it carefully and took a demure sip, returning her smiling gaze to Andrew.

'Whisky for Father... and?'

'Er... what do you have?'

His father's lips pursed at the question. 'It's not a bloody RAF mess bar, you know – we've got sherry and we've got whisky.'

'Whisky then, please, thank you.'

His father handed Andrew a large whisky, sat down on the sofa and talked about the goings-on in the town. Over the course of two further whiskies, Andrew was brought up to date on who had married whom and how many children they'd had; which businesses had opened, closed or changed hands; on the number of deaths, the manner of dying and the size of the funeral. Throughout his mother nodded and chuckled but said nothing.

Anthony looked at his watch. 'Fish and chips for tea, Andrew. Let's go and fetch them.'

Andrew stood to follow his father out the door. He paused by his mother's chair.

She drained the last of her sherry. 'Thank you for coming, Andrew,' she said and nodded.

Anthony and Andrew walked back to the harbour through the darkening evening. The wind had subsided and with it the rain. The town's lights threw garish reflections on the wet road. There was no one else in sight.

'Is she all right?' Andrew asked.

'She's ill and she thinks she's dying. She relies on the sherry to dull the pain. She doesn't get about much and not a lot gets done unless I do it. Come on.' He strode on.

'What does the doctor say?'

His father ignored the question. Andrew reached out a hand and touched his father's shoulder.

'The doctor, Dad. What does the doctor say?'

His father stopped. 'She doesn't want to bother the doctor. She's scared of what the doctor might do; she doesn't want an operation.'

Andrew persisted: 'And you, Dad? What do you think?'

'I think she has cancer.'

13th February, 1936

Andrew put on his tweed suit and wrapped one of his father's long scarves around his neck. Lighting a cigarette to clear the smell of sherry from his head, he left the cottage to go in search of Peter.

Andrew warmed up with the brisk walk to the Ellis household. He found Peter tidying up fallen leaves in the front garden. Peter's face beamed with pleasure at his friend's arrival and he set Andrew to work pruning the overgrown shrub roses that lined the path.

'It's not something my Dad is very hot on, gardening,' Peter said in an apologetic tone. 'I'm glad you volunteered for the pruning because I have absolutely no idea what that's about.'

'My father does little else these days,' Andrew explained. 'I've never pruned anything in my life before; he'd never let me near his precious roses. But I've watched him and listened to him often enough to know the principle.'

'I suppose the important thing is to make enough weaving room for my Dad on his landing approach.'

Both men laughed.

'How is he?'

Peter sighed: 'Asleep, probably still drunk. Finally got him to bed at three this morning. His nightmares are really bad at the moment. I'm wondering if it's not my fault for joining the army and forcing him to dredge it all up again.'

Andrew paused in his pruning. 'Look, Peter. You can't be responsible for the last war, largely because I suspect they will make us responsible for the next one.' Andrew lit a fresh cigarette.

'Do you think it will really happen?' Peter paused in his work, leaning on his rake. 'Even with the League of Nations and all the politicians and everything?'

'Hitler's a politician. Mussolini's a politician. Stalin's a politician.' Andrew sighed a lung full of smoke out into the crisp air.

'Yes, but they're soldiers as well,' said Peter.

'So, my dear boy, are you.' Andrew arched his eyebrows. 'What time does the pub open?'

'Round about now, I suppose.'

The previous evening's storm had dragged behind it clear skies and still air. The watery, late morning sun dried the puddles from the road as the two men strolled down to the quayside and on to Bakery Road.

They arrived at The Anchor just as the doors opened. Andrew ordered two pints of mild ale and they sat in a window seat facing across the road into the crush of buildings and narrow alleys opposite. Sipping his ale, Andrew spotted a small boy run down an alley onto the pavement. The boy carried a crude toy pistol carved from a tree root.

Andrew nudged Peter: 'Watch this.'

The boy moved along the pavement and slipped into the shadows of a doorway. After a few moments another boy carrying a broom-handle rifle advanced gingerly down the alley onto the pavement. The second boy glanced one way and then the other. He moved cautiously in the opposite direction to his hiding enemy. The first boy peeped out from his hiding place and in an ecstasy of triumph leapt out, pumping three imaginary bullets into the back of his foe. 'Bang! bang! bang!'

Andrew barked a laugh into the pub's quiet, fuggy atmosphere. 'That boy would make an excellent fighter pilot. Here, fancy a game of darts?'

18th February, 1936

Andrew sat on the wooden bench outside the station, the morning newspaper folded on his lap. Peter sat next to him and they both stared across the road at the small, wet meadow where half a dozen horses grazed. The paper brimmed with stories about the Socialist election victory in Spain two days before and the shockwaves caused by the unexpected result. Already the Spanish politicians moved to deny the victory and prevent the formation of the Socialist government. The front page bore a photograph of Franco, the figurehead of right-wing opposition. Cold determination ran through the man's strong face.

'I'm scared.' Peter's voice sounded small.

'What's there to be scared of?' Andrew spoke around his cigarette.

'I'm scared sick of people like him having the power to affect my life.' Peter stabbed at Franco's photograph with his finger. 'I mean, if *we* don't like a new government we just bloody well wait for the next election. We don't go starting a bloody war.'

'Come on now, Peter. No one's started a war.'

'Yet!' Peter erupted with emotion, 'No one's started a war *yet*.' He turned wild eyes to stare at Andrew. Abruptly the wildness softened with welling tears and his voice dropped to little more than a whisper: 'We talk about it all the time. Europe with its bloody dictators. But no one ever really thought it would happen.' For a moment he fell silent and tears dropped from the end of his nose, splashing on the toes of his polished boots. He drew a great shuddering breath: 'And now the bloody stupid Spaniards have made it all more likely.'

Andrew remained silent.

'I'm signed up for five bloody years, Andrew. Five bloody, stinking years and there's no way out. The French will soon be surrounded by fascists. And those bastards can't fight their way out of a wet paper bag on their own. I'm first in the bloody queue for the trenches and thanks to my bloody father I know exactly what's going to happen to me.'

Peter dropped his face into his hands and melted into the sobs that wracked his chest.

Andrew put his arm around Peter's shoulders: 'Come on, my friend. It's still a long way from that.'

'Fuck it!' Peter's hands muffled his voice. 'Oh, fuck it!'

The steam whistle cut through the air and Andrew checked his watch.

'I've got to go, Peter. Listen to me.' Andrew pulled Peter's head up, cradling the other's cheeks in his hands. 'If and when we get dragged into whatever happens, you and I will be old hands. We'll be bloody professionals. What you know... what you've been taught, will protect you. Do you understand me, Peter?'

Peter nodded through his misery.

Andrew stood up, grabbed his bag and spun on his heel in one fluid motion. Striding towards the train, he called back over his shoulder: 'Goodbye, Peter. I'll see you again soon.' He didn't look back and he heard no reply.

Andrew climbed into the carriage and hoisted his bag onto the overhead rack. He stood transfixed for a moment, a hard knot of emotion tightening at the base of his throat. The prospect of war and the raw emotion of his friend's fears excited him, made him aware of the pulse of his blood and the tingling surface of his skin.

Breathing deeply, he sat down near the window. Through the billowing steam he spotted his friend walking away up the hill towards the town. He walked back to his father and his father's nightmares.

'God bless you, Peter my friend,' Andrew whispered under his breath.

CHAPTER 7

Initium

28th February, 1936

Gerry scanned the blackboard for his next pupil, groaning when he found the name. Mr Beamish had taken dozens of lessons and was still a way off flying solo. Gerry wanted to dump Beamish, but Max viewed him as regular income so the lessons continued.

Gerry zipped up his overalls and walked out towards the old Brougham cabin plane. Mr Beamish stood by the wing waiting, fidgeting with excitement.

'Gerry, my good man. Hello, wonderful day for flying,' he called.

'Good morning, Mr Beamish. Yes, wonderful.'

As Gerry walked across the grass, Max drove between him and the Brougham in the airfield truck. Max waved, the pipe jammed in his face spewed a dancing plume of smoke behind him. Gerry paused as the truck careered out through the main gate towards town. Max would be away for at least half an hour. Gerry looked back at Mr Beamish and made a decision.

Gerry strapped himself into the seat of the plane next to Mr Beamish. He waggled the joystick on his side of the cabin and made certain his pupil's dual control duplicated the motion. He did the same with the rudder bar.

'Okay, Mr Beamish, let's do the pre-flight checks.' Gerry watched the big man go through the routines he'd learnt by heart.

'Switches off.'

'Petrol on.'

'Throttle closed.'

'Brakes on.'

The mechanic forced the propeller round three turns to prime the engine. Standing back, he gave Beamish the thumbs-up. Beamish cooed with delight and shouted 'Contact!' as he pulled the starter ring. The starter cartridge fired with a sharp bang, kicking the engine into life. Beamish, chuckling and murmuring, let the engine run at quarter throttle until the oil temperature rose sufficiently. He glanced at Gerry.

Gerry nodded.

The big man melted with pleasure. 'Chocks away,' he shouted.

The mechanic ran clear, pulling the chocks behind him on long ropes. Beamish released the brakes and taxied to the end of the runway. He swung the plane into the wind and turned to Gerry.

'You know what to do, Mr Beamish.'

Beamish sagged in his seat and his smile paled. A tremor crept into his hands. He licked his lips and cast a fevered look over the dials. Finally he centralised the control column and threw the throttle forward.

As the plane moved across the grass the nose crept out to the left. Normally Gerry would correct this with the rudder control on his side of the cabin. This time he let the aircraft drift. Beamish darted his eyes from one dial to the next as if he'd lost something.

Gerry's foot hovered over the rudder.

Beamish glanced up and saw the swerve. He kicked the rudder, over-compensating. The nose swung to the right and the starboard wing dipped towards the ground. Beamish kicked opposite rudder. The plane wallowed back to a straight course and picked up speed.

Beamish glanced down at the airspeed indicator. Satisfied he had sufficient speed, he eased the column forward to raise the tail. Gerry eyed his pupil's trembling hands; an exaggerated move would drive the nose too far down and put the propeller into the ground. Beamish held his nerve and the tail rose off the grass. He eased the column back and the main wheels followed. He'd moved too early and the wheels dropped to the grass again. Beamish let the speed build a bit more before lifting the machine off the ground and staying airborne.

As they gained height Gerry looked at his pupil. Beamish had stopped trembling and fidgeting, he'd stopped cooing and chuckling. The rapt concentration on the big man's face suggested Mr Beamish had become a flyer. Gerry smiled and relaxed. The first part of the gamble had paid off.

'Okay, Mr Beamish,' Gerry shouted over the engine's din, 'let's take her round in a wide left-hand circuit and land her.'

His pupil's face stayed rock solid but his eyes darted sideways at Gerry in trepidation.

'Come on, Mr Beamish,' Gerry shouted, 'you've spent long enough enjoying your flying lessons. It's time to enjoy being a pilot.'

Beamish gave a stiff nod and turned into the circuit. Gerry sat back, his muscles tightened in apprehension. He'd instructed Beamish on the procedures for landing many times, but the man had never landed without assistance.

Grim concentration creased the pupil's brow as the plane banked into the landing approach.

'Relax into it, Mr Beamish. You are part of the machine.'

Beamish throttled back and lost height, settling into a shallow glide. He dropped the flaps as he crossed the airfield's boundary. Correcting a slight yaw with a touch of rudder he allowed the plane to sink to within a yard of the ground. Easing back on the column he held the plane off until it stalled and sank to the grass. Gerry released a deep breath as Beamish brought the plane to halt.

'Well done, Mr Beamish. Let me get out and you can do it all again on your own.'

Gerry smiled into his pupil's pallid face, undid his straps and opened the door. Once clear, Gerry gave Beamish a wave and watched him taxi back to the end of the runway. The engine pitch gunned higher and the Brougham ran into the wind for a smooth take off.

The sound of the plane's engine mingled with another and Max pulled up in the truck, a tin of coffee on the passenger seat. He squinted skywards at the climbing trainer.

'Who's that?'

'Mr Beamish,' Gerry replied.

Max shook his head: 'Gerry, either you really are a genius or you'll be buying me a new plane tomorrow.'

Gerry looked back to the sky as Beamish lined up for his first solo landing.

24th May, 1936

Every 20 yards across the field a white pole stuck up from the grass. Atop each pole sat two horn-shaped loudspeakers, each bedecked with red, white and blue ribbons. They spewed out marching music in a haunting, tinny register. Between each pole white rope hung looped at waist height.

Behind the rope stood a bank of spectators ten deep, all dressed in their Sunday best. Families had picnics laid out amongst the throng, couples stood arm in arm sharing binoculars, and small groups of uniformed servicemen mingled throughout the crowd. Just in front of the rope a line of small boys sat cross-legged or lay prone with chins cupped in hands, staking out the best view possible. Away and beyond them stretched Biggin Hill airfield and its runway. In the distance, at the end of the runway, stood six silver fighter planes. Their engine noise drifted across the field, causing a ripple of anticipation to run through the crowd.

The ghostly marching band was interrupted as a man's voice crackled over the Tannoy:

'Ladies and gentlemen, boys and girls. Good afternoon and welcome to our Empire Day air pageant for 1936. To begin today's flying exhibition we have members of 64 Squadron who, until recently, served as sentinels of the Empire stationed in Egypt, bravely guarding British possessions against the menace of Italian invasion. Let's give them a round of applause, ladies and gentlemen please, as they take off in their Demon fighters.'

Andrew, leading the second section of three aircraft, sat in the vibrating cockpit with eyes fixed on the control tower. Nerves nibbled at his stomach. On his port side sat Alan Gold, on his starboard side, George Anders, both watching him intently. The seconds ticked on and the oil temperature crept higher. At last a flare launched from the control tower's balcony and barrelled skywards leaving a spiral of black smoke drifting across the sky. The flare curved lazily at the top of its trajectory and blossomed into a bright green ball – the signal to go.

Andrew eased the throttle forward and held his left arm straight in the air, his anxiety melting with the sudden ability to act. He fixed his attention on Squadron Leader Fenton at the head and centre of the section of three Demons ahead. Fenton also had his left arm raised. He glanced left, then right and dropped his arm. Fenton's three fighters surged forward across the grass. Andrew sat clenched in his cockpit, his aircraft straining against its brakes.

Seeing the leader's arm fall, Andrew began his countdown: 'One, one thousand. Two, one thousand. Three, one thousand.'

Andrew dropped his own arm, released the brakes and pushed the throttle fully open. His section charged across the grass, tight on the tails of the others.

****

Molly Lloyd tottered on tiptoe as the engine noise grew louder, but could see nothing. She stood a little over 5ft tall and was stuck behind the wall of spectators. Suddenly three silver aircraft surged into the air above their heads, moving fast from right to left. She gasped as three more bi-planes followed them.

The racket of aero-engines intensified as the tight-packed formation banked to starboard away from the crowd. Molly stood rapt at the impossible spectacle and her back tingled with excitement. She watched the planes bob and drift in their places, sweeping through a wide climbing turn. As the formation wheeled further to the right and out of sight, Molly elbowed her way through the press of people.

'Ladies and gentlemen' – the Tannoy sounded feeble after the aural assault of six radial engines – 'the squadron will now demonstrate the fate awaiting any enemy bombers who dare to venture into their territory. The first section will play the part of the enemy bombers and the second section will be our defending fighters.'

Andrew raised his arm into the buffeting slipstream, then dropped his hand back onto the controls to peel his section off from the formation and lead them into a full-power climb away from the airfield. The remaining three fighters in the leading section throttled back and formed up in line astern. Reaching the pre-planned altitude, Andrew levelled out his formation and circled.

'There they are, ladies and gentlemen' – the Tannoy rang out – 'the fighter section has mounted a standing patrol to defend the innocent civilian population from the ravages of indiscriminate enemy bomber attack.'

Molly reached the rope barrier and gazed up at the silver shapes circling overhead.

'What's this, ladies and gentlemen? Look out, here come those bombers!'

Andrew waved his hand in a circle above his head. Alan and George dropped out of their V formation and reformed in line astern behind him. Looking down he picked out the three mock-bombers approaching the far end of the field. Judging his moment, Andrew rolled his bi-plane onto its

'How can it be?' Andrew leant forward onto the card table: 'We talked for no more than a minute.'

'So what's the flap? Forget her.'

'That's the problem, Bryan.' Andrew lit a cigarette. 'She keeps barging her way into my thoughts.'

Bryan collected the cards from the table. 'You can borrow my car anytime, you know,' he said, shuffling the pack. 'Go and see her. Clear your head.' He stopped shuffling and arched an eyebrow: 'You might even get a haircut.'

****

The telephone jangled on the wall, catching Molly halfway through rolling a curler into her customer's grey hair. The telephone fell silent for a second and jangled again.

'Just a moment, just a moment…' Molly panted through a mouthful of hairpins. She finished the curler and impaled it into position with a pin. Dropping the other hairpins onto her tray she grabbed the telephone from its cradle halfway through the fourth ring.

'Hello, Lloyd's hairdressing, Molly speaking. How can I help?'

A momentary silence crackled at the end of the line before an unfamiliar voice spoke up.

'Is it all right to visit your shop even if I don't need a haircut?'

Molly frowned: 'Why would you want to do that, sir?'

'I got the impression you would quite like me to.'

Molly's back stiffened.

'Who's calling, please?' This time the answer came immediately.

'My name's Andrew. You gave me your card when we spoke at the air pageant. I'm so sorry if I've misunderstood, only I've got some leave to take and I thought I might drop by and take you to lunch or something. I'm so sorry if—'

'No' – Molly's heart raced – 'no, really. That would be wonderful.'

Molly's half-finished customer eyed her quizzically in the mirror. Molly turned her back on the woman and lowered her voice.

'When were you thinking of?' she asked.

The voice on the telephone relaxed: 'This weekend. I'll borrow a car and drive across. Is there an inn or something where I can stay?'

'Yes. The Crown. They always have space.'

'All right, Saturday it is.'

'I work in the morning, but we close at one.'

'Excellent, I'll see you then.'

'Yes. Goodbye.'

Molly put the telephone back into its cradle and leant against the wall. A single minute had changed everything: a man from a daydream had suddenly become real. Long moments passed as she breathed heavily and enjoyed the buzz of her happiness. A polite cough from behind her brought her back to her senses. She wheeled on her heel and grabbed the hairp: from the tray.

'Right, where were we?'

4th July, 1936

Andrew set off early in Bryan's Humber, grinding the gears as he d out of the aerodrome gates. It was well over 100 miles from the squa 's airfield in Suffolk to Biggin Hill in the outer reaches of south London.

Making good time, he skirted the town of Ipswich, crossed the bridge and pointed the car south-west down the A12 to London. The road atlas flapped on the passenger seat as he leant on the open window and relaxed into the driving.

First Colchester, then Chelmsford rolled by. Half the journey completed and a sudden twinge of panic gripped his stomach. He really knew nothing about Molly, apart from her hairdressing trade, the name of the village where she plied that trade and the fact he'd kissed her soft, warm hand.

It was enough.

The thought of seeing her again transformed the mundane road trip into a flight of fancy, its dangerous excitement equal to the buffeting rush of a low-level barrel-roll taken at full throttle. His elation gripped him and he whooped his joy through the open window into the tree-lined fields beyond.

Heading into the East End sobered Andrew's mood. The traffic crushed in around the car, forcing him to concentrate on driving. Gradually the buildings became grander and he broke through the City onto the north side of the Thames.

Crossing the river by Tower Bridge he stole a glance over to the Tower of London before heading south to Croydon and searching out signposts for Biggin Hill.

Andrew spent the last eight miles to the aerodrome collecting his thoughts: 'Just be yourself, old man'.

The RAF signpost came up ahead and he took the dog-leg turn onto the northerly road running parallel to the runway. Over to his right a bright yellow Anson trainer hauled into the sky and banked away.

Andrew pulled onto the verge next to the aerodrome's main gate and a uniformed airman emerged from the guard hut to peer at him.

'I'm looking for the village' – he glanced down at Molly's card in his hand – 'Leaves Green?'

'Carry straight on, sir. Four hundred yards, you can't miss it.'

The road continued north, lined with densely-leaved trees which hid the hangars and runway from view, then curved left past The King's Head pub. The trees melted away as the road bisected a sprawling green surrounded by shops and houses. At the northern end of the green Andrew turned off into the Crown Inn's car park.

****

Molly cut and dried, curled and lacquered as the clock ticked on the wall. At half-past-eleven her last customer came in. While the woman settled herself in the chair, Molly looked out over the green, past the boys playing football, to the road where the traffic cruised by. She wondered where he might be. He must be close.

'Quiet in here today, love,' her customer broke into her musing.

'Yes, I'm meeting a friend this afternoon. You're my last booking.'

'How lovely, dear. What sort of friend?'

'Um, friend of the family,' Molly lied.

'Oh, how nice. What's her name?'

****

Andrew threw his suitcase and duffel bag onto the bed. There was no wardrobe in the cramped single room. But at least the door sported two coat hooks. He smoothed out his blue pilot's uniform and hung it with his clean white shirt behind the door. He placed his cap on the small dresser and retrieved a pair of gleaming shoes from the duffel bag, setting them down by the bed.

'That's more like it,' he muttered, 'just like home.'

He took his toilet bag into the small connecting bathroom and peered into the mirror. He dashed hair-tonic into his palm and plastered down the damage done by the car's slipstream. Washing the remnants of tonic from his hands, he splashed cold water onto his face, spluttering at the shock. Drying off on a crisp white towel, he returned to his critical appraisal in the mirror. Refolding the towel, he straightened his tie and looked his reflection in the eye.

'Tally-ho,' he smiled to himself.

****

Molly cleared up her pins and combs and took payment from her customer.

'Have a lovely afternoon, dear,' the lady said, tying her head-scarf, 'see you next time.'

The door banged shut. Molly threw the latch and walked back to the mirror. She fell to plumping her hair with a brush, tutting as she worked. A movement caught her attention and she gazed into the mirror, over her reflected shoulder and across the green.

A figure meandered across the grass in a brown tweed suit and mustard waistcoat, puffing a cigarette as he skirted around the footballing boys. Exhaling a long breath to steel her nerves, she grabbed her jacket and handbag from the coat-stand and left the shop. As she locked the door, she heard Andrew call out: 'Molly? Hello, Molly?'

She turned, smiling: 'Hello, Andrew.'

Andrew flicked away his cigarette and hurried over, bending to kiss her lightly on the cheek.

'I hope I'm not late. Is there somewhere we can get tea?'

'The King's Head stays open until three, I'm sure we could get something there.'

They walked off along the footpath at the edge of the grass. This far from the traffic the birdsong weaved around them undisturbed. Andrew talked about his journey and Molly informed him he was supposed to be a friend of the family called Alice.

Chuckling together they pushed open the doors and passed into the smoky bar of The King's Head. The drone of conversation dipped in volume for a moment as the regulars turned to weigh up the newcomers. Andrew led Molly to the bar.

'Hello, sir,' the barman greeted him. 'What'll it be?'

'Erm, tea. Do you do—'

Molly interrupted him: 'Tea for one, please' – then to Andrew – 'you must be gasping for a proper drink.'

'Oh, yes. Thank you,' he smiled at Molly. 'Tea for one and a pint of bitter, please.'

Andrew paid and they took their drinks to a table by the window. Molly stirred the pot of tea and poured a cup. Andrew lit a cigarette, taking the chance to study Molly's face. Sensing his gaze, she looked up from the tea and smiled.

'It's nice to have the chance to talk to you without an impatient wingman dragging me off,' he said. 'Still, he was good enough to lend me his car. Bryan. That's his name.'

Molly giggled as Andrew stumbled through the small-talk.

'You're a very good pilot,' she rescued him. 'You must love it very much.'

'Oh, yes.' Andrew hunched forward and took a swig from his beer. 'There's nothing quite like it. Even motorbikes don't come close, Molly. On a motorbike you are still a prisoner of the road. In an aeroplane you are absolutely free.'

'Isn't it dangerous, though?' she asked. 'They train pilots on the aerodrome up the road and it seems every other week something goes horribly wrong and someone ends up in hospital.'

'No more dangerous than motorbikes really.' Andrew exhaled a long stream of cigarette smoke through his nostrils. 'Except we've got guns strapped to our planes, which ups the risk level a bit, I suppose.'

'Are you worried about what's going on in Spain?' She sipped at her tea. 'The Germans. Are they a danger?'

'Their planes look a lot better than anything we've got.' Andrew pursed his lips, 'But I expect our boffins are hard at work on their drawing boards as we speak.'

Apprehensive silence hung between them for a moment.

Then Andrew brightened. 'It could be my chance to become a test pilot,' he breathed. 'Imagine.'

'Just imagine,' she mimicked with a laugh in her voice.

'I would be a real hero, Molly.' Andrew warmed to his subject: 'I'd leap into the cockpit of someone else's engineering theory, ride it into the crucible of the sky and put the contraption to the test with a series of dizzying manoeuvres.'

'Bravo!' Molly clapped her hands in playful applause.

'Then I'd wrestle the unruly beast back to the ground, tell the designer how it should be improved and stride off for a magnificent lunch.'

'Hurrah!'

'And when I slept, my rest would be like the sweet slumber of innocence, because tomorrow I might be…'

The silence dropped again, this time with more weight.

Andrew cleared his throat. 'Sorry,' he mumbled, 'got carried away.'

Molly smiled. 'You're not wrong, Andrew,' she said quietly. 'Maybe we should all eat, drink and be a bit merrier while we've still got the time.'

They left the pub and walked back around the green to Molly's shop.

'I promised you lunch,' Andrew said, 'and all you've had is a measly cup of tea.'

'We could take the bus to Croydon this evening, if you like,' Molly suggested, 'have something to eat there. And there's bound to be a dance we could pop into somewhere. It's Saturday night, after all.'

'That would be wonderful.'

'The bus-stop is right over there.' Molly pointed. 'Meet you at six to catch the five-past.'

****

Molly arrived at the bus-stop a few minutes early. The late afternoon sun still held some warmth and she closed her eyes as it bathed her face. Suddenly a shadow blocked the sunlight.

'Hello.'

She opened her eyes to look into Andrew's face, solid and handsome beneath his blue RAF cap. Her eyes dropped to his chest where his pilot's wings glittered with silver threads and the crested buttons gleamed.

'Ooooh.' She looked back up to his eyes: 'You're here.'

The bus pulled up behind Andrew, he pushed the door open and the couple jumped on.

The evening whirled around Molly's head like a dream. They bought pie and chips in a high street cafe, washed down with steaming mugs of tea. Then on to a pub where Molly allowed herself a gin and lemonade. They followed a crowd from the pub to the dance hall where they waltzed and two-stepped for a couple of hours – all of it filled with laughter and easy conversation.

The last bus home pulled into Leaves Green at a half-past midnight and the pair stepped down to the pavement, softly calling their goodnights to the driver.

'Thank you for a wonderful evening, Molly.' Andrew looked down into her face. 'Now, I should get you home before your parents call the police.'

'My parents live on the south coast. They're retired.' Molly returned his gaze. 'They had me late in life,' she explained. 'I live alone in the flat above the hairdresser's.'

'Oh.'

'Shhhsh.' Molly reached up and drew his face to her kiss.

5th July, 1936

Bryan Hale heard his Humber crunch onto the shingle outside the mess.

'Hail the conquering hero,' he murmured under his breath and strode out through the door towards the car.

'Bryan,' Andrew called, halfway out of the car-seat, 'thank you so much, my friend. I've had a wonderf—'

'Andrew,' Bryan interrupted, 'your father's been on the phone. It's your mother, old boy. I'm afraid she's passed away.'

Andrew slumped back into the seat. 'When?'

'About ten-thirty last night.'

10th July, 1936

Winston washed out the coffee mugs in the canteen sink. 'What are your plans for the weekend, Gerry? Where are you taking the lovely Devline?'

Gerry didn't raise his head from his newspaper: 'Nothing planned.'

'Oh, big mistake, Mr Donaldson. You've gotta' treat 'em special if you want to keep 'em happy.' Winston returned to the table with the clean mugs. He sat down opposite Gerry. 'That bothering you?' he nodded at the newspaper.

Gerry looked up and frowned: 'It's a civil war, Winston. People are being bombed out of their homes, people are getting killed. Of course it bothers me.'

Winston screwed up his face: 'It's in Spain, right?'

Gerry nodded.

'So if Washington particularly want you to get involved I'm sure they'll ask the President to let you know.' Winston poured two mugs of fresh coffee. 'So up to, and until, you get a call from the President, you have the perfect right to enjoy your life here and now… and tomorrow.' Winston smiled and sipped his coffee. 'So call Devline and tell her what you're doing together on Saturday night before she walks out on you for a man who keeps his head at home.'

Gerry flipped the paper around to show Winston the double-page spread.

'Have you ever seen aircraft like this?' Gerry pointed to a huge double-engine bomber formation.

'Or this?' He pointed to another picture, this one showing a gull-winged dive-bomber.

'Or this?' He pointed to a robust monoplane fighter with squared-off wing tips.

Winston looked from one to the other and scratched his chin.

'They're German planes, Winston. German planes fighting on the side of fascism in Spain. They're clawing the Spanish bi-planes out of the sky. And the best thing about it? The French and British have nothing but the same bi-planes to stop the Germans when they've finished in Spain and want to play war somewhere else.'

Gerry's voice had risen. He cleared his throat and continued in a normal tone: 'I'm sorry if all of that bothers me, but that's the way it is.'

PART 2

Arduum

CHAPTER 8

Amans

3rd September, 1939

'...and I have to tell you that no such undertaking has been received. Consequently this country is at war with Germany. You can imagine...'

Click.

The sound of the switch reverberated into a virgin silence immediately shattered with shouts of outrage from the assembled pilots.

Bryan turned to confront the complaints: 'What does it matter what else he says? It's on, lads, that's all that matters. It's bloody well on.'

Two airmen pushed Bryan aside and the radio crackled back to life behind him.

Bryan walked over to where Andrew sat fiddling with his box camera. Leaning over his friend, Bryan chewed his lip with relish. 'It's on, Andrew. Bloody official this time. It's bloody well on.'

'I heard,' Andrew said without looking up.

'Come on, take a picture of me in front of my aeroplane. One for the album, what do you say?'

Andrew got up, following Bryan out towards the Blenheims lined up outside the readiness hut. The dun green, double-engine aircraft stood impassive, blunt noses pointing skywards.

Away from the noise of the hut, Andrew stopped. 'This is a day we need to remember, Bryan. This is the last ever day of its kind.'

Bryan slapped him on the shoulder. 'Bog-rot,' he said, and jogged towards his aircraft. 'Let's get this photograph taken before the Germans invade.'

Andrew smiled and walked after him.

He stumbled to a halt as a cacophonous roar ripped through the still afternoon air. A Blenheim tore through the treetops at the far edge of the airfield. A panel peeled away from the underside, spinning from the craft in a spiral of duck-egg blue. The port undercarriage swung loose and the engines screamed with an urgent ferocity as the pilot fought to drag his plane higher. The stricken machine clattered over Andrew's head, dragging behind it a swirling vortex of leaves and twigs.

'Look out!' Andrew shouted into the maelstrom.

Bryan spun in mid-stride, his momentum carrying him over onto his bottom, and he flopped flat on his back as the plane zoomed overhead.

The pilot gained only enough height to take out the tops of the trees on the opposite side of the field. The impact jolted the nose up and the plane hung in haughty indignation at the top of its stall before swooping into the beet field beyond the copse. They heard a crunch of rending metal and the resounding *thunk* of engines abruptly halted by heavy soil. Black smoke crept up over the shattered tree-line and a flock of starlings rattled around the sky in the sudden silence.

'Bloody hell!' Bryan gasped, still lying on his back. 'He got that a bit wrong.'

'Come on Bryan, let's help the poor bastards!'

Bryan clambered to his feet and chased Andrew through the trees, over the shallow perimeter ditch and into the field beyond. Both men stopped in horror.

The Blenheim had hit a brick farm-building and the wreckage of both intermingled in a chaotic swathe across the field. One wing blazed with the sharp odour of aviation fuel. An engine lay stripped of its cowling, ticking as it cooled and bleeding thick, black oil into the earth.

The two men skirted the wreckage and came across a body.

'Flying alone, do you think?' Andrew murmured.

Bryan nodded: 'Courier type, I suppose. Delivering a new kite. Anyway, there aren't any bits big enough to hide anyone else.'

The pilot lay at the apex of the wreckage pattern, face down in a furrow, the breeze tugging at his hair. A twisted propeller rested across his legs and behind him one wing lay broken and stripped like a huge sea creature washed up on a beach.

'Two trees and a brick shithouse,' Bryan said in mock admiration. 'And we've only been at war for three minutes.'

The bell on an approaching ambulance jangled.

'I'll go and tell them there's no hurry.'

Bryan sauntered back around the brick-strewn wreckage and disappeared into the trees. Andrew raised the camera to his eye.

****

Andrew sat back on his haunches watching the ambulance crew lift the pilot onto a stretcher. The limbs flopped around their shattered bones. In places blood seeped into the uniform and a large wet patch soiled the man's trousers. The stretcher-bearers turned the pilot to lie on his back and Andrew looked into his face. The coarse soil had scoured the skin from his forehead and the impact had crammed his eye sockets with earth. Striations in the flesh, gouged by sharp fragments of stone, oozed a clear liquid that glistened against the dirt. The man's broken jaw sagged onto his chest, leaving his tongue-less mouth agape. Yet still the breeze tugged at his hair.

Andrew stood as the ambulance crew hefted the stretcher. A glint of sunlight flashed on the dead man's wedding ring as they carried him away.

Andrew switched his gaze to the fire crew dousing the wreckage with foam. The Blenheim's fuselage lay like a shattered torso, brittle bones piercing its aluminium skin. The trunking and wiring coiled across the ground like twisted intestines, bright and colourful in the autumn sunshine. Scorched and burnt perspex lay scattered around like pork crackling and the sordid stench of burning rubber hung heavy over the scene.

Andrew flew this same type of aircraft. This is what happened when one of them fell from the sky. He walked back through the trees to the readiness hut.

For the next hour Andrew tried to write a letter. For much of the time he stared at the blank writing paper. No words would sit well on the page:

'Dear Molly, I've just witnessed a terrible crash…'

'Dear Molly, now we're at war there's every chance I shall be killed…'

'Dear Molly…'

Defeated, he sat and stared out across the field at the Blenheims until the squadron came off readiness.

****

Avoiding company, Andrew walked to the aerodrome gates and the telephone box just outside. While he waited for the operator to connect his call a smile crept across his face for the first time since the crash.

'You're through now, caller.' The operator's impassive voice cut through his thoughts.

'Hello, Molly Lloyd here.'

Andrew's smile broadened: 'Hello Molly. It's Andrew. Listen, darling, I love you. I want us to get married and have a baby…'

A moment's silence stretched down the line. When Molly answered he could sense tears in her voice: 'That would be wonderful.'

'Are you all right, Molly? I'm sorry this is a bit sudden, it's just—'

'I heard on the radio,' Molly cut across him. 'I heard that things… might get difficult. I hoped you'd call. Andrew, if you hadn't asked me I might've asked you. I want to spend the rest of my life with you…'

The line fell silent while each of them caught up with what they'd said.

Andrew broke the silence: 'Go and see the vicar, darling. I've got three days' leave at the end of the month. I'm sure they'll still let me go. Talk to the vicar and let me know what he says.'

'I will, darling. Bye, bye.-' Molly's voice sounded far away and lost.

Andrew listened to the buzz of the disconnected line for a few moments before he hung up the receiver.

Walking to his room, his thoughts drifted back to the dead pilot. The man's wife wouldn't be told about the crash until tomorrow or even the next day. Andrew pictured this faceless woman preparing her evening meal, maybe putting her child to bed. Certainly she'd heard the news of war, but perhaps she'd taken comfort in the thought that her husband worked as a ferry pilot. That's safe enough, she'd think to herself as she closed her eyes to sleep tonight. But tomorrow they'd tell her. Tomorrow or the next day.

****

Vincent sat in his room. With his father in the house he couldn't relax, but being alone helped. A voice on the radio wafted up from the sitting room, but Vincent couldn't make out the words. The radio stopped and his father's voice took over. His mother's voice sounded next, raised in protest, cut short by the slap of hand on flesh.

A commotion broke out at the foot of the stairs, his mother's sobs grew louder accompanied by his father's rasping breath as he dragged her up the staircase. His mother landed on her iron bed, the force of the impact clattered the bedhead against the wall.

Vincent clawed open his door and lurched out onto the landing.

'Stop it! Please… Stop it.'

Samuel's back stiffened and he turned to face his son. With his left hand he loosened his belt; with his right he grabbed Vincent's face and pushed the boy back into his room. Vincent's head banged against the door and he sprawled out on the floorboards, coming to rest with a jolt against the chest of drawers. The door bounced back on its hinges and swung shut.

After a moment's silence there came a tearing of fabric and the rhythmic clanking of bed against wall.

Vincent clambered to his feet and stared out of his bedroom window, his hands pressed over his ears. The clanking continued, undercut by his mother's gasping sobs. Vincent could taste his own fear. It was too much.

He pushed some clothes into a duffel bag and retrieved his saved wages from the sock drawer. Opening his bedroom door carefully, he slipped across the landing and crept down the stairs. As he pulled his coat from the hook and opened the front door, the noises behind him approached a crescendo. Biting his lip until the oily taste of blood filled his mouth, Vincent closed the door on his family and hurried down the street towards the railway station.

4th September, 1939

The train pulled into Liverpool Street station and the passengers stood, retrieved briefcases and shuffled to the doors. Vincent remained huddled in his seat. For the last few hours the train had done his running away for him and he'd sat passive in its grip. Now he looked at the terminus platform with abject trepidation.

A cleaner moved through the carriage. 'Are you all right, son?'

Vincent nodded: 'Just tired.'

Vincent stepped down from the carriage and closed the door. The station's noises and smells crashed in on his senses. The rushing of steam and the sweet, pungent scent of the engines filled the vast space around him. Vincent wandered down the platform, handed his ticket to the collector at the gate and walked onto the main concourse.

He'd never seen so many people, all hurrying about their business. Many men in different service uniforms departed or arrived with their mothers or girlfriends crying or smiling. Policemen stood around the periphery, watching and waiting. Porters weaved their way through the crowd and hawkers shouted above the din selling newspapers full of the news of war.

A swathe of bunting tied across the front of a trellis desk caught his eye. Above the desk a sign read: 'Join the RAF here.'

15th September, 1939

Andrew found Bryan in the mess reading a newspaper.

'Hello, Bryan. How would you like a promotion?'

Bryan folded the paper and looked at Andrew through narrowed eyes.

'I'd accept nothing less than wing commander, but I fail to see what you could do about that.'

'I need to promote you from Chauffeur to Best Man. I've just received a note from Peter saying he can't make it, but he can't tell me why.'

'Ah, dear boy, that's exactly why it's called "Best Man" rather "Best Friend".' Bryan tilted his chair backwards and lit a cigarette. 'And I consider myself eminently qualified, so the answer is 'yes" – he blew out a stream of blue smoke – 'as long as you buy me a pint.'

When Andrew returned to the table with two pints, Bryan tossed the paper onto his lap.

'Looks like the Government is sending your friend Peter off on a little trip to France with the British Expeditionary Force' – Bryan paused in mock reflection – 'you'd think they'd change the name after the shambles the last one got into.'

Andrew scanned the article. 'Peter's dad took part in that shambles. He's hardly been sober for a day since he got back.'

'At least he got home. How many of these young scrotes are likely to survive a garden party with the whole German Army?'

'Well hopefully, now we've got soldiers on the ground, the Nazis will stay their side of the Maginot Line.'

'I admire your optimism, Andrew. Now Hitler's got Austria and Poland, he'll likely want France as well' – Bryan took a swig of beer – 'wherein lies the tragedy.'

Andrew shook his head: 'Which tragedy are you talking about?'

'I don't expect Hitler really wants war with England. But we've just sent our entire bloody army to stop him taking France.'

'Meaning?'

'Meaning, when he's killed or captured the whole of the Glorious BEF, a defenceless Britain will look a whole lot more attractive.'

'Come on, Bryan. Surely the British Army has at least an evens chance of winning this one?'

Bryan took a deep draw on his cigarette: 'Let's say they're shipping out 400,000 troops, more or less. Obviously the French Army will sit in their lovely safe bunkers and gun emplacements on the Maginot Line. So the only place they'll have left to put our poor bloody infantry is in a long thin line along the French-Belgian border.'

'But Belgium is neutral' – Andrew trailed off in thought – 'so instead of attacking the Maginot Line you think the Germans will go through Belgium?'

'If it's obvious to me, it's obvious to Hitler.' Bryan took another deep draught from his glass. 'Punch a hole through the British lines and drive as much artillery as you can in a straight line to Paris' – Bryan grimaced a sickly smile – 'lob a couple of hundred shells towards the Eiffel Tower and the French will be falling over themselves to surrender. Which puts the British Army firmly up shit creek.'

Andrew slumped back in his chair, frowning.

'So,' Bryan chirped up, 'enough of advanced military strategy, let's talk about this Best Man lark.'

30th September, 1939

Andrew's eyes wandered over the whitewashed walls and up to the ancient oak beams of the roof. He stole a glance at his watch.

'How can she be late?' he hissed, 'she only lives a mile down the road.'

Bryan raised an eyebrow: 'Did you not pack a parachute?'

'I do *not* need a parachute. Thank you, Bryan.'

'Looks like it's too late to bail out anyway.'

The vicar emerged from the vestry, taking up his position in front of the two men, and the ancient organ ground out the opening bars of the *Wedding March*.

'Atten-tion!' Bryan muttered under his breath and craned his head over his shoulder for a look at the bride.

'Good Lord,' he murmured, 'well done, old man.'

Andrew held his gaze fixed at a point over the vicar's left shoulder until a bustle and sway of fabric announced Molly's arrival at his side. He turned to look at her as her father retreated to the front pew.

Molly gazed up at him, unveiled. Her cream cap-sleeved gown was covered with a delicate pattern of leaves. The fabric hugged her figure to just above her knee and then flared out to the ground, forming a small oval train behind her. The neckline looped down under her throat and the fitted bodice accentuated the rise and fall of her breathing. In her hands she carried a bouquet of small sunflowers.

'Hello darling,' he whispered.

Molly smiled and turned to face the vicar.

****

The village hall thrummed to the musical murmur of happy conversation as the wedding guests tucked into sandwiches, cakes and tea. Andrew spotted Bryan talking with Mr and Mrs Lloyd and sauntered across to their group.

Andrew shook Mr Lloyd's hand and smiled warmly at his mother-in-law: 'Thank you both for coming up and helping us with the spread.'

'Don't mention it, Andrew, you're family now,' the older man said. 'I was just asking Mr Hale what he thought about the situation in France.'

'Oh, dear—'

'He seems to think the British Army will stop the Huns in their tracks and it will all be over within the year.'

Andrew glanced at Bryan who smiled and nodded sagely.

'Well, Mr Lloyd, I hope that is the case,' Andrew said. 'I'd prefer not to get into a bun fight with the Luftwaffe.'

Andrew and Bryan drifted back to the buffet.

'So, now you think the British Army will stop the Germans in their tracks?'

'Of course not,' Bryan snorted, 'but it's not my place to scare the old folk, especially on a day like this.' He picked up a plate and browsed over the food: 'The fact is, sometime in the next six months or so, you and me could very well find ourselves floating face-down in the channel with our arse on fire.' He wolfed down a cucumber sandwich. 'Which is why' – he nodded across the room – 'you need to concentrate on that.'

Andrew followed his gesture and saw Molly chatting and laughing with his father.

'She is beautiful, isn't she?' he breathed.

'Which is why,' Bryan said around a mouthful of cake, 'you must leave her to me in your will. Just in case you get your arse burnt off first.'

87

CHAPTER 9

Totum

14th December, 1939

Andrew pulled his greatcoat closer around his chest and tucked his chin down further into his muffler. He glanced at Bryan's sallow features and turned back to watch the fitters manhandle the wood-burning stove into place in the corner of the dispersal hut.

'Can we light it yet?' The freezing air compressed Bryan's flat tone.

'No, sir. Not yet. We have to fit the chimney,' one of the fitters smiled in apology.

'Shall I kill him, Andrew?'

Andrew shook his head: 'No, I think he's doing his best.'

Andrew spoke through the vaporised breath rising around his face: 'Give him another 20 minutes.'

Bryan threw a cigarette into Andrew's lap and lit one for himself. 'Do you remember the last flap we were invited to attend?' Bryan screwed up his face in mock concentration. 'Camels… lots of sand…'

'Egypt.' Andrew lit the cigarette and held his fingertips over the still-burning match. 'That was Egypt.'

'Yes.' Bryan brightened. 'Egypt' – he nodded to himself – 'I seem to remember we did fuck-all fighting there. Just like here' – he wagged a finger in Andrew's face – 'except—'

'It was too bloody hot in Egypt,' Andrew intoned.

'Exactly.' Bryan relapsed into his seat, hunching deeper into his overcoat. 'And d'you know what?'

'What?'

'I'd rather do fuck-all fighting against the bloody Italians in the warm than do fuck-all fighting against the bloody Germans in the freezing bloody cold.'

'Come on, Bryan. You can hardly expect the Germans to invade in this weather.'

Bryan raised an incredulous eyebrow: 'We declared war on them two-and-a-half months ago, and what have the Luftwaffe done since then?'

'Nothing.'

'Precisely. The bastards.'

29th December, 1939

Bryan dropped the keys into Andrew's hand: 'Don't bend her. She's not much, but she's all I've got.'

'Don't worry, Bryan. It doesn't go fast enough to get bent.' Andrew climbed in and gunned the old Humber's engine. 'Thanks again, old man. I'll see you on the 2nd. If me and Molly don't get snowed in,' Andrew winked and pulled away.

Bryan watched him drive through the aerodrome gate and accelerate down the road. 'Oh, I forgot to tell you, the heater doesn't work.'

****

Dusk gathered in dense shadows as Andrew reached London. The snowbanks along the sides of the country roads gave way to pools of grimy slush on the city streets. The blacked-out capital surrendered to the fall of darkness and Andrew's progress slowed to a crawl amongst the dark shapes of pedestrians hurrying through the cold.

Once across the river he upped the pace as much as he dared and soon took the familiar dog-leg turn past Biggin Hill and cruised along the last stretch to Leaves Green. Pulling up outside the hairdressing shop, he grabbed his suitcase from the back seat and stepped out carefully onto the frozen tarmac.

After a couple of knocks, Molly appeared at the bottom of the stairs. Flicking on the shop lights, she unlatched the door and opened it wide.

'In!' she commanded. 'Hurry, it's freezing.'

'I know,' Andrew chided, 'that bloody tin box doesn't have a heater.'

Molly swung the door closed and Andrew leaned down to kiss her.

'Your nose is cold,' she said.

'So is everything else,' he smiled.

'Good,' she smiled back, 'then I have just the thing for you.'

She took his hand and led him up the stairs to the flat. In the living room the log fire popped and crackled, warming the air with a fragrant heat. In front of the fire stood a large tin bath, steam rising in lazy curls.

'That's for you,' Molly said. 'I've got more hot water on the stove.'

'You're an angel,' he said, unbuttoning his coat. 'I don't deserve you.'

'You probably don't deserve the pheasant and roast potatoes I have in the oven either' – she stood on tip-toes and kissed the end of his nose – 'but you're the best I've got so I'll let you have some.'

Andrew took his case through to the bedroom and undressed, laying his clothes out on the chair. The cooler air made him scamper back to the warmth of the fire.

As he lowered himself cautiously into the hot water, Molly came and knelt by the bath. She handed him a glass and took a sip from her own. Andrew raised an enquiring brow.

'Scotch and green ginger,' Molly said, 'Daddy's present to us both "before the rationing starts to bite".' She smiled and raised her glass: 'Happy belated Christmas, darling.'

Andrew sipped his drink and gazed into the fire: 'What hope is there for a happy new year?'

'Who knows,' Molly sighed, 'but we must make of it what we can.' She brightened: 'I think people feel a bit safer now the army has gone out to France. At least the Germans will see we mean business.'

'The trouble is they have to wait for Hitler to make another move and the longer we leave him to his own devices, the stronger he gets.' Andrew traced the line of Molly's chin with his fingers.

'There's a good chance he'll not settle until he has France at least.' Andrew sipped his drink. 'I'm beginning to think we should've hit him hard and fast in September.' he looked into Molly's eyes: 'We might have lost this war already, Molly. What's to become of us?'

Molly reached out, smoothing his frown with her thumb: 'Well, we can't change yesterday, because that's gone forever. We don't have tomorrow, because that doesn't yet exist. So that leaves us with today.'

'So what do we do with today?' Andrew smiled.

'Well, I've got you, you've got me, and we've both got roast pheasant.' Molly drained her glass. 'What do you want first?'

14th January, 1940

Andrew and Bryan stamped their feet against the cold. Above them the Hurricane squadrons circling Martlesham in the early morning haze broke up into sections of three and swooped in to land. It took ten minutes to bring the 36 fighters safely to the ground. As the last section of three touched down, the two men walked out to dispersal for a closer look.

They approached the nearest Hurricane just as its pilot climbed down from the wing.

'What's the flap, chum?' Bryan called out.

The pilot pulled a cigarette packet from his flying overalls. 'Administration cock-up,' he grimaced. 'Our forward station isn't ready yet, but we were airborne before they bothered to tell us. They thought we might be safer sitting here for a few hours rather than stooging around an undefended field in France.'

'You're off to France?' Andrew asked.

'You lucky buggers.' Bryan flicked his lighter and held the flame to the pilot's cigarette. 'Mind if we have a look over your kite?'

'Be my guest.' The man blew out a plume of smoke: 'I'm off to find a brew.'

Andrew and Bryan walked around the squat, solid fighter.

'This knocks spots off the carts they've given us to fly,' Bryan whistled. 'Eight machine guns, Andrew. Imagine the mess those will make.'

Climbing onto the wing they pulled back the canopy and peered in.

'That all looks very cosy,' Andrew murmured, running his fingers along the armour plating on the back of the seat.

'No bloody navigator farting in the cockpit, no gunner moaning about the cold.' Bryan waggled the stick and watched the ailerons move up and down. 'That would suit me fine.'

Andrew laughed and jumped down from the wing.

'Seriously, Andrew,' Bryan clunked the canopy shut and followed him, 'If I'd wanted to fly a boat complete with its own jolly little crew, I would've joined the Navy,' he waved his arm back at the Hurricane, 'I want of one those. Even if I have to demand a transfer to get one.'

'You wouldn't leave the squadron, would you?'

'They treat me like a bus driver, Andrew. I'm a fighter pilot, why won't they let me fight anyone.'

The two men trailed across the grass towards the mess.

11th February, 1940

Molly crunched her way across the stony beach, arm in arm with her mother. The impassive white facades of Eastbourne's guest houses faced out across the grey channel waters. Along the top of the beach soldiers unloaded scaffold poles from trucks while their comrades bolted them together in an ever-lengthening barrier along the front.

Florence Lloyd paused to watch the white-topped waves rear and fall into noisy collapse amongst the shingle.

'I love this beach,' she said. 'It's such a shame to think of what it might become. But I suppose we must abandon these things for the time being, in order to get on with war.'

Molly squeezed her mother's arm: 'We should keep moving. It's too cold for dawdling.'

'Do you think they would've come already, if it weren't for the weather?'

'They've got the British and French armies to deal with first, Mother. So you needn't worry yourself about them just yet.'

The older woman nodded at the tank-traps: 'Somebody, somewhere is worried about them.'

They headed back up the beach and climbed the steps to the road. Drab green lorries laden with scaffold poles growled past them as they walked the short distance to a cafe.

Sitting at a table in the window, two cups of steaming tea between them, Molly reached out to grasp her mother's hand.

'I have some good news, Mum,' she smiled. 'I'm going to have a baby.'

'That's wonderful. What does Andrew think?'

'I haven't told him yet.' Molly squeezed her mother's hand: 'I wanted to tell you first.' A grin flashed across her face: 'I'm saving it up to tell him on Valentine's Day.'

Florence's smile dropped and she looked down into her tea: 'It's not the best time to have a baby though, is it dear?'

Molly leant back into her chair: 'I've never told you before, but I was seeing Andrew for well over three years before we got married.'

'I guessed, dear,' her mother smiled. 'Your happiness was so' – she cast around for the right word – '*loud*, so I knew there was a special reason for it. What better reason than a handsome lover?'

Molly blushed at her mother's candour. 'So what I mean to say is, the pregnancy is very much planned. Andrew always talks about having children, so, what with everything else, we thought we'd better get on with it.'

Florence took a sip of her tea and gazed through the window. The grey smudge of the late-winter sky hid the coast of France from her view.

13th April, 1940

Andrew walked into the briefing hut, spotted Bryan in the front row and took the seat next to him. The room filled behind them.

'What's the gen, Bryan?'

Bryan pursed his lips: 'Who knows? Maybe we're off to bomb Wales by way of some practice.'

'It can't be an operational briefing,' Andrew swivelled his head to scan the crowd, 'there's only pilots in the room.'

'Must be a committee meeting to organise my leaving party.'

'What?'

'I told you, Andrew. I'm fed up with driving a bus. I put my transfer request in this morning.'

Andrew opened his mouth to protest but Squadron Leader Fenton entered the room and chairs scraped the floor as the assembled pilots stood to attention. Fenton walked to the dais and regarded them for a few moments across the silence.

'As you were, gentlemen,' he began, 'I won't keep you long. I have what many of you will regard as good news.' He smiled around at the expectant faces. 'Over the next couple of days we will be taking delivery of 18 factory-fresh Spitfires.'

'Bugger!' Bryan breathed to himself.

'A couple of bods from operational training will be staying with us for a week or so to get you all converted. Then, as soon as everyone's settled into flying the new kites, we'll be moving down to Kenley to become part of No. 11 group's defensive fighter screen for London.'

A ragged cheer broke out amongst the pilots. Bryan sank his head into his hands.

'For the duration of home defence operations, 64's code-name will be 'Bluebird'. Harry will give you details of the training timetable and hand out copies of pilot's notes for you to read at your leisure. Any general questions?'

The room remained quiet.

'Right then, I'll hand over to the adjutant' – he paused – 'Pilot Officer Hale?'

Bryan looked up: 'Yes, sir?'

'Don't look so miserable, old chap, I've already torn it up.'

'Yes, sir!' Relief flooded Bryan's face. 'Thank you, sir.'

The adjutant handed out the technical notes and gave a brief lecture about the capabilities of the new fighters. He fielded a few questions and dismissed the group. As he strode out, the whole room burst into excited conversation.

'Bloody Spitfires, Andrew!' Bryan's elation reddened his face. 'What could be better than bloody Spitfires?'

'Kenley!' Andrew exclaimed, 'Kenley is only ten miles from Molly!' He grabbed Bryan's cheeks between his thumbs and forefingers: 'We've hit the bloody jackpot.'

10th May, 1940

'Break camp! Come on lads, get it packed up, we're on the move,' the platoon sergeant yelled his way down the line of tents.

Peter crawled out into the early morning daylight.

'Jump to it.' The sergeant moved closer: 'Pull your fingers out.'

Peter stepped forward, saluting: 'Good morning, sarge,' he said as his sergeant strode past. 'Where are we off to?'

The sergeant spun on his heel. 'Ah' – his eyes narrowed and he leaned into his words – 'good morning, private. I trust you slept well?'

'Well, yes—'

'I'm pleased to hear it!' The sergeant's voice dropped to a low, menacing tone, 'There are hundreds of German paratroopers dropping out of the sky all over Belgium' – he waved his arm at the east – 'so me and the King thought you and the rest of the girls might like to go and have a chat with them.'

The sergeant stalked off, shouting as he went.

'What's happening, Pete?'

Peter turned to see his friend Angus hopping up and down, pulling on a boot.

'The war just stopped being phoney.' Peter's voice sounded brittle in his own ears. 'The Germans have invaded Belgium.'

The battalion's marching boots threw up a desultory haze of dust from the road. The column marched four abreast on the side of the road to allow the vehicles streaming north to overhaul them. A group of soldiers riding in the back of a truck jeered at their comrades trudging along on foot.

'What's up with those jokers?' Angus snorted. 'Anybody would think we were still fucking about on Salisbury Plain. This is one party I'm happy to walk to.'

'I can't believe it's happening.' Peter shook his head against the rhythm of the march: 'After all this time waiting for it, I still can't believe it's happening.'

'Oh, I can believe it's happening,' Angus said, 'I just can't believe they sent us across the channel to get caught up in a German invasion of bloody Belgium.'

'Better here than England.'

'Really?' Angus glanced around the surrounding fields and hedges. 'Where are they? Where are the bloody Germans?'

Peter nodded in the direction of the march: 'Up there somewhere.'

'Aye,' Angus retorted, 'setting up machine-gun nests and digging gun emplacements, no doubt.'

Peter swallowed hard but said nothing.

'I'd much rather be shooting them while they're trying to climb out of their boats on Brighton beach,' Angus continued, 'with a stack of ammunition by my side and all day to use it.'

'Column halt!' The order echoed down the road. 'Fall out. Ten minutes' rest.'

The soldiers sunk onto the grass verge, shedding their packs and rubbing their shoulders. The signpost across the road pointed the way to Ypres. Peter lit a cigarette and blew smoke into the sickly silence.

12th May, 1940

Andrew picked up his suitcase and kit-bag and made one last sweep of his room. Satisfied he'd forgotten nothing he strode out of the mess. An airman took his bags, hoisting them onto a truck already laden with dozens of cases.

'Thank you,' Andrew said. 'See you in Kenley.'

'Yes, sir,' the airman smiled. 'I expect you'll get there first though, sir.'

Andrew clumped his way across the field in his flying boots and overalls, heading towards the Spitfires lined up next to the grass runway. He spotted Bryan climbing into his own machine. Andrew whistled through his teeth and Bryan turned, flashing a ferocious grin from under his flying helmet.

Andrew reached his Spitfire and climbed onto the port wing. He took his parachute from the ground crew and placed it on the seat. Climbing into the cockpit he sat on top of the parachute and fastened the harness straps. He pulled on his leather flying helmet and plugged in the wireless lead. Adjusting the cockpit harness a notch tighter, he fastened it, testing his weight against the straps. He reached out to turn the petrol cocks on and checked the throttle lever had sufficient friction to keep it set where placed. He centred the elevator, rudder and aileron trims.

Andrew flicked the wireless to transmit: 'Bluebird Yellow Three to Homebrew Control, wireless check, over.'

The answer crackled back: 'Homebrew Control to Bluebird Yellow Three, receiving you loud and clear. Are you receiving me, Bluebird Yellow Three? Listening out.'

'This is Bluebird Yellow Three to Homebrew Control, receiving you crystal clear. Thanks for everything, Homebrew. Good luck.'

As he spoke Andrew checked the petrol gauge showed full and the oxygen container was full and working.

The mechanic hunched down by the starter battery next to the fighter, thumb hovering over the button. Andrew switched on the petrol tap, flipped the two magneto switches up and pumped the primer three times. Sticking a thumb up to the mechanic he jabbed both starter buttons. The propeller whined its way through three turns before it coughed into life and blue exhaust streamed past the open cockpit. The mechanic leant in under the fuselage, disconnected the battery lead and pulled away the chocks.

Andrew opened the throttle to taxi towards take-off.

Alan was assigned as Yellow Two and Bryan was section leader. Andrew rolled over to the starboard side of Bryan's plane and waited for Alan to tuck in on the other side. Bryan looked back over each shoulder and waved a signal from his open cockpit. Andrew eased his throttle forward and the section moved across the grass.

Andrew concentrated on the leading aircraft as it gathered speed. Bryan's wheels left the ground and he felt his do the same. He moved his left hand from the throttle to the stick to free his right hand to pump the wheel retraction lever backwards and forwards. He heard the wheels lock into place with a click and a red light glowed in confirmation on the panel.

'Bluebird Yellow Leader calling Yellow Section,' Bryan's voice crackled onto the wireless. 'Climb to Angels ten, vector two-two-five. Tighten up, Yellow Section. Let's make it look good.'

****

Molly leaned her bicycle against the wire fence and pulled her thermos flask from the carrier basket. Sipping her tea, she gazed across Kenley airfield. She knew Andrew would disapprove if he found out, but she could hardly see her bump and certainly didn't feel pregnant since the morning sickness had eased. She closed her eyes and let the spring sunshine warm her eyelids as she waited.

The distant rumble of aero-engines trembled in the air and Molly searched for the source. Three black specks appeared against the white backdrop of clouds, growing bigger as they barrelled towards the airfield.

The three Spitfires roared over, breaking into a climbing turn to starboard as three more approached, buzzing the hangars and following their climb. She squinted her eyes against the sky and six more planes came into view.

****

Andrew saw the three sections ahead of them buzz the field and climb away as Bryan led his section across the airfield and straight over the control tower, barely clearing the wireless mast on its roof before hauling into a climb to join the rest of the circling squadron.

The wireless clicked into life: 'Beehive Control to Bluebird Leader. When you've quite finished playing silly buggers, you're clear to land in sections.'

'Bluebird Leader to Bluebird Squadron' – a hint of affection tinged Fenton's voice – 'let's do what the nice man says.'

CHAPTER 10

Silva

14th May, 1940

Peter lay prone behind the chalky ridge, pine needles prickling under his elbows. The trees rose straight above him, stark and skeletal against the blue sky. The boom of distant guns drifted in on the breeze, not yet loud enough to disturb the chattering birds. Occasionally small groups of planes he couldn't identify traversed the clouds, intent on a different target.

He looked out over the flat fields scored with dykes, perfect ground for killing infantry with machine-gun crossfire and a barrage of rifles.

'Where are they, Angus?' Peter breathed. 'We've marched for three days without a single sniff.'

'I don't know where they are, lad,' Angus sighed. 'It could be a hundred yards, it could be a hundred miles.'

'Shouldn't we be digging trenches?'

'I suspect we'll be moving forward soon. If the Belgians are still holding their line, they'll need our help.'

Peter gazed out over the flat fields to the tree-line in the middle distance. 'It could be a hundred yards.'

A commotion erupted around the wireless operator and a soldier called out for the platoon sergeant. Peter couldn't make out the short, tense exchange that followed as the sergeant dropped to a squat by the wireless pack and spoke into the transmitter. His head sagged and he covered his eyes with his hand. Recovering his composure he handed the transmitter back to the operator and stood up.

'Right, lads,' he shouted, 'the Dutch have surrendered! Which means our left flank is exposed.' A low murmuring undulated amongst the soldiers on the ridge. 'And the Germans have broken through the Ardennes forest into France, on our right flank, with many Panzer divisions.' He paused to let the news sink in. 'At the best, we can hope the German armour will push south, away from us, straight towards Paris. If that happens we have a fighting chance here. For a while. At worst, the Panzers will head north and attack from our rear.'

Shouted questions burst from a few of the soldiers.

The sergeant waved them silent. 'Dig in here until I find out what we're to do.' A wry grimace crinkled his face: 'But don't dig too deep, lads. Be ready to move at a moment's notice. Pass it down the line.'

Peter sat pinching his nose between thumb and forefinger: 'We're in a bloody rat-trap.'

'Aye.' Angus unhitched the entrenching tool from his pack. 'So it would seem.'

They scratched and chopped at the dry, lumpen soil for the rest of the afternoon, cursing the stringy, shallow roots of the pine trees. As the sun westered, each soldier lay in his own shallow scrape, munching on dry rations.

A corporal moved down the line, pausing to talk with each group of troops. As he moved on, the soldiers roused and busied themselves sorting their packs. The corporal reached Peter's group.

'The French are withdrawing on the right flank, so we're moving back in line with them,' he hissed. 'Keep it quiet. No naked lights. No smoking.' He pointed away over his left shoulder: 'We're heading west.'

****

Bluebird squadron sat waiting in the briefing hut. A red thread pinned to the map on the wall traced out a route from East Anglia to the Kent coast where it veered south-east across The Channel to Northern France.

'What the bloody hell is that all about?' Bryan muttered.

'There are plenty of bomber fields in East Anglia,' Andrew answered. 'Maybe it's a bomber flight plan?'

'Good Lord,' Bryan breathed, 'why are they attacking forests?'

Squadron Leader Fenton came in and took his place in front of the map.

'Sit down, chaps.' He waited for the commotion to subside. 'I hope you're all nicely settled in and busy running up your mess tabs.'

A ripple of laughter washed around the room and someone threw a pencil stub at Bryan's head.

'Well, it's time for the real work to start.' He placed his notes on the dais. 'As you may be aware, the Germans have invaded Holland and Belgium. By all accounts the Belgians are putting up quite a show; the Dutch are not doing quite so well.

'But you may not know that the Germans have also invaded France. They've skirted the western end of the Maginot Line and come south through the forests of the Ardennes. Lord knows how they got their tanks through that little lot, but they did. Luckily the River Meuse is slowing them down a bit.

'Three squadrons of Wellingtons are on their way to bomb the German bridgeheads. Our French-based Hurricanes will be looking after them over the target, but we've been asked to pick them up on their way back, rendezvous Amiens.'

He stabbed a finger onto the map halfway along the red thread's route back to The Channel.

'By that time they'll be at the extreme edge of German fighter range. If you do happen to see any 109s, please do not chase them east.' He glanced around at his pilots: 'Let's get airborne. Good luck, Bluebird.'

****

'Bluebird Leader to Bluebird Squadron. Continue climb to Angels ten.'

Andrew looked down at the unfolding green blanket of The Weald rolling away beneath them.

'Bluebird Leader to Bluebird Squadron. That's Hastings. Set course one-three-five.'

The green countryside gave way to water as Bluebird arrowed out into the Channel. Merchant ships ploughing through the swell cut glittering white wakes in the grey-green monotony.

The French coast flashed by as the squadron levelled out at 10,000ft. Andrew fell to scanning the sky.

Minutes passed, then Bryan's voice crackled over the wireless: 'Bluebird Yellow One to Bluebird Leader. Many aircraft dead ahead and below.'

'Thank you, Yellow One. 'A' flight follow me to Angels eleven, we'll take top cover. 'B' flight, go down and watch their tails.'

Six Spitfires soared into a climb while the other six dipped into a shallow dive to meet the twin-engine bombers.

Andrew pushed his stick forward and followed the 'B' flight leader in a wide arcing turn. The Wellington formation lumbered by and the Spitfires banked around to follow them. There were no other planes in the air.

Andrew looked up to see the other half of the squadron settle in 1000ft above them. He turned his attention to the bombers droning along in front and flipped the wireless to transmit.

'Bluebird Yellow Three to Bluebird Leader. There should be three squadrons. I count only twenty-two planes.'

'Bluebird Leader to Yellow Three.' The squadron leader spoke in a measured tone. 'It looks like the big boys play rough.'

Andrew's Spitfire bobbed around in the bombers' slipstream. 'Fourteen planes missing. Six men on each.' The thought chilled him.

The Channel stretched out in front of them and the top cover Spitfires descended to sit in front of the bombers. Minutes later Hastings beach rolled away underneath.

'Bluebird Leader to Bluebird Squadron. Let's go home.'

The Spitfires banked away to the north-west.

15th May, 1940

Gerry watched Devline walk across the airfield towards his office. The sway of her hips threatened to break his resolve. He moved away from the window and sat behind his desk. Devline knocked once and breezed in.

'Hello, sweetheart,' she said, 'I brought you a piece of cake for your coffee break.' She put a paper bag on his desk and leaned over to kiss his forehead.

'Sit down, Dev,' Gerry said, 'I need to talk to you about something.'

Devline straightened up, looked from Gerry's face to the newspaper on his desk and back again. She settled into the chair and regarded him with a steady gaze.

Gerry looked down at his clasped hands to escape the disruptive power of her eyes. 'A travelling salesman dropped by today. His company sells spark plugs for aero-engines all the way up the east coast, even as far as Ontario—'

'Uh-huh!' Devline's interjection drew his eyes back to hers.

'Anyway,' he held eye contact, 'he said the Canadian Air Force are recruiting pilots to go to Europe.'

Devline unlocked their eyes and reached for the newspaper on the desk.

'Germany invades Holland and Belgium.' She read out the headline. 'British and French armies advance in counter-attack.'

She dropped the newspaper onto the floor and a tear welled in her eye: 'You do know that I love you, Gerry?'

Gerry reached across and took her hand: 'I love you too, Dev, but—'

She looked up sharply and the tear dropped away from her jaw. 'But what, Gerry? Why does there have to be a 'but'?' Her voice grated along the hard edge of her outrage. 'If you were defending America it might be different. We'd all be in it, everyone would give up their man.'

'Don't you see, Dev,' Gerry implored, 'I *will* be defending America?'

Devline pulled her hand from his and stood up, clattering the chair onto the floor, 'You're the only one that thinks that way. You'll be alone.' She choked out a sob: 'And I'll be alone too.'

'There are people losing their homes and families, Dev. I have to do something for them, I just have to.'

Devline stalked to the door and pulled it open. 'You're doing this for nobody else but yourself,' she hissed.

The wooden wall of the hut reverberated with the slam of the door. Through the window Gerry watched Devline walk away.

****

'I'm sorry, Mom' – Gerry held her hand across the kitchen table – 'but it's the right thing to do.'

'I know, son.' Tears escaped onto her cheeks. 'And I'm very proud that you're standing by what you believe. I knew my good boy would grow up to be a good man.'

Bob paused from stirring the stew. 'Anyway, Mary, there's nothing to say the Canadians will take him on.'

'You take that back.' Mary's eyes stayed on Gerry's face. 'My son is the best pilot in the state,' she smiled through her tears. 'They'll snap him up.'

Bob served the stew and sat at the table. Mary dried her eyes and said grace.

'What happens next, Gerry, in Europe I mean?' Bob sprinkled salt onto his meal.

'It depends on how fast the German army moves.' Gerry took a mouthful of stew and chewed. 'If the British and French dig in where they are, then I guess we're back to 1917.'

His father nodded.

'If the Germans push them into the sea,' Gerry continued, 'then the French coast becomes the front-line.'

'And the Germans invade Britain?'

Gerry paused in thought. 'They might risk it.' He pursed his lips. 'I'm sure the Royal Navy would put on a pretty big firework display if they tried.' Gerry shook his head. 'I think the Germans are more likely to offer peace terms.'

'So,' his mother brightened, 'it could all be over before Christmas?'

'I suppose that depends on the British and how much they trust Hitler's respect for treaties. In any event, if the Germans capture France, their bombers will be in easy range of England, probably with fighter escorts' – Gerry paused, looking down into his stew – 'which is why they need more pilots.'

Bob threw a nervous glance at his wife: 'Well, Gerry's a flying instructor, so if I was the British I'd put him to work training those new pilots.'

'Yes, sir,' Gerry nodded, 'that's what I'd do too.'

19th May, 1940

Peter trudged west, his platoon wedged near the front of a long khaki snake of marching soldiers. His pack bit deep into his shoulders and he hefted it continuously, seeking respite. Angus plodded beside him, humming around the stub of a cigarette, solid and indefatigable.

The road widened and broke out from the woodland shade onto a plain of open ground. The late afternoon sun dipped in the sky in front of them; prickles of sweat broke out on their foreheads.

Peter squinted ahead. The road crossed open fields for a mile before diving into the cover of more woodland. He scanned the terrain to the north, nothing moved except a swirling flock of crows circling an isolated stand of trees. To the south a black smudge stained the horizon, too dark for storm clouds. He nudged Angus and pointed.

His friend grunted: 'Something's well ablaze.'

'How far away?'

'Too far to bother us just now.' Angus lit another cigarette. 'Let's just keep going.'

'The Panzers turned north, didn't they.' Peter swallowed a moment of panic. 'They're coming for us.'

'Aye,' Angus blew a long line of smoke over his head, 'so it would seem.'

The sweat trickled down Peter's temples. He fixed his gaze on the shaded shelter of the trees 500 yards ahead.

A faint drone tickled the edge of Peter's hearing. He looked back over his shoulder, expecting to see motorbikes on the road. There was none. But the column rippled as some of the marching men faltered. The engines grew louder.

Peter turned back as two black shapes emerged from the sun's glare. The column erupted into shouts around him as the shapes resolved into fighter planes, flattening out from a shallow dive. The men in front of him parted like a bow-wave, scrambling to get off the road.

Peter stood transfixed by the yellow noses rushing towards him, their noise clattering to a deafening crescendo. Then their wings sparkled.

The air above and around Peter ripped like tearing canvas. The two fighters roared over, 30ft above his head, large black crosses incongruous against their impossibly blue undersides. The machine-guns' rattle and the thumping of cannon played a rhythmic counterpoint to the cacophony of engines.

Peter screwed his head to follow the planes and the blast of their passing whipped dust and grit into his face. He blinked his eyes clear, buckling to his knees at the sight revealed before him.

The column was cleaved apart. Two furrows ploughed by cannon-shells curved along the road and onto the grass verges. Around these scars lay the bloodied bodies of soldiers, some still, many writhing or crawling. Peter gazed at one man, thrown onto his back in a ragged pentangle by the force of his own evisceration.

'Peter!' Angus beckoned from a roadside ditch: 'Get over here, man. They're coming round again.'

Peter crawled off the road, rolling into the ditch. The two fighters climbed away in a banking turn to the right. The second plane slotted into formation with his leader. Their path took them round and over the road but they made no move to attack.

'The bastards,' Peter breathed. 'They're taking a look at what they've done.'

The staccato popping of rifle fire followed the planes as they accelerated away to the east.

The ringing in Peter's ears subsided, replaced by the gentle ebb and flow of moans and coughs from the wounded.

Peter and Angus climbed from the ditch. 'We were right there,' Peter's voice cracked, 'we were walking right there…'

The platoon sergeant's voice broke through the miasma: 'Move out! Give the medics space. Let's get under the trees in case those bastards come back.'

Shouts echoed down the road and the column shifted again, flowing through and around the human wreckage scattered along the path.

22nd May, 1940

Peter lay behind a log, peering into the woods opposite. Over to his right the platoon's Bren gun team set up behind a bush. Angus dropped down next to him.

'Looks like we stand here, Peter.'

Peter wriggled deeper into the leaf-mould and settled with his rifle resting on the top of the log, the weapon's butt snug against his shoulder. The thick moss on the bark bled its moisture into his battledress.

The warmth of the sunlight waxed as the morning wore on. Silence fell over the waiting troops, broken only by the occasional rustle and clink as soldiers fixed bayonets onto rifles.

Peter caught a flicker of grey against the gloom of the woods, then another. The movement resolved into a ghostly human shape, flitting across the ashen sunlight filtering between the trees. The movements multiplied, cascading into small groups of men until the whole wood rippled with advancing soldiers.

A cold fear descended on Peter as he watched and waited.

The first German stepped out from the tree-line pausing to look over his shoulder for his comrades. More grey-clad soldiers broke the cover of the trees, blinking against the sun.

'Open fire!'

Echoes of the shout drowned in the rolling barrage of rifle fire. The grey-clad soldiers in the open bucked and crumpled, the trees behind them spitting splinters over their bodies.

The barking recoil of Peter's rifle clanged against his steel helmet and rang like fury in his ears. The deeper mechanical thunder of the Bren gun rattled and paused, rattled and paused.

Peter loosed a round into an emerging German and one more into his corpse as it hit the ground. Raising his aim, he fired blindly into the gap between two trees and another dark figure slumped forward.

The machine-gun swept back and forth, chewing bark away from the trees. Peter fired at random through the gaps between the trunks, moving left and right until his empty rifle clicked with impotence. Twisting urgently, he grabbed a fresh magazine from his belt and jammed it into the gun.

Turning back to the tree-line he paused. Nothing moved.

'Cease fire!' The order rippled down the line. 'Cease fire!'

Uneasy silence settled over the scene. A low moaning drifted across from the trees. Shattered bodies littered the grass at the edge of the woodland, grey uniforms seeping into red around ragged tears and gashes.

'Peter?'

Peter stared into his friend's face.

'Are you all right?' Angus reached out to squeeze his arm.

'We killed them,' Peter breathed. 'They didn't even shoot back.'

The heavy air rumbled to a new vibration; a deep-throated engine gunned and strained, underpinned by the clanking of caterpillar tracks.

'Christ,' Angus whispered, 'Panzers.'

A thunderous boom rolled over the ground followed by an explosion 50 yards away in the woods. Three trees sagged over to tangle in the branches of their neighbours. Shrapnel skittered against the leaves and sang through the air over Peter's head.

'Fall back! Fall back!' The platoon sergeant's shout released them. 'Let's get out of here!'

Peter and Angus rolled to their feet and jogged away north with the rest of the platoon.

CHAPTER 11

Receptus

26th May, 1940

Andrew held Molly's hand and toyed with her wedding ring. The wooden pew felt hard against his buttocks and the sparse stone church retained an echo of winter's severe chill.

The vicar's voice trembled in the still air: 'We have all admired the courageous bearing of the British Expeditionary Force during the intense and difficult fighting of the last two weeks in Belgium and France. We can be proud of the gallantry they are displaying against a determined foe, gallantry which will be written with honour in the annals of the British Army. Hold our magnificent troops in your hearts and minds as we dedicate our prayers to them in their hour of peril.

'Our Father, which art in heaven…'

****

Andrew and Molly crunched over the churchyard gravel through the shadows cast by the lichen-spattered gravestones.

'You should move to Norfolk, Molly,' he said. 'My father would be glad to look after you.'

'No. I prefer to be close to you. Look after myself.'

'It won't be long before the Germans start chucking bombs around.' Andrew stopped and turned her to face him. 'And you live just outside the fence at Biggin Hill.' He took her face between his palms. 'It's just too dangerous.'

'Please let's not argue about it.' She walked on. 'It's far more dangerous for you.'

Andrew opened his mouth to reply but she cut him short.

'Like the vicar said, today we should be thinking about the soldiers in France. We should be thinking about your friend Peter.'

Andrew sighed. 'Poor old Peter. I told him his training would keep him safe. I don't believe that's true anymore. The enemy he was trained to fight no longer exists.'

Molly grabbed his hand and squeezed it tight. 'Today is supposed to be a day of hope,' she said. 'What is your hope for Peter?'

Andrew grimaced: 'To be honest, I hope he got captured in Belgium. It wouldn't be pleasant, but it would be better than being driven into the sea.'

'Will it be that bad?'

'Yes, I believe it will.'

****

Molly ladled the steaming soup into Andrew's bowl. 'Will you stay tonight, darling?'

'I shouldn't. I'm on readiness tomorrow morning at six.'

She smiled: 'I have an alarm clock.'

'All right, but we should spend the time planning where you're moving to.'

'I thought I'd made it plain I'm going nowhere.' She sprinkled salt onto her soup. 'For goodness sake, my dear old mother is refusing to leave Eastbourne. You can probably see the Germans from there on a clear day.' She reached across and touched his wrist. 'I know it comes from your heart, but we're all involved in this war and we all have to find our own ways of fighting it.

'My mother fights her war by taking daily walks along a beach covered in tank traps, as if everything is normal. I fight my war by cutting hair and chatting with my customers, as if everything is normal.' She looked into his eyes. 'I can't bear to think about the way you fight your war. Which is why I have to stay close to you. Because then I can spend as much time as possible by your side,' she smiled, 'as if everything is normal.'

'But... what about the baby?'

'She feels the same.'

****

Peter sat on the roadside. French civilians trailed past in carts, on bicycles and on foot – a never-ending centipede of misery searching for safety in a country that offered no sanctuary. When the platoon marched out of Belgium the refugees flowed with them. Now they marched north to the coast, the flood of humanity washed down the road against them.

Peter had no cigarettes. His head ached with a dull, sleepless throb and his hands trembled without respite.

'On your feet, lads.' The platoon sergeant worked his way down the roadside. 'Dunkirk or bust,' he winked at Peter as he passed.

'Bloody hell.' Angus bent to help Peter to his feet. 'What a shambles.'

They stepped into the jostling stream of refugees, unheeding of the people they bumped and deaf to the curses thrown at them. Behind them, British trucks tangled in the human tide blared their horns in an unending litany.

Peter gazed out to his left where black smoke broiled a long column into the heavy sky.

'Where's that, Angus?'

'That'll be Calais.'

'How far is Calais from Dun—'

Peter's words were drowned in the whoosh of a descending shell. The ground bucked with a thunderous explosion 100 yards behind them. Two more shells hit in quick succession, stitching death across the crowded road. A moment of silence sucked away Peter's breath and debris pattered down around him.

The soldiers straightened up, adjusted their packs and walked on through the screaming, crying crowd that pressed around them. None looked back.

27th May, 1940

The landward horizon lightened with the first fingers of the still dawn as Peter stumbled through the dunes. Everywhere dark figures huddled around in small groups, their outlines blurred by the swaying marram grass.

The platoon found a space on the beach below the dunes and the men sank into grateful repose.

The sergeant called for silence: 'We're not finished yet, lads, so watch your weapons in this sand.' He nodded towards the looming shadows of cruisers in and around the docks: 'We can get a lift with the Navy back to Folkestone from here, but we might need to keep the Krauts off the beach until we do.'

'Stay here. I'm off to find the beach-master, see if he's got a plan.'

Angus wiggled the butt of his rifle into the sand until the weapon stood on its own. Taking off his helmet he hung it over the barrel and scratched his head with vigour.

'I hesitate to point this out…'

Peter glanced at him: 'But?'

'There's an awful lot of fish in this barrel.'

****

The chill lifted from Peter's flesh as the sun climbed above the horizon, chasing away the wisps of mist from amongst the dunes.

Men and vehicles packed the beach. The light breeze whipped along snatches of conversation and the occasional shouted command. In the distance soldiers moved in small groups towards the harbour.

'We need to dig in, Angus.' Tension reverberated in Peter's voice: 'What if they send fighter planes.'

Angus grabbed a handful of sand. Grimacing, he let it trickle through his fingers, 'There's no use, lad' – he gestured at the crowded men around him – 'and there's no space. It's like Margate Beach on a bank holiday.'

An artillery shell tore a tunnel through the air, striking the beach at the water's edge. Wet sand and water erupted in a torpid plume. Men ran and staggered away. Another struck further along, then another, walking a path of destruction through the sprawling soldiers towards the docks.

Again and again the explosions pounded into the shoreline, the concussions rolling up the beach, popping Peter's ears with pressure. Men pressed faces into the sand, writhing and wriggling in an agony of exposure. There was nowhere to run.

The last explosion echoed away off the harbour walls and a numb silence dropped across the sands, violated by the cries of shattered men and the shouts of soldiers.

Peter stood. Driven by the need to help, he took a few urgent steps towards the carnage by the water. Hopelessness strangled his movement and dread smothered his courage. He turned away, tears welling into his eyes.

The drone of aero-engines crept into his senses. He wiped away the tears and looked along the length of the beach. There in the distance, six shapes dived in low and fast. The noise expanded and the shapes became twin-engine bombers, their shiny glazed noses sparkling like the heads of malevolent insects. The middle one raced straight at Peter, bomb-bay open.

Terror tore a cry from his throat: 'Daddy!'

The stick of bombs fell away from the plane, wobbled in the air and dropped towards him.

****

'Bluebird Leader to Bluebird Squadron. Climb to Angels fifteen. We cross south of Boulogne and head due east to Saint-Omer.'

The promontory of Dungeness slid away under the climbing squadron, their shadows flashing down the wide shingle beach and out over the flat calm water that reflected the innocent blue of the early summer sky.

Andrew studied the French shoreline away to his left. Rippling banners of black unfurled from Calais like bookmarks of destruction. The smoke roiled across the water obscuring the coast beyond from view. Ahead of the squadron, Boulogne sat under its own smoky haze of demolition. Both ports lay under German occupation.

As they skirted Boulogne, a few flak shells blossomed in the sky to the left and below the speeding Spitfires; their pristine white smoke hung against the dull green landscape and drifted sullenly seawards. Andrew ignored them, scanning the sky for hostile aircraft.

'Bluebird Leader to Bluebird Squadron. That's Saint-Omer. Set course zero-six-zero. Break up into sections and patrol parallel to the coast. Don't go near the beaches or the bloody Navy will shoot you down.'

The squadron drifted apart in groups of three.

'Yellow One to Yellow Section.' Bryan's voice sounded flat and calm. 'Alan fly wingman for me, Andrew cover our tails. Let's hunt some Germans.' He eased the section into a gentle climb.

The sun bore down through the perspex canopy and the sweat beaded on Andrew's forehead. He scanned and squinted, searching for danger above and behind.

'Yellow One to Yellow Section,' Bryan called, 'bandits below at 2 o'clock, heading west. I count nine. Heinkels. Can't see any escort. Tally-ho!'

The enemy formation rumbled its way across their path as Bryan led the section into a shallow diving turn for a rear attack. Accelerating into the dive Bryan flattened out and opened fire; Alan, on his right, fired moments later.

Andrew's vision sparkled with clarity as he stabbed his firing button in turn. The gun smoke from the Spitfires' ahead of him spiralled away in their

111

slipstreams. Flashes decorated the bombers' tails where German gunners rattled their retaliation. His tracer lines chased and penetrated the Heinkel formation, groping at the air and striking the bloated bodies of the lumbering planes.

Then a flicker of yellow. Bullets whipping close overhead. Andrew jammed the transmit button.

'109s!' he yelled. 'Break right!'

He followed Bryan and Alan as they hauled into a tight right bank. Two yellow-nosed Messerschmitts flashed over, still firing.

Their tight turn brought the three Spitfires onto the tails of the 109s as they barrelled due east in a run for home. Bryan levelled out into a chase. The Germans split up, one heading north-east in a climb, the other diving south-east.

Bryan climbed after the first one. 'Stick with me Yellow Section.' The excitement stretched Bryan's voice: 'Let's nail this bastard!'

Black smoke coughed from his exhausts as Bryan engaged full boost. Andrew checked above, behind and below. All clear. The second 109 had not turned back to threaten them.

He saw Bryan open fire and hits danced along the enemy's right wing towards the fuselage. Crystal shards erupted from the shattering canopy and the plane bucked, flipped onto its back and dropped into a spiralling power-dive to the ground.

'Reform on me, Yellow Section.' Bryan's voice chimed like ice: 'Let's get back to the patrol line.'

Andrew banked to port, following the other two onto their original heading. Past his lowered wing he could see the thick, oily smoke spiralling up from the burning core of the wrecked Messerschmitt.

They levelled out and Bryan's voice broke through on the wireless.

'Yellow Leader calling. Bandit below, 3 o'clock, Stuka I think. Silly sod is all on his own. Line astern, line astern.'

Andrew eased out to the left while Alan slid in behind and below Bryan's plane, then he manoeuvred in behind and underneath them both.

'Loosen up as we go down. Break right after attack. Tally-ho!'

Andrew dropped back 20 yards. The extra space gave him the chance to look for the enemy aircraft.

He saw it below and to the right. Dark against the landscape, its gull wings giving it an air of prehistoric menace.

The Stuka jinked from side to side as the Spitfires curved down in a shallow dive. The German pilot thrashed the engine for all the speed he could muster and black smoke streamed from its exhausts.

Bryan closed on the fleeing dive-bomber. Flashes blossomed from the back of the German canopy and the rear-gunner's tracers spiralled up and through their formation. At the same moment Bryan stabbed a two-second burst, tearing fragments from the German's tail. As Bryan pulled away to the right, Alan closed in, already firing.

The Stuka exploded in a violent flowering of red flames and black smoke. The blast sucked away the bomber's momentum and Alan's Spitfire flew into the collapsing enemy. The two planes arced away like crumpled birds in a last desperate embrace before the Spitfire's fuel tank detonated with a flare of orange and the whole tangle dropped away towards the fields.

Andrew heaved the control column back into his stomach and careened through the black smoke, fragments pattering along his fuselage.

His tight turn brought him around on his starboard wingtip and he regained sight of the doomed planes just as they hit the centre of a vineyard, spreading fingers of burning fuel out into the trellised vines. He levelled out and looked around in shocked confusion.

'I'm above you' – Bryan's voice broke through – 'on your starboard quarter.'

Andrew located the other Spitfire and curved up to drop in behind its starboard wing.

'What the hell happened there, Bryan?'

'Looks like he still had his bomb on board. Keep your eyes peeled. Let's get out of here.'

****

Andrew climbed out of his cockpit. Hauling his parachute after him he jumped to the grass. His engineer stood nearby.

'Any luck, sir?' the man asked.

'We damaged a couple of Heinkels... Bryan got a 109 confirmed...' He paused searching for the right words. '...and a Stuka got destroyed...'

'Good show, sir.'

'...but we lost Yellow Two...' His voice sounded alien in his head. 'Pilot Officer Gold...' He swallowed against his dry throat. '...Alan.'

'Green Section came back one short too, sir.' The man's face softened with sadness: 'It's been a rough old day for the Bluebirds.'

Andrew gazed at him for a moment: 'It's not even 8 o'clock in the morning.'

CHAPTER 12

Circumvorto

28th May, 1940

Gerry rocked gently in his seat as the train clattered over the points outside Michigan Central Station. Soft pillows of steam rolled past the carriage windows as the engine slowed alongside the stone platform. With a final wheeze the train staggered to a halt and Gerry stood to retrieve his holdall from the overhead rack.

Passengers bunched around the open doors, jostling to get out. Gerry stepped back, waiting for the crush to dissolve, savouring the hot, brassy smell of the steam engine wafting in on the fresh breeze.

Stepping onto the emptying platform he walked into the station building. The spectacle of ranked colonnades and huge tiled arches slowed his steps. He paused, sitting on one of the long wooden benches, gazing around at the splendid interior.

'Are you okay, sir?' A porter leaned over him.

'It's… big…'

'Yes, sir, it is. Where are you going?'

'Windsor,' Gerry smiled, 'that's in Canada.'

'Yes, sir, it is. Take a right out of the station on Dalzelle Street, then south on Twelfth Street. You'll see the bridge.'

The man hurried away. Gerry lingered a few minutes longer, enjoying the ring and resonance of the cavernous space, before following the directions.

Emerging at the end of Twelfth, Gerry's hair ruffled in the stiff breeze from the river. A broad smile creased his face as he remembered: 'You'll see the bridge.'

A mile-long bridge spanned the Detroit River. It hung from two metal towers tall enough to scrape the sky; cables and cantilevered trusses festooned its length. Following the road up to the bridge he walked out along the pavement over the water.

Trucks ground backwards and forwards and a few pedestrians hurried passed him, crossing back to Detroit in business suits.

Gerry stopped halfway across, leaning on the railings to watch a cargo steamer emerge from under the bridge. Looking down the river towards the Great Lake beyond, he sensed a moment of passing. Thoughts of Devline rippled a wave of sadness through his chest. He couldn't expect her to wait, better to think of it as over.

Gerry turned away from Detroit and strode into Canada.

****

'Walker Airport,' the driver called.

'That's me,' said Gerry, 'thank you.'

The bus pulled away and Gerry walked up the curving drive to the airport terminal. The whitewashed building had the air of a tiny battleship. The squat, single-storey structure, no longer than two railway carriages, was bisected by a control tower bristling with radio masts.

Gerry walked through the double doors to the main desk.

'I need to talk to someone from the RCAF, please.'

The receptionist smiled: 'Please take a seat.'

Gerry sat down. The girl made a brief phone call and a minute later a door opened across the waiting room. A man in a dark blue uniform leant through the opening and peered across the space over round spectacles.

'Son,' he called, 'son, over here.'

Gerry walked across to the open door. The man returned to his desk and busied himself shuffling through some papers.

'Come in, sit down. What can I do for you?'

'Thank you, sir.' Gerry sat. 'I've come to join the Air Force.'

The man looked at Gerry over the top of his glasses: 'Are you from Windsor?'

Gerry bit his lip, but the lie died in his throat. 'No, sir,' he sighed, 'I'm from Minnesota.'

The man went back to his papers. 'It's called the Canadian Air Force for a reason, son.'

'I'm a flying instructor.' Gerry pulled out his log-book, placing it on the desk between them: 'I have good experience.'

The man flipped open the book, leafing through the pages. Silence hung in the room. The man looked up at Gerry and back to the log-book. He reached for the phone and dialled. The faint buzz of the distant ringing chafed in the air, cut short by an indistinct voice at the other end.

'Hello, Don,' the man said, 'I've got a volunteer sitting with me here at Walker...

'He's a flying instructor...

'No. Minnesota...

'I know that, Don. I said exactly the same thing...

'Don, wait...

'Don...

'Listen...

'He's got over 1800 hours in his logbook...

'Eighteen...

'Various types...

'Ok, Don. Will do.'

He clicked the receiver back into its cradle.

'I'm putting you on the afternoon flight to Ottawa. There'll be a car at the other end to meet you. You've got a flight test tomorrow.' The man stood to shake Gerry's hand. 'God luck, son.'

29th May, 1940

Vincent hooked a square of oiled flannel onto the cleaning rod and plunged it down the machine-gun barrel. The smell of cordite sizzled in his nostrils as he moved along to the next gun-port. The wing wobbled under the armourer's tread as he cleaned and oiled the breech blocks from above. They both paused at the sound of approaching engines. Dropping towards Gravesend airfield came three Spitfires, one trailing a line of white smoke.

'Looks like trouble,' Vincent said.

'At least he got back,' the armourer growled. 'We've got two poor sods missing this morning already. I'm ready for the ammo, Vincent.'

Vincent stowed his cleaning rod and grabbed an ammunition magazine. Swinging under the wing he passed the fixing strap up to the armourer through the open panel. Vincent lifted the heavy box into place and the armourer secured it.

'Panels on, lad. Then onto the next one.'

Vincent screwed the blue-painted panel back into place, grabbed a second magazine and shifted along to the next gun.

117

'Do you think they'll invade?'

The armourer peered through the wing past the gun mechanism at Vincent: 'Do you really want to know what I think?'

Vincent passed up the fixing strap, nodding.

'Well, once they've shot down this little lot' – he tapped the Spitfire's wing for emphasis – 'which, at the rate they're going, won't be very long, I reckon Mr Churchill will have a look round for a Plan B.'

'Plan B?' Vincent offered up the magazine.

'Once he's lost the Army *and* the Air Force, he'll be in no mood to lose the Navy. Mr Churchill's got a soft spot for the Navy. And he won't want the Germans getting hold of our ships. So I reckon him and the King will up sticks with the Royal Navy and sail to Canada.'

'Run away?'

'Tactical retreat, more like. Panels on.' The armourer's face disappeared as he replaced the top wing panel. 'You see, from Canada he'll have a better chance of persuading the Americans to join in.'

'Where does that leave us?' Vincent bit his lip as he screwed on the lower panel.

'Did they teach you to use a rifle in basic training?'

'Yes.'

'Well, there you have it.'

****

Vincent knocked on the office door.

'Come.'

Vincent gulped back his nerves and entered the room.

The station commander's fountain pen scratched his signature on a letter. Vincent stepped forward to stand in front of the desk, snapping to attention.

'Aircraftman Vincent Drew, sir.'

The commander looked up: 'Stand easy, Drew.' He regarded Vincent's oily face: 'You're on ground crew?'

'Yes, sir. Armourer's mate, sir.'

'Must've been hard work of late,' the man smiled. 'What can we do for you, Drew?'

'I'd like to apply for pilot training, sir.'

30th May, 1940

'Quiet please, Bluebird.'

The murmur of voices tailed away.

Squadron Leader Fenton continued: 'It seems the nation's prayers are being answered, gentlemen.' He smiled: 'I have never seen the Channel stay so calm for so long. In fact, the good weather means even the smallest boats fancy their chances at making a round trip.

'The Germans are playing true to form. According to the Navy, their 109s are strafing and sinking the small boats as they're leaving the beaches. In order to discourage this nasty behaviour, Group wants a continuous fighter presence over Dunkirk during daylight hours.

'So we'll take off in sections of three, 20 minutes apart. Exit over Dover and stay low – let's make sure our boats see we're there for them.

'The Germans will be over the beach in numbers, so there'll be plenty for us to go at. Patrol for 20 minutes or until ammunition is expended. Back to base, refuel, re-arm and back at them again. Keep the kettle boiling, so to speak.

'There are three other Spitfire squadrons running the same relay today, so make sure you identify what you're shooting at before you shoot at it.

'My section off first, then Yellow, Red and Blue in that order. Good luck, Bluebird, happy hunting.'

Chairs scraped the floor as the men stood and shuffled out of the hut towards dispersal.

'Did you notice?' Andrew said.

Bryan and George walked either side of him.

'Eighteen pilots in the room,' George muttered. 'They've got six on the reserve bench for today's game.'

'You'd be silly to dwell on it,' Bryan breezed. 'Come and look at this.'

The roar of engines swashed across the field as the first section climbed away into the early summer sky.

Bryan walked over to his Spitfire, pointing at the cockpit: 'Ta-dah!'

On the door underneath the canopy's rim sat a small painted swastika.

'Are you sure that doesn't breach King's Regulations?' Andrew chided.

'The King?' Bryan rounded on him in mock dismay. 'When the King has shot down a bloody 109, he can start telling me what to do.'

Bryan climbed into his cockpit for final checks. Andrew and George walked on in sombre silence towards their own machines.

****

Dover dashed away under their tails and Andrew glanced up at the white flash of the chalk cliffs receding in his mirror. Ahead a trail of small ships dotted the course leading to the rolling smoke over Dunkirk.

Some boats plied west to England, packed with soldiers, their faces upturned to watch the fighters streaking overhead.

Halfway across the water Bryan's voice broke the silence: 'Let's get a tad more altitude Yellow Section, we don't want to get bounced at this height.'

The three planes lifted their noses and the boats sank away below.

Andrew could make out several large vessels standing off the coast. The beach appeared black with soldiers.

'Eyes peeled, Yellow Section. Andrew, watch our tails.'

They levelled out, Andrew weaving back and forth, scanning the sky. The beach approached, the blackness resolved into men standing in lines snaking out into the water, small boats pressed against the sand, taking on their human cargo.

'Bandits at 3 o'clock.' Bryan's voice glittered with anticipation: 'Ju88s. Tally-ho!'

A pair of twin-engine bombers raced towards the beach from right to left. Bryan led the section into a banking turn to port as the bombers tore past their noses.

'Hold your fire until they're away from the beach.'

Andrew straightened out, resting his thumb on the firing button. Black objects fell from the underside of the German planes and they bucked higher in the air. Andrew eased his stick backwards as the bomb-blasts wobbled his tail.

The bombers split up, one banking right over the docks, the other banking left over the sea. Andrew clung onto the seaward plane, closing the distance. The German pilot flew straight and level. No fire came from the rear gunner…

'*Straight and level.*'

Andrew flicked his eyes to the rear-view mirror. Two black shapes closed on him. He hauled the stick back and to the right. His Spitfire stood on its starboard wing, tilting the coastline across his vision. Tracer whipped by over his left shoulder and two loud bangs reverberated down his port wing.

He held the turn until the distant English coast wheeled into view. Levelling out he pushed the throttle into full boost, running for home.

Blinking away the sweat, Andrew peered into the mirror with dread. Sunlight flashed on a canopy as the two 109s peeled away from the chase and headed back to France. Slumping under a wave of relief, Andrew throttled back to cruising speed.

He switched to transmit: 'Bluebird Yellow Three to Yellow Section. Where are you, Yellow Section?'

The wireless remained silent.

Ahead and above, Andrew spotted a single Spitfire. Wary of flying alone he pushed his throttle to catch up. A thin, white stream of coolant trickled away from underneath the other plane.

Andrew glanced at his compass. The damaged Spitfire flew due north, a course that would miss the east coast completely.

Andrew gunned his throttle to pull up along the other's port side. He didn't recognise the lettering on the fuselage; the plane wasn't from Bluebird. Edging closer, Andrew gazed across at the pilot.

The man slumped forwards in his seat, his head resting on the perspex amidst a dark smudge of smashed skull and gore. The slipstream flapped through the top of the shattered canopy, streaming blood along the cockpit's length like a rippling banner of scarlet anger.

Andrew's prop-wash tipped the ghost fighter into a shallow, curving dive towards the sea. Andrew peeled away, setting course for Kenley.

****

Andrew ran his fingers around the ragged holes in the wingtip. The rigger standing with him whistled in appreciation.

'You been getting up close and personal, sir?'

Andrew squeezed a wan smile onto his face: 'I got jumped by two 109s.'

The rigger squinted at the damage: 'Machine-gun bullets. Lucky they weren't cannon-shells. Cannon-shells would have your wingtip right off.'

Bryan and George taxied into dispersal. Andrew wandered over towards them as Bryan slid back his canopy and shut off his engine.

'Andrew, old son.' He clambered out of the cockpit. 'How very nice to see you again. Did you go to a different party?'

'You could say I followed the wrong girl home, yes.'

'Well, me and George had a lovely time, didn't we, Georgie?'

George joined them and the group walked towards the dispersal hut for debriefing.

'It turns out those 88s burn very nicely when you stoke 'em properly.' Bryan flashed a fierce smile towards Andrew. 'One chap even bailed out on us. But the poor dear didn't quite have enough height for his parachute to open.'

'Are you all right, Andy?' George asked. 'You look a bit pale.'

'I got bounced and shot up' – Andrew's voice caught at the edges of his throat – 'my own fault. It won't happen again.'

Bryan put his arm around Andrew's shoulders: 'As long as it's them today, it won't be us until tomorrow, old boy. Let's go tell the boffins what we've been up to.'

****

Molly ran down the stairs and flicked on the shop light. She smiled to see Andrew's face pressed up against the glass. Skipping across, she opened the door.

'What a lovely surprise!' She kissed his lips. 'I wasn't expecting you tonight, come in.'

'Bryan's taken a car-full to The Crown for a celebration.' Andrew followed her up the stairs. 'He bagged another one today.'

'You should be over there with them,' she chided. 'They'll think I've got you under my thumb.'

'I needed to see you, Molly' – he laid his palm on her pregnant belly – 'I wanted to tell you I love you.'

'I know you do—'

Andrew cut her short with a finger on her lips. 'I got shot up today. I was a few seconds away from being killed. I let them creep up on me. Two of them. I saw them just in time, just before they opened fire.

'And on the way back across the Channel' – he closed his eyes for a moment as the image of the ghost pilot drifted across his vision – 'I tried to remember the last thing I'd said to you. I tried to imagine how you'd remember me.'

Molly leaned into his chest and hugged him close. He cupped her face in his hands and looked into her eyes. 'I came to promise you I'd be more careful, that I'd always try to come back,' he smiled. 'When you answered the door just now it was a simple joy to see your beautiful face. One day you might answer the door to someone else. You might answer the door to the officer they've sent to tell you what happened to me.'

Molly shook her head in mute denial.

'Will you promise me something, Molly?'

She nodded through fresh tears, 'Anything, darling.'

'Will you promise to forgive me?'

CHAPTER 13

Trajectus

3rd June, 1940

The port of Montreal receded in its wake as the *Duchess of Atholl* steamed seawards down the St Lawrence River towards Quebec City. Gerry strolled along the passenger deck past large groups of uniformed infantry, sprinkled with a few blue-clad officers and men of the Canadian Air Force. Reaching the prow, he pulled his jacket collar closer around his neck to ward off the freshening breeze.

'Mister Donaldson?' A young man in a Canadian Aircraftsman uniform stood before him. 'The senior officer wants to see you, sir, follow me.'

The young man led Gerry off the deck and down the steps to a corridor lined with cabin doors. Stopping at one, the young man knocked, waited a moment and swung the door open, gesturing Gerry inside.

The man sitting at the desk smiled and rose to shake Gerry's hand.

'Hello, Gerry. My name is McIntosh.' He sat down. 'Wing Commander McIntosh. Take a seat, son. I understand you're a strange bird.'

'I'm an American,' Gerry offered, 'if that's what you mean.'

McIntosh laughed: 'Well, son, quite a few Americans have joined us, but none of them, except you, is on this boat. They're all in basic training and if they get through that, they'll go for flight training.

'What sets you apart is your flying hours. You have more than the average Air Force pilot. Why waste time teaching Grandma to suck eggs? We need to get you into a cockpit as soon as possible so you can start making a difference.

'So you've been given a commission.' He pushed a package across the desk, 'You're a pilot officer.'

Gerry pulled back the tissue paper to reveal the folded uniform.

'There's a mistake, sir,' he stuttered, 'the wings on this tunic say RAF—'

'No mistake, Gerry,' the older man smiled again. 'When London heard about you they wanted you for their own. The sooner they get an American into combat the better.'

'Combat?' Gerry's voice snagged with excitement. 'I thought I'd be a flying instructor stationed in the wilderness somewhere.'

McIntosh shook his head: 'As I understand it you'll be met by RAF officers in Liverpool and taken for immediate conversion to fighters. From there you'll go to operational flying in southern England.'

4th June, 1940

Andrew flexed his shoulders into his flying overalls and sat down to pull on his fur-lined boots.

Bryan walked in and yanked open his locker door: 'Did you hear what that bloody chump had to say on the radio this morning?'

George took the bait. 'Which chump are you talking about?'

'Winston bloody Churchill,' Bryan rounded on him, 'the biggest chump of all.'

'Careful, Bryan,' Andrew chided, 'Winston might consider that treason.'

Bryan ignored the reproach. 'He said that we'll "fight them on the beaches",' he held out his arms in supplication. 'Now, correct me if I'm wrong, but I thought the army had just spent the best part of last week fighting them on the bloody French beaches. And we got our arses kicked.'

Andrew stood up and stamped his boots home. 'Winston's got a job to do. Just like us. We can't be seen to be giving up.'

'Hitler can keep the beaches in France for all I care,' Bryan ground out the words through clenched teeth. 'He'll get nowhere near the bloody English beaches if I have anything to do with it.'

12th June, 1940

The telephone jangled and a few moments later the orderly stuck his head out of the hut window: 'Yellow Section Scramble!'

Bryan, Andrew and George sprinted to their Spitfires. Engines coughed into life and the fighters taxied to take-off. As they manoeuvred, George's plane lagged and the propeller slowed.

'Yellow Two here.' George sounded annoyed. 'My oil pressure has just dropped to zero. It's looks like I won't be coming out to play.'

'Got that, George,' Bryan answered, 'we'll see you at tea-time.'

The remaining pair roared down the grass runway and climbed into the summer sky.

'Bluebird Yellow Leader to Beehive Control. Yellow Section are airborne. Listening out.'

Climbing steadily, Andrew tucked his fighter behind Bryan's starboard wing and began the routine scanning of the sky. They reached 10,000ft and the controller's voice cut through the static.

'Beehive calling Bluebird Yellow Section. Vector one-one-zero. Patrol Maidstone Angels twelve. Lone bandit heading east.'

Bryan accelerated and increased the climb. Andrew stayed with him.

'Beehive calling Bluebird Yellow Section. Bandit should be crossing your vicinity now.'

'Bluebird Yellow Leader to Beehive. I see him. A big fat Heinkel. Tally-ho!'

Bryan banked to starboard into a shallow dive. Following him, Andrew spotted the target, 500ft below and one mile away, heading due east.

'Stick by my wing, Andrew.' Bryan's voice held a steely tension: 'Watch my tail.'

The two fighters screamed down behind the bomber. Andrew saw Bryan open fire, squeezing out three long bursts before banking away to port. The bomber flashed across his windscreen and Andrew loosed a brief spurt of fire.

As they wheeled for another attack, black smoke trickled from the bomber's port engine. The German pilot jinked in a desperate zig-zag across the sky, disrupting return fire from his top and side gunners.

Empty cartridges streamed from underneath Bryan's wings as he opened up with another sustained burst. The two Spitfires flashed over the top of the German bomber and peeled away to port racing ahead of their target.

'Damn it,' Bryan cursed, 'I'm out of ammunition.'

'I still have plenty,' Andrew answered. 'Keep an eye out for trouble while I have a go at him.'

The Spitfires curved around in front of the bomber. Bryan continued to orbit while Andrew peeled off to attack the bomber's port side. Waiting as long as he dare, he fired a short burst; his bullets ripped across the trailing edge of the wing and peppered the side gunner's position.

The bomber dipped into a steeper dive as the North Kent coast rolled underneath, flattening out at sea-level. Andrew followed it down, jinking from left to right to avoid haphazard fire from the dorsal gunner.

Andrew closed the distance with a burst of throttle and fired from astern. Bullet-strikes sparkled along the top of the fuselage and the gunner fell silent. Andrew roared over the bomber, climbing away in a slow bank.

The Heinkel's tail hit the crest of a wave, then another. It propellers ploughed into the surf and it lurched to a halt, settling into the water.

Andrew circled. Three aircrew climbed onto the wing and inflated a dinghy. One needed help to board the small craft and slumped into the bottom of the boat as the other two paddled away from the sinking bomber.

'Well done, Andrew.' Bryan paused: 'Have you got enough ammunition to finish the job?'

The question hung in the ether for long moments as Andrew circled the dinghy. The bomber's tail reared like a flagpole, the large, white-edged swastika plainly visible, before sliding out of sight under the waves.

'Yellow Three to Yellow Leader' – Andrew found refuge in wireless protocol – 'suggest we return to base.'

****

Bryan dipped into his landing approach. Andrew peeled away to do another circuit. The adrenalin throbbed through his system. The excitement of hurling damage across the sky still danced over his skin. As soon as he rose from this cockpit, as soon as his feet touched the ground, it would catch up with him. But while he still flew he could outrun the reality of the killing.

Throttling back onto the glide-path he pulled the canopy back, enjoying the cough and chafe of his idling engine. His wheels bumped to the ground and the tail settled. He swung off the landing strip and taxied to dispersal.

Andrew unhooked his harness and swung out of the cockpit. Sliding down the wing to the grass, he walked across to where Bryan waited.

'What's wrong with you?' Bryan hissed. 'Those aircrew were sitting ducks.'

'They were beaten, Bryan. For the sake of humanity—'

'Humanity?' Bryan cut him short. 'When did humanity enter the equation? Those people are trying to enslave us. You saw them bombing

127

defenceless soldiers at Dunkirk. Beaten soldiers. Men with nowhere to hide. They're butchers, plain and simple. Forget your chivalry, forget your honour, forget your humanity. Take every opportunity you have to kill the bastards. Every single opportunity. If only for Molly's sake—'

'Molly?' Andrew shouted. 'If we get through this alive we will have to live with what we've done. I will not make my child's father a murderer. Not for you, not for the King, not for anyone.'

'I say, chaps' – George strolled over – 'what's the flap?'

'Nothing,' Bryan chirped, 'just a disagreement about tactics.' Bryan looked into Andrew's eyes and nodded: 'Nothing to worry about.'

13th June, 1940

'Disembarking now.' The shout echoed down the corridor. Gerry knotted his tie and stepped back from the mirror. The pressed blue-grey uniform fitted him well and the RAF wings glittered under the dressing table light.

Gerry grabbed his holdall from the bed and strode down the corridor. Stepping out onto the deck, he merged into the crowd shuffling along towards the gangplank. The ship sat alongside a quay, hemmed in on all sides by tall red-brick warehouses. Large multi-paned windows dotted their walls, lending them the demeanour of prisons.

Smoke and steam from the vessels shunting around the dock dirtied the blue square of sky between the buildings and the gulls' absonant cries split the air around his head.

Gerry walked down the gangplank, scanning the quayside. Disembarked soldiers formed into columns and marched away to the shouted orders of platoon commanders. More soldiers spilled onto the quay, jostling to get into formation and follow their comrades. At the edge of the khaki-clad river of soldiery Gerry spotted a man in a dark blue uniform standing next to a staff car.

Gerry stepped onto the quay and weaved through the crush of soldiers towards the car. The uniformed man stepped forward to shake his hand.

'You must be Pilot Officer Donaldson,' the man smiled in greeting. 'My name is Day, Gordon Day. I'm one of Dowding's adjutants.'

'Dowding?'

'Hugh Dowding.' The adjutant raised an eyebrow. 'AOC of fighter command.'

'AOC?'

'Top brass,' Day smiled again, 'did the Canadians teach you nothing?'

'They did, sir,' Gerry replied, 'they taught me how to play bridge.'

Gerry put his holdall in the boot of the car and climbed onto the back seat next to the adjutant. The man leaned forward and tapped the driver on the shoulder. The engine growled into life and they crawled forward through the crowds.

'It's a five-hour trip to London.' Day took off his cap and scratched his scalp. 'So please call me Gordon.' He pulled a flask out of the foot well. 'Tea?'

Gerry shook his head. Gordon poured a tea for himself and juggled the cup while he retrieved a pencil and pad from a briefcase.

'So tell me about your history, your family and suchlike.'

'Why would you want to know that?' Gerry asked. 'It's not very exciting, I promise you.'

Gordon fixed Gerry with a quizzical look through the steam from his tea: 'You do know you're the first American to enter the war? The guns in your fighter will fire the first American shots against the Axis Powers. That makes everything about you interesting.'

'I never thought about it that way.'

'Nevertheless' – Gordon licked the end of his pencil – 'the papers are going to write something. If we don't give them the story, they'll just make one up themselves.'

15th June, 1940

Andrew and Bryan sat on a hard wooden bench in the cavernous concourse of King's Cross station. People flowed past, the trub of their conversation settled in the air around them.

'I don't even want to go on leave' – Bryan sat hunched like a disgruntled crow – 'let alone go on leave to bloody Norfolk.'

'You need it, Bryan. It's only three days.' Andrew lit two cigarettes and passed one over. 'And you couldn't stay on base with the squadron buzzing off on patrol without you. Besides, you'll like it up on the coast, it's… bracing.'

Higher-pitched noises pierced the background mire of voices; the serrated squeals of children ricocheted around the walls.

An elderly woman walked past trailing behind her a line of young evacuees. Each child carried a suitcase or bag and every one wore a gas-mask box slung over their shoulder. A brown parcel-tag tied to their clothing bore their name in large letters. Their excitement at the grand adventure was uncontainable, and the long line trooped past in noisy elation. Bringing up the rear, detached from the others, a small boy stumbled along, his tear-streaked face filled with fear and misery. He locked imploring eyes on the two pilots as he passed. The boy's parcel-tag read 'Peter'.

****

Andrew and Bryan stepped out from Wells-on-Sea station. Andrew's father waited to greet them.

'Hello, son.' He hugged Andrew.

'Hello, Dad. This is Bryan. He flies in my section.'

'Actually, Mr Francis' – Bryan stepped forward to shake hands – '*he* flies in *my* section.'

****

After a late lunch the two pilots emerged from the Francis household into the afternoon sunshine and set off for a stroll. Skirting around the edge of the town they found themselves outside the graveyard.

'Do you mind if' – Andrew nodded at the gate – 'my mother?'

They walked through the arch and along a path lined with graves. Andrew stepped off the path and moved along the rows of stones.

'Ah, here she is.' Andrew crouched on the grass. 'Dad keeps it immaculate. These roses are from his garden' – he touched the fresh open blooms in the stone vase on the grave – 'and he does love his roses.'

Bryan nodded: 'That's nice.'

Andrew stood up and the two men walked back to the gate.

'What about your parents, Bryan?' Andrew asked. 'I've never heard you talk about them.'

'That's because I never have.'

'Why?'

Bryan shook his head: 'My parents didn't love me.' He threw a flat glance at Andrew. 'They weren't beastly to me, you understand, they just didn't love me.

'They never encouraged me, never praised me, never really understood anything I did or said. I never went hungry or cold, they always looked after me, but they did it in the manner in which you might look after a neighbour's dog. You feed it, make sure it doesn't hurt itself, try not to lose it anywhere—'

'I'm sorry, Bryan,' Andrew stammered, 'I should mind my own business.'

'Don't be sorry,' Bryan patted him on the back, 'now I've come to understand it, I can cope with it.'

'Are they still alive?' Andrew asked.

Bryan stopped. 'Come to think of it, I don't know.'

The two men walked in silence back to the centre of town. Andrew bit back the urge to apologise once more, instead he allowed the uneasiness to diffuse itself in their wordless walking.

When they reached the top of the main street Bryan brightened. He browsed in the shop windows and smiled at passers-by. They made their way down to the quayside and stood watching the tide flood into the harbour.

'You were lucky, Andrew,' Bryan murmured. 'Growing up here must've been fun.'

'Yes, it was.' Andrew pointed at the edge of the quay wall: 'Me and my best friend Peter would catch shore crabs right there.'

'Ah,' Bryan mused, 'your pongo friend. Went to fight the Bosche in France to avoid buying you a wedding present.'

Andrew nodded: 'I've heard nothing from him since.'

The flowing tide dragged in the fishing boats. One by one they wound down the narrow channel, most stacked with crabs and whelks in wooden boxes. Amongst them a yellow-painted trawler chugged into the harbour and pirouetted to face the flow before manoeuvring towards its moorings.

The boat settled against the wall and Andrew spotted a ragged bundle on the deck. He nudged Bryan to follow him and walked closer.

The bundle was a bloated body dressed in British aircrew uniform. The man's face, eaten away by fish and gulls, hung in strips around the grinning teeth of his exposed skull. His hands, also stripped, curled like claws at his side and his lower body and buttocks were black and charred.

16th June, 1940

Bryan sat out in the garden studying the Sunday papers in the morning sunshine. Andrew stepped out of the house, shrugging into his jacket.

'I'm just off to see someone,' he said. 'I shan't be long.'

Bryan peered over the top of the paper: 'Not a hometown floozy, I hope.'

Andrew laughed and headed for the gate.

Memories crowded around Andrew's head on the short walk to Peter's house and he let them ebb and flow through his mind as he strolled along the road.

In the Ellis's dishevelled front garden the roses straggled on long legs and the half-open gate sagged on its hinges. Andrew pushed through the gate and walked down the path to the front door. He knocked and waited.

'What do you want?'

Andrew started at the voice and turned to see Donald Ellis walking down the path behind him.

'Hello Mr. Ellis,' he said. 'You remember me… Andrew… I'm an old friend of Peter's'

Donald brushed by him and fumbled his key into the door: 'What do you want?'

'I came to find out if you had any news about Peter. I wondered if he may have written you a letter.'

The door swung open. 'He might've.' Donald stepped into his house. 'There might be one in that lot,' he nodded at a pile of unopened mail behind the door.

'Would you mind?' Andrew asked.

The older man shrugged and walked down the hallway to the kitchen beyond. He took a bottle of wine from one jacket pocket and a bottle of gin from the other. Setting them on the table, he reached into the sink and retrieved a tin mug.

Andrew stepped inside and shut the door. The air in the house carried a clinging sourness that stung his nostrils deep under the bridge of his nose. He crouched by the pile of mail, leafing through the envelopes. From the kitchen he heard the pop of a wine cork leaving the bottle.

Andrew came across a brown envelope bearing a regimental crest. Standing, he dropped the others to the floor around his feet. He flipped the envelope over and loosened the flap with his thumb. Unfolding the letter, he walked slowly to the kitchen as he read the typed words.

He halted by the table. Donald Ellis looked up from his drink.

'Peter is dead, Mr Ellis.' He placed the letter on the table next to the bottles. 'Dunkirk. I'm very sorry.'

Andrew turned and walked back down the hallway, over the scattered envelopes and out the door.

CHAPTER 14

Patris

18th June, 1940

The gruff voice crackled into the air above the silent pilots in the readiness hut.

'*...the whole fury and might of the enemy must very soon be turned on us. Hitler knows that he will have to break us in this island or lose the war.*

'*If we can stand up to him, all Europe may be freed and the life of the world may move forward into broad, sunlit uplands.*

'*But if we fail, then the whole world, including the United States, including all that we have known and cared for, will sink into the abyss of a new dark age...*'

'Bloody hell,' Bryan burst out, 'are we honestly still listening to that man?'

Several pilots made frantic shushing noises and leant closer to the wireless.

'Shush, yourself.'

'*...let us therefore brace ourselves to our duties, and so bear ourselves, that if the British Empire and its Commonwealth last for a thousand years, men will still say, This was their finest hour...*'

'I'm just back from the seaside,' Bryan shouted over the rising protests, 'can't we listen to a bit of Arthur Askey?'

'How does he get away with it, Andrew?' Bryan's voice dropped back to a conversational level. 'He sold Dunkirk as a victory, and now we've got old men marching up and down with broomsticks, he's calling it our finest bloody hour. If it wasn't for the English Channel we'd already be in the same boat as the Frogs.'

'We've still got the navy,' Andrew said. 'They'd make a pretty mess of an invasion fleet before they even reached the beaches.'

'The navy is no use against bombers. When fighter command has shot its bolt, the bombers will have free rein. Factories, barracks, refineries – all of them bombed flat. And then they'll parachute their army in, not a single wet foot amongst them.'

'Well,' Andrew slapped him on the knee, 'we need to 'brace ourselves to our duties' and make sure that doesn't happen.'

Bryan gazed steadily at Andrew's smiling face: 'You should go to work for Arthur Askey.'

****

A door opened at the end of the corridor and a uniformed figure stepped out.

'Pilot Officer Donaldson,' he called, 'would you like to come down, please?'

Gerry recognised Gordon Day. He stood and walked towards the open door.

'Welcome to the Air Ministry, Gerry, please sit down.' Day shuffled through some papers, holding one up: 'This is very impressive. Converting to a Spitfire in less than 20 hours, well done.'

Gerry blushed at the compliment: 'It's a very beautiful aeroplane, sir. A pleasure to fly.'

'Well, I've got your transfer orders here' – Day brandished a brown envelope – 'but I need to have a chat about some other things before we get to that.'

'Yes, sir.'

'I take it you heard Winston's speech on the radio today, with the somewhat pointed reference to America?'

Gerry nodded.

'Winston is a realist,' Day continued, 'he knows Germany will not be defeated without America's involvement. He also knows the Americans are not keen to get drawn into what they see as a European war.

'So Winston is very interested in the possibilities you represent. He sees your presence here as a 'moral quest' that transcends your national loyalties. He sees you as an example to hold up to the American people, something they can measure themselves against.'

Gerry shook his head: 'I came because it's the right thing to do, not so I'd become any sort of example.'

'Which is precisely why you *have* become an example.' Day smiled his reassurance: 'Don't worry, we don't need anything too onerous. We'll send your story to the *Evening Standard* tomorrow. I expect that will attract some

135

attention from American journalists. They'll have to come through us of course, so it's probably best not to speak to anyone we haven't cleared.

'And Winston would be very pleased if you could write about your experiences. Something we could make into a pamphlet.'

Gerry remained silent.

Day picked up the brown envelope: 'And in return you get to have your very own Spitfire.'

19th June, 1940

The two soldiers stood atop the sand-dunes looking out across the North Sea. Stretched across the sand in front of them, the coils of barbed wire already showed spots of rust. Behind them the fenced-off grazing meadows lay empty of animals. A warm southerly breeze teased at their tunics.

'Are the bastards here yet?' The cry drifted from the other side of the meadow at their backs.

The soldiers turned to see a man in civilian clothes approaching the meadow fence. One of the soldiers brought up his binoculars.

'Stone me,' he breathed, 'he's got a bottle in one hand and a service revolver in the other. Looks like he's three sheets to the wind.'

The soldier ran down to the meadow perimeter and cupped his hands around his mouth.

'Do *not* climb over the fence!' he shouted across the expanse of grass. 'This is a minefield. Turn around and go back the way you came!'

Donald Ellis paused at the fence, took a swig of gin and put the still-opened bottle back into his jacket pocket. He placed his right boot on the lower strands of wire and hoisted himself up the fence. Barbs pricked into his hands and body as he rolled over the top and landed heavily on the other side. Rising unsteadily to his feet, he lurched towards the sand-dunes.

'Stay where you are!' the soldier screamed. 'Do not move—'

The explosion sucked the man off the ground, curving his bulk through the air. The body twisted and fell flat on its back. The second explosion, muffled by the man's dead weight, threw the ragged corpse a few feet vertically before it slumped to soggy rest on the smoking ground.

20th June, 1940

The taxi pulled up by the guard hut at Kenley aerodrome as the dusk deepened to darkness.

Gerry leaned forward in the back seat: 'How much do I owe you?'

'On account, guvnor,' the driver answered, 'Air Ministry.'

'Oh,' Gerry fumbled in his pocket, pulling out an unfamiliar coin. 'Take this.'

The driver's eyebrows raised in surprise: 'Thank you, sir. Most kind.'

Gerry climbed out as the driver retrieved his holdall from the boot. The guard emerged and checked over Gerry's papers. Satisfied, he stepped back and saluted.

'I need to report to the Squadron Leader Fenton. I've just joined Bluebird,' Gerry said, 'where do I need to go?'

The guard looked at his watch. 'If the squadron leader is still on station, I imagine he's in the mess, sir,' the guard replied, 'just up there, to the left.'

Gerry hefted his holdall and trudged up the road towards the dim outlines of buildings. Squinting in the thickening darkness he made out the words 'Officers' Mess' and pushed at the door. It opened straight into a thick curtain and Gerry struggled to push his way through.

'Put that light out!' The shout was followed by raucous laughter. 'Don't you know there's a war on?'

Gerry untangled himself from the black-out curtain and stepped away from the door. A dozen faces regarded him flatly for a moment and turned away. A dark-haired man detached himself from the bar and walked over.

'Hello, I'm Andrew.' He shook Gerry's hand.

'Gerry Donaldson, I'm joining Bluebird Squadron.'

They walked back to the bar. 'That's us.' Andrew gestured at the room. 'Forgive them, they're not being unfriendly. It's just difficult being pleased to see a replacement—'

'Yes, I understand.'

'Anyway, this is Bryan,' Andrew continued. 'You'll find he really is slightly unfriendly.'

Bryan turned on his barstool to look at the newcomer, cocked an eyebrow and went back to his newspaper.

Andrew winked at Gerry: 'Would you like another pint, Bryan?'

'Is Hitler a Nazi?' Bryan drawled.

'Right,' Andrew beckoned the steward, 'three pints of bitter, please.'

'I don't really drink…' Gerry began.

'You really ought to have a drink tonight,' Bryan announced, 'because you might not have a chance tomorrow night.'

'Anyway, it's a special occasion.' Andrew slapped Gerry on the shoulder. 'You've just joined the best squadron in the RAF.'

Bryan leant over to one side and broke wind. Several beer-mats skimmed in from around the room, bouncing off his back.

The steward placed three pints on the bar.

Andrew took a swig. 'Whereabouts in Canada are you from?'

'Oh, I'm not Canadian.' Gerry shook his head. 'I'm American.'

'Hang about' – Bryan straightened in his barstool – 'there's something here in *The Standard* about an American pilot. Is that you?'

Gerry blushed: 'I think it could be.'

Bryan swivelled on his stool to address the room. 'Lads,' he called out, 'America has joined the war.'

A ragged cheer rose from the other pilots as Bryan downed half his pint to toast his announcement.

'No, hold on' – he squinted at the paper in his hand – '*an American* has joined the war.'

Hoots of mock disappointment rang around the room and more beer-mats sailed over the bar.

'A Yankee in a Spitfire, eh?' Bryan shook his head. 'Whatever next?'

'I'm supposed to report to the squadron leader,' Gerry said.

'He lives off-station,' Andrew replied, 'he'll be in the briefing hut tomorrow morning. Bluebird is on readiness at 7 o'clock. The dorm rooms are down that corridor. The steward' – he nodded towards the man behind the bar – 'will give you a key for an empty room.

'You'll need to report to Flight Lieutenant Harry Stiles too. He's the adjutant for Bluebird, affectionately known by some as 'Madge'. But don't try him until at least 10 o'clock, he's not really a morning person.'

'So, Yankee' – Bryan leant forward to interrupt – 'when is America going to step up and give us some help?'

'I don't know' – Gerry smiled – 'but at least I've turned up.'

'Surely they realise,' Bryan persevered, 'once we've been wiped out, they'll be next?'

Gerry picked up his pint in both hands and took a sip. 'They're beginning to accept that. But they don't want to send their boys to die on foreign soil.'

Andrew shook his head: 'So they'd prefer to fight on American soil?'

Gerry nodded: 'I've had a hundred conversations, and yes, that's the way they're thinking.'

'What about their families,' Andrew asked, 'their children?'

'Their towns and cities,' Bryan added. 'Take a look at Calais the next time you fly past it.'

Gerry took a larger sip of beer. 'They see it in the same light as 1917. They question what good the last war did for them.'

'Ha,' Bryan laughed, 'what kind of America would you have if the Kaiser had controlled Britain and Canada?'

Gerry shrugged: 'All they remember is the amount of money it cost them.'

Bryan swivelled back to his newspaper. 'I hope the lovely American people and their piles of dollars will be very happy under their impending German government.'

Andrew leant on the bar. 'You're in for a lot of that, I'm afraid.' He pulled a thin smile. 'It's not really fair. I suppose it always looks different from the sharp end.

'You see, when we come into land we often fly over a village ten miles to the east of here. My wife lives in that village, she's carrying our first child. Everything about this war is personal to us, and that sometimes makes it seem a bit desperate.'

Gerry nodded: 'The last time I saw my mother she was sobbing her heart out. The last time I saw my sweetheart she was walking out of my life.' He took another swig of beer. 'It's personal for me too.'

21st June, 1940

A pall of cigarette smoke drifted into the rafters of the briefing hut. Squadron Leader Fenton walked in and took the dais.

'Good morning, gentlemen,' he smiled into the upturned faces, 'things have been a bit slow over the past few weeks, which I know has been a great disappointment to many of you. But don't fret, the Germans have not gone away. They've just been occupied moving their airfields to the

Channel coast. Once they've got settled in, no doubt they'll turn their attention on us again.

'When they're ready, it's likely they'll start with the closest targets. That means our supply convoys in the Channel will be first on their list. This gives us a wee bit of a problem. Our RDF stations can't give us enough warning to get airborne and intercept short-range bomber attacks before they happen. As you will appreciate, chasing the Germans home after they've sunk our merchantmen isn't going to win the war. So that means standing patrols over the Channel.'

A low groan came from the assembled pilots.

'I know, I know,' the squadron leader chuckled, 'we might get lucky, we might not. I'm particularly keen myself to have a crack at a Stuka after seeing what they did at Dunkirk. We'll see what happens.

'But remember, every bomber strike is likely to have escorts. The 109s are a lot closer to their bases than they were at Dunkirk, so they'll have a lot more fuel to mix it up in a scrap. And don't chase them too far inland in case you run into some of their mates on their way out.

'It will be no surprise to you that the Luftwaffe outnumbers us quite heavily. So, text-book squadron or section attacks are no longer applicable against large formations. We need to get as many guns to bear as quickly as possible to disrupt the bombers before they reach their target. So once you hear the 'Tally-ho', choose individual targets.

'One more thing before we take off. Pilot Officer Gerry Donaldson joins us for the first time today. Gerry has come all the way from America to lend a hand. Back home he worked as a flying instructor, which is why he converted to Spits in around 20 hours, so he knows what he's doing in the cockpit. Gerry will be less familiar with King's regulations, mess bills and cricket, so help him out where you can.'

Laughter smattered the room.

'You'll fly as my wingman, Gerry.' The squadron leader picked up his helmet and gloves: 'Let's go to war, gentlemen.'

****

Molly's head rested on Andrew's shoulder. The pale skin of her pregnant belly pressed against his waist. He pulled the bed clothes up and over her hips.

'You're not to get cold,' he said, 'put something on.'

'No, not yet,' Molly murmured, 'it's such a relief to be naked. Nothing I have fits properly anymore.'

Andrew stroked her abdomen, delighting in its curve. 'How are feeling? Is everything going well?'

'How would I know? I've never done this before,' Molly laughed, 'but my ladies in the shop have been very helpful. Apparently the backaches and trapped wind are perfectly normal.'

Andrew craned his neck to kiss the top of her head. 'I received a letter from Dad today; Peter's father has been killed in an accident.'

Molly twisted to look at Andrew face: 'Accident?'

'He walked into a minefield.'

'Oh Lord,' she breathed, 'where will it end?'

Andrew shuffled onto his side, took Molly in his arms and squeezed her gently: 'I'm afraid it's only just beginning.'

5th July, 1940

'Beehive Control to Bluebird Leader, I have bandits on their way home. Climb to Angels fifteen. Patrol Dover.'

Gerry's skin tingled with a sudden excitement.

'Bluebird Leader to Bluebird Squadron. Angels fifteen. Buster, buster.'

Gerry sat behind the squadron leader's port wing. Fenton's Spitfire reared into a steep climb, bucking away with acceleration. Pushing his own throttle through the gate, Gerry leapt after him.

Taking a deep breath, Gerry pulled the guard off the red firing button and swivelled the ring from 'Safe' to 'Fire'. The deliberate nature of the act cemented his resolve. He flicked his gunsight on and checked his oxygen valve was fully open.

'Beehive Control to Bluebird Leader. Vector one-three-zero. Climb to Angels twenty.'

Halfway across the Channel the Spitfires levelled out at 20,000ft, throttling back to cruising speed.

The squadron banked into a long shallow turn to port. A flash of movement down to his right caught Gerry's eye. A small silhouette raced along at lower level, heading straight for France. He reached for the transmit button, but an urgent voice stopped the motion.

'Bluebird Leader to Bluebird Squadron! Bandits at 11 o'clock. Tally-ho!'

Gerry glanced to his left and spotted the aircraft his leader had called out. He counted five black dots heading towards them. As the squadron wheeled left to intercept them, Gerry made a snap decision. He peeled away to the right to chase the lone aircraft the others hadn't spotted.

The nose of his Spitfire dipped into a vicious dive as he pushed the throttle fully open. Trading altitude for velocity, the air-speed indicator ticked up towards 400 miles an hour.

Gerry eased back on the stiffening control column, pulling out of the dive in small increments, fighting the g-force threatening to drain the light from his vision and the thoughts from his mind. Flattening out to level flight, he spotted his target, still some distance ahead but travelling slower.

Gerry's thumb hovered in readiness over the firing button. 'What if it's a British fighter?' he thought.

He eased his Spitfire up slightly to get a better view. The blue-grey fighter plane ahead of him flew on squared-off wings which bore large white-edged crosses.

Gerry bobbed back down behind his target, took a glance in the rear-view mirror to check his tail and pressed the firing button. The Spitfire shuddered with violent recoil, then Gerry jolted in his seat as his plane bucked in the enemy's slipstream.

His windscreen was suddenly empty. Cursing his carelessness, Gerry scanned the sky, catching sight of his quarry at the bottom of a diving turn. Rolling his Spitfire over, Gerry dived in pursuit.

Gaining again, the French coast slid beneath him. Over home territory, the German stopped running, swinging into a tight turn to engage his pursuer. Gerry hauled round to cut inside the other plane's circle.

Trapped inside the wider curve, the German could only hold the turn. His plane edged closer to the centre of Gerry's gunsight.

Boom!

A detonation clanged through the airframe behind Gerry. He hauled back on the stick, throwing his plane into an opposite turn. A huge shape flashed past his machine, banking to pursue him.

Gerry screamed into a climbing turn to come around into a firing position on his assailant. Another huge shape flashed over him. His original opponent returned to the fight. Gerry stuck with his turn, inching his nose onto the second 109's tail.

The dark silhouette grew larger. As Gerry prepared to fire, his stomach lurched in horror. The electric gunsight was dead and dark. Grappling to stay in place behind his target, he thumped the base of the gunsight with his gloved hand, shouting in frustration.

White fingers of tracer curled over his right wing, dashing away ahead of him, their trails pumping closer to his cockpit. Swallowing panic, Gerry pulled into another violent turn that flung his shuddering Spitfire into a tailspin.

Dropping away from the combat, Gerry kicked the rudder to correct the spin and nose-dived to regain airspeed before levelling out. His compass spun wildly. Looking about to get his bearings, a thin white line on the horizon lent him a clue.

Gerry turned to threaten the 109 that was still in view. It banked away to the east. Gerry turned back to the west and the thin strip of Dover chalk. He rammed the throttle into full boost and dived for home trailing black exhaust smoke across the water.

****

Gerry taxied in next to a knot of pilots talking and gesticulating amongst themselves. He was the last to land. The ground crew waved him into place and he shut down the engine. Pulling off his helmet and gloves, he climbed out of the cockpit.

As he hit the turf his legs threatened to buckle beneath him and he reached out to steady himself against the fuselage with his left hand. He hung his head forward to stretch neck muscles that were locked like steel cables at the base of his skull, wincing against the pain. Despite the sunshine bathing the airfield, cold shivers crept up his spine.

'You really ought to look at this.' Andrew's voice came from the other side of the fuselage. 'You picked up a cannon-shell'.

Gerry walked around the tail to join him. There, just below the roundel, a ragged hole breached the aluminium skin of the aeroplane. Gerry crouched next to Andrew as he peered into the cavity.

'Looks like a couple of battery connections have been cut,' he said.

'That explains why my gunsight stopped working.'

'But look at this.' Andrew put his fingers behind two control cables at the bottom of the fuselage. Against his pale skin it was easy to see both were nearly severed. 'That's your elevator and that's your rudder. You're lucky you brought this crate home.'

Gerry looked away into the sky, sucking in a deep breath. Without a rudder or elevators there would be little chance of staying alive against two 109s.

'Good Lord, Yankee,' Bryan's ebullient voice jarred Gerry's reflection, 'what have you done to the King's Spitfire?'

'Bryan has just scored his third victory.' Andrew stood, helping Gerry to his feet. 'So the beers are on him tonight.'

'Well done.' Gerry forced a smile. 'What did you get?'

'Oh just a cheeky little 109. Confirmed, mind you.' Bryan leant forward: 'Do you know the best way to get a 'confirmed'?'

'What's that?'

'Keep firing until the canopy shatters,' Bryan grinned, 'because if the canopy goes, the bastard's head goes with it.'

CHAPTER 15

Mater

19th July, 1940

Eileen Drew pushed her straggling hair away from her eyes and bent to scrubbing the kitchen table. The knock on the door echoed along the hallway and she froze mid-stroke, waiting. The knock came again. She glanced at the clock, shaking her head as she thought: 'Must be a salesman'. Tutting, she wiped her hands on a tea-towel and walked down the hall to open the door.

Eileen's hand flew to her mouth: 'Vincent!' She threw her arms around him and squeezed.

'Hello, Mum.'

'Come in, boy, come in.'

Vincent peered warily over her shoulder.

'He's at the slaughterhouse until six, then he'll go straight to the pub. Come in, son.'

Vincent walked down the hall to the kitchen and sat down at the still-damp table. Eileen closed the door and followed him.

'I've missed you, Vincent,' she smiled through fresh tears, 'it's so good to see you again.'

Vincent took her hand in his: 'I came back to say I'm sorry, Mother. I'm sorry I didn't have the courage to stay and help you. I'm sorry I ran away without saying goodbye.'

He reached out to wipe Eileen's tears away with his thumb. 'I took the train to London. The RAF were recruiting at the station. I just fell into it, really.' His own tears welled. 'I'm sorry, Mother.'

'No,' Eileen shook her head, 'you shouldn't be sorry, Vincent. No boy should have to see his mother treated like a sack. It isn't you who should be sorry.'

'Is he still...?' Vincent didn't know how to finish the sentence.

'He has another woman somewhere.' Eileen pushed her hair away from her brow. 'A younger woman I think. She takes the brunt these days. There's still a little left for me, but it's not that often anymore.'

She walked to the stove: 'Would you like some tea?'

Vincent watched his mother's back as she filled the kettle and warmed the teapot. She spooned tea-leaves into the pot and paused. Her head sagged forward as she leant on the stove's edge. Without turning she spoke: 'Did he ever touch you?'

Vincent swallowed against the sudden dryness in his mouth. 'No, Mum. Never,' he lied.

Her shoulders relaxed. She retrieved two cups from the draining board and placed them on the table. 'So, my lovely young man, what is it you do in the RAF?'

'For the first few months I helped the armourers, loading and cleaning the guns in the planes.'

Eileen smiled over her shoulder: 'That sounds like an important job.' She poured boiling water into the teapot and stirred. 'Certainly a bit different from baking bread.'

She brought the pot to the table and sat down. The first few months?'

'For the last six weeks they've been teaching me how to fly the planes.'

Eileen's face froze: 'What sort of planes?'

'Fighters,' Vincent smiled, 'Spitfires. They're the best, Mum. At the end of next week I'm joining a squadron on the south coast.'

'Fighters...' Eileen poured the tea. '...*fighters*.'

'The Germans are banging hell out of our merchantmen in the Channel,' Vincent continued. 'I'm going to help stop them.'

'Six weeks?' she murmured. 'They taught you to fly a plane in six weeks? Vincent, it takes longer than that to learn how to drive a car.'

'There's a war on, Mum.'

29th July, 1940

'Beehive Control to Bluebird Leader. Many bandits massing north of Calais. Fifty-plus. Vector one-one-zero.'

'Bluebird Leader to Bluebird Squadron, one-one-zero. Buster, buster.'

Andrew pushed his throttle forward. Excitement thrilled up his spine. After days of slogging up and down the Channel without a sight of the enemy, their luck had changed – Bluebird was airborne at the same time as the raiders.

Folkestone slid away underneath the Spitfires' wings. The black shapes of the convoy they'd come to protect slunk slowly through the waves, heading south-west. Another squadron flashed over the coast to their left.

'Bluebird Leader to Bluebird Squadron. Hurricanes at 8 o'clock. Let them have the bombers. Let's get some altitude for the fighters.'

The Spitfires lifted into a climb. The Hurricanes, flying level, overhauled them.

Andrew watched the squat fighters vanish beneath the back edge of his wing then fell to searching the sky ahead.

Bluebird Squadron levelled out, dropping to cruising speed. Andrew could see the Hurricanes ahead and below – four little V-shaped formations barrelling towards battle. Squinting against the reflective glare of the clouds, Andrew could make out the tiny black dots of the enemy formation.

'Bluebird Leader to Bluebird Squadron. Bandits 12 o'clock. More fighters than bombers by the looks of things. Stay in sections until they play their hand. Tally-ho!'

Andrew glanced up at the fighter cover, but his gaze was drawn back to the 12 Hurricanes. They flew head-on towards 30 or more twin-engine bombers. Suddenly gun-smoke streamed away from the Hurricanes as they opened fire.

The concentrated violence of 96 machine-guns shattered the spell. The bombers broke formation, swerving out of the path of their attackers. One slumped over on to its back and fell into a vertical dive towards the sea, trailing smoke from its port engine.

'109s coming down now!'

The German fighters sliced down in a steep dive, firing as they swept past, scattering Bluebird Squadron in its turn.

'They're going for the Hurricanes, Bluebird. Let's get after them.'

Andrew rolled his machine onto its back and pulled into a dive. Ahead, the Hurricanes broke away from the disarrayed bombers as the 109s ploughed into the combat.

One Hurricane banked into a climbing turn away from the melee. Behind him, unseen below his tail, a 109 skidded into position to open fire. Andrew hauled his Spitfire around until the German filled his windscreen. He squeezed out an un-aimed burst of fire. Strikes blossomed on the 109's wingtip and the plane broke away, diving for the sea.

Andrew kicked the rudder and careered after the fleeing German. The speed of the dive stiffened his controls. By main force Andrew pulled the target to the centre of his gunsight. Jabbing the firing button he loosed two long bursts into the rear of the German fighter.

Flames burst from under the 109s engine cowling, washing along the sides of the cockpit and back along the fuselage. The plane bucked in its dive, like an animal in spasms of pain.

Andrew checked his tail, throttled back and pulled out. Banking round he watched the falling torch of wreckage plunge into the sea, spewing out a plume of white foam from the water.

Scanning the sky Andrew spotted a plane above him. He watched its approach with caution until he could make out the roundels on its underside. The Spitfire drew up next to him and Andrew recognised Gerry.

'Where did everyone go?' The American's drawl sounded strange in his headset.

'It appears the bombers thought better of it. Let's go home.'

Gerry gave him a thumbs-up: 'I can confirm your 109 when we get back. I saw it all.'

Gerry's Spitfire slid into formation on Andrew's right wing. Andrew pulled back his canopy to let the slipstream buffet his face while he tried not to imagine fire in the cockpit.

1st August, 1940

'Hell,' Bryan shaded his eyes, squinting into the sky, 'that'll make it even more difficult to get a comfy chair in the mess.'

Two Hurricane squadrons circled Kenley, dropping section by section into the glide-path to land.

'The whole place will be overrun with bloody tractor drivers.'

Andrew hissed a sharp intake of breath: 'Hold on, Bryan. It wasn't so long ago you were lusting after one of those Hurricanes.'

'My dear boy' – Bryan levelled his gaze at Andrew – 'one's affection for a bulldog cannot be expected to last when one has raced a greyhound.'

'Hello guys.' Gerry sat down on the grass between them. 'I'm on your section this morning.'

'Good grief, Andrew,' Bryan chuckled, 'the teacher's pet has come to play with the naughty boys. Shall we let him stay?'

Gerry shook his head: 'Squadron Leader Fenton thinks I might learn something flying with you two. So far all I've learnt is that you're an ass, Bryan.'

'Stop it you two,' Andrew chided, 'let's enjoy the peace while it lasts.'

'Ass?' Bryan muttered to himself. 'Is he talking about a donkey?'

The last of the Hurricanes taxied in and switched off. Silence settled over the field.

In the hut the telephone jangled once. The pilots on readiness froze in mid-movement. A head emerged from the window.

'Bluebird Yellow Section scramble. Lone intruder off Eastbourne.'

Andrew, Bryan and Gerry burst into motion, running for their planes. A minute later three engines choked into life and Yellow Section climbed into the air.

Andrew finished cranking up his undercarriage as Bryan's voice cut through the ether: 'Bluebird Yellow Section to Beehive Control. We are airborne. Listening out.'

'Beehive calling Bluebird Yellow Leader. Vector one-five-seven, Angels five. Lone bandit stooging around off Eastbourne. Take a look will you?'

Bryan accelerated, Gerry and Andrew tucking in behind him. The fields rolled away beneath as they levelled out at 5000ft.

Eastbourne appeared, a dark smudge banded by beach, then they were over the sparkling wave-tops.

'Beehive Control calling Bluebird Leader. Bandit due east of your position, heading for home.'

Bryan banked them onto the new course and Andrew searched the sky.

'There it is,' Gerry's voice came over the air, 'dead ahead. But it's white... why is it painted white?'

The three Spitfires gained rapidly. Andrew saw they were chasing a white bi-plane with large floats, lumbering along a few dozen feet above the surface.

'Yellow Three to Yellow Leader,' Andrew called, 'those are red crosses on the wings, Bryan. It's a rescue plane.'

'Yellow Leader to Yellow Section.' Bryan ignored Andrew's transmission. 'Tally-ho!'

The leading Spitfire peeled off into a dive after the bi-plane. Andrew and Gerry flew on straight and level.

'Yellow Three to Yellow Leader,' Andrew's voice rose, 'I repeat, it's a rescue plane. It's marked with red crosses.'

'They're all bastards...'

Bryan opened fire, a great swathe of bullets slashed into the water next to the float-plane, churning the sea to maelstrom. The bi-plane wallowed left and right to evade the attack.

Bryan's second burst bracketed the aircraft. Black holes and rents peppered its white body and wings. The bi-plane's nose sagged and its floats hit the waves. The machine somersaulted twice, wrenching its wings into tatters, and landed on its back in the water.

Bryan flew low over the sinking flotsam, dipping a wing to examine it as he passed.

'Yellow Leader calling.' Bryan's voice held a peculiar flatness. 'Regain formation, Yellow Section. We're going home.'

Andrew and Gerry banked down to take position behind Bryan. No one broke the silence on the flight home.

The three Spitfires circled the aerodrome and Bryan led them down to land. Each pilot taxied to their station in dispersal and shut down their engines.

Bryan walked to the readiness hut for debriefing; Andrew and Gerry trailed after him.

The stifling air in the hut hung heavy over the trio as they sat down before the intelligence officer's desk. Fagan, a slight and thoughtful man, looked up over his spectacles at Bryan: 'Any contact?'

'Yes,' Bryan nodded, 'control directed us onto a lone raider. We caught up with him about ten miles off Eastbourne.'

Fagan nodded as he typed. 'Did you identify the raider?'

'It was a Heinkel float-plane.'

Gerry couldn't contain himself: 'It was a Red Cross rescue plane.'

Fagan held up his hand to silence Gerry, 'Any other markings?'

'Yes,' Bryan glanced at Gerry, 'a ruddy great swastika on its tail-plane.'

Fagan looked at Andrew and then Gerry. Both remained silent.

'Did you engage?'

'Two three-second bursts from dead astern. The raider hit the sea and sank very quickly.'

'Can you confirm this?' Fagan looked up again at Andrew and Gerry.

'Yes,' Andrew said, 'that's exactly what happened.'

'Well done, Hale,' Fagan smiled, 'another confirmed kill.'

2nd August, 1940

Vincent checked over his Spitfire with the rigger.

'Everything is sound. This little lovely has been out on a few patrols already so I'm sure she won't be springing any surprises on you, sir.'

The man strode away to the next fighter and Vincent stood alone surveying the aircraft. He walked back to the readiness hut battling with conflicting emotions. The thought of flying into combat for the first time filled him with dread. Under the dread lay a desperation to get it behind him, to prove to himself he could do it.

He slumped into a deckchair and breathed deeply to calm his fluttering heart.

'For Christ's sake, Kingfisher Squadron, get off the deck!'

Vincent leapt to his feet. The voice came from the field rather than the orderly in the readiness hut.

The squadron leader sprinted past, struggling into his flying jacket as he ran, 'Kingfisher, scramble!' he shouted over his shoulder. 'They've dropped us in it this bloody time!'

Vincent gazed into the sky beyond the airfield. A large bomber formation cruised towards them at about 15,000ft.

Vincent grabbed his flying jacket from the back of the deckchair and ran into the melee of pilots and mechanics.

Climbing into his cockpit he glanced back at the approaching formation. A sudden lurch of terror gripped his throat. There wasn't time! They'd be blown to hell before they could get off the ground.

Gunning the Spitfire's spluttering engine, Vincent swallowed his panic and taxied away to the runway. The first flight of six raced across the grass in front of him, lifting into the air.

Vincent looked around in desperation. He formed up with four other members of 'B' flight, but couldn't see the leader. Craning his neck, he caught sight of the missing plane. The propeller windmilled on the power from the starter battery but refused to catch.

Vincent's panic forced a whimpering moan through his throat. He screwed his head round to the approaching raiders, trying to calculate where they would release their bombloads in order to hit the aerodrome. It couldn't be long.

Gritting his teeth, he fought the desire to take off alone and fixed his gaze back on his leader. The reluctant engine coughed plumes of blue smoke and fired up. The mechanics pulled away the chocks and the Spitfire lurched forward towards the waiting flight.

Vincent twisted his head round to check the bombers. They flew directly overhead with bomb-bays closed. Their target lay elsewhere.

The flight surged across the grass and bucked into the air. With undercarriages locking into place they curved away to port in a steep climbing turn to the north.

'Kingfisher 'B' flight calling, where are you 'A' flight?'

'Hello, Kingfisher 'B' flight, we're due north of base, Angels four. Climbing like bastards. Pull your finger out.'

Kingfisher Squadron climbed at 3000ft a minute towards the enemy formation. The bombers lay in front but still above the climbing Spitfires. Kingfisher 'A' flight flew at full throttle boost and black streams of oily vapours swept away from their exhausts.

'Kingfisher 'B' flight. Full boost, chaps, we don't want to miss the fun.'

Vincent throttled back, pushed the small red boost lever fully forward and opened up the main throttle once more. The aircraft leapt forward, jarring him back into his seat. The engine vibrated with noise and black smoke from Kingfisher 'B' flight joined the trail of their comrades.

Reaching the height of the bomber formation the squadron closed up.

'Mandrake Control to Kingfisher Squadron. How far are you from contact? Listening out.'

'Kingfisher Leader to Mandrake. What the bloody hell do you think you're playing at? I've had contact with these bastards since they showed up at my airfield unannounced. I can *see* them. Get off the air and learn to stay awake, stupid clots.'

Kingfisher Squadron levelled out at 16,000ft. They flew behind and to the starboard of the bomber formation. Vincent beheld the enemy for the first time. One hundred bombers, stepped up in ten ranks of ten from front to rear; 5000ft above the bombers he spotted the vapour trails of at least twenty escorting 109s.

'Kingfisher Leader to Kingfisher Squadron. That's a bloody hornet's nest of rear-gunners down there. So we'll take 'em head-on. Stay tight, Kingfisher. Buster, buster.'

Black smoke belched from the exhausts as the squadron pushed their engines once more into boost. As the Spitfires overhauled their target, the bombers receded over Vincent's left shoulder. He judged they'd gained about three miles when the wireless crackled to life again: 'Kingfisher Leader to Kingfisher Squadron. Throttle back, prepare for attack.'

A moment later the leader led the squadron around in a steep turn to port. Vincent slipped the safety off and rested his thumb on the firing button. The horizon filled with ugly black shapes punctuated by sparkling canopies careening towards him at incredible speed. He jabbed the firing button without aiming and his machine vibrated with the furious recoil of eight machine guns.

From the corner of his eye Vincent caught the leading Spitfires breaking left and dropping below the first rank of bombers. Vincent held the firing button for a second longer.

The perspex nose of a Heinkel 111 loomed, a helmeted figure threw his arms across his face. Vincent wrenched the control column to the left and back, kicking full port rudder. Blackness crashed down on his vision and a huge jolt reverberated down the airframe from the tail.

The crushing weight of gravity pushed him further into the cockpit, dragging down the flesh on his cheeks and compressing his blinded eyes back into his skull.

Shudders wracked through the Spitfire as it stalled at the top of its uncontrolled turn, hung for a moment in space, then dropped into a sickening spin. Vincent's vision returned to see the countryside carouselling from left to right.

He pushed starboard rudder to stop the spin and let the plane dive to increase airspeed before wrenching back into level flight.

Panting, he checked his tail in the rear-view mirror. It looked intact and the air was clear behind him. He scanned the sky searching for the bomber formation and the battle he'd dropped away from. They had moved on out of sight. Flying straight and level in the empty sky, Vincent became aware of a clinging wetness on his legs and a pungent stench filling the cockpit.

CHAPTER 16

Ignis

5th August, 1940

'What's going on over there?' Bryan murmured.

Andrew raised his head to see Gerry deep in conversation with Squadron Leader Fenton and a civilian in an ill-fitting suit. Fenton shook the suited man's hand and strode away.

Gerry and the stranger walked towards the readiness hut. As they got closer their conversation drifted over on the gentle summer breeze.

' …came in through Ontario, took a flight test and joined right there. Shipped over on a troop liner and arrived in Liverpool about seven weeks ago,' Gerry said.

'How many Americans are flying with the RAF?' The stranger spoke with an American accent. He held a pad of paper, making notes as they talked.

'I've heard there are a few in training. But I believe I'm the only one on operations.'

'Ok,' the man licked his pencil, 'I'll put 30.' He wrote a few words. 'Now, when do you normally take off?'

The pair reached the chairs grouped on the grass outside the readiness hut. Gerry motioned for the man to sit down. Andrew and George put down their reading matter and Bryan lit a cigarette.

'We have a control system to tell us when to take off,' Gerry explained. 'When they detect a raid they call on the phone and tell us where to intercept it.'

'Detect?' the suited man frowned.

'It's called Radio Direction Finding. They bounce radio waves off the incoming planes and observe them on a screen.'

'Fascinating.' The man scribbled in his pad. 'And this is a British invention?'

Gerry nodded.

The man leant forward: 'Have you been in combat—?'

'Yes, he has,' Bryan interrupted, 'he nearly got his *ass* shot off.'

Gerry smiled: 'These are some pilots from Bluebird Squadron' – he gestured towards the suited man – 'and this is Mr Renton, war correspondent for *Collier's Weekly* back in the States.

'In answer to your question, yes,' Gerry turned back to the journalist, 'I've been in close combat with a pair of 109s, and, as Bryan suggested, I did pick up some damage on my Spitfire.'

Renton narrowed his eyes: 'Were you scared?'

'I'm scared all the time, Mr Renton,' Gerry said. 'I don't necessarily see that as a bad thing.'

Renton turned his body to include the other pilots: 'When do you expect to beat the Luftwaffe?'

George snorted a burst of laughter. 'We don't.' He leant forward in his deckchair. 'No force outnumbered this badly has the right to expect anything of the sort.'

Renton's pencil scurried across the page. 'So, why do you carry on fighting?'

'We've heard what they've done in France,' Andrew said.

'The Germans are fighting a total war,' Gerry continued. 'Negotiated surrender terms will mean nothing to Hitler once he has control of this country. This has to be a fight to the death.'

'Yes,' Bryan intoned, 'a fight to the bloody, unpleasant death.'

Gerry stood up: 'Would you like a look round a Spitfire, Mr Renton?'

The two men walked away towards the dispersed fighters.

6th August, 1940

'The squadron leader will see you now, Drew,' the adjutant nodded towards the office door.

Vincent stood and went through, snapping to attention before the desk. The adjutant followed him in, moving to stand at one side of the desk.

'Stand easy, Drew.' Kingfisher's squadron leader regarded Vincent over inter-woven fingers. 'I'm told you failed to take off with your section this morning.'

'Yes, sir.'

'The adjutant says your ground-crew found you unconscious in the cockpit after the others had taken off.'

'Yes, sir.'

'What's it about, Drew?'

'I believe I had a seizure, sir.'

'A seizure?'

'Yes, sir,' Vincent nodded. 'I had a couple when I was younger.'

'You realise how bloody dangerous this is, don't you, Drew?' The squadron leader leant forward 'A ruddy great Spitfire parked in the middle of the runway while its pilot has a fit.'

'Yes, sir. It hasn't happened for nearly five years, sir.'

The adjutant spoke up: 'Drew had a bit of a close shave with a German bomber on his first operational patrol. By all accounts it' – the adjutant paused, striving for delicacy – 'had a profound effect on him.'

The squadron leader chewed his lip: 'Listen, Drew, we can invalid you out of the service. You could go home and not worry about any of this anymore.'

'The diagnosis, sir?'

'It would have to be "Lack of Moral Fibre".'

Vincent flushed: 'But that's not true, sir. I want to fight. I want to make my mother proud.'

The adjutant leaned forward again: 'I could talk to the medical officer. Maybe a short stay in hospital… an assessment… something like that.'

The squadron leader nodded: 'Yes, let's try that. All right, Drew, go back to your quarters and wait for instructions. Don't leave base and don't go anywhere near a plane. Dismissed.'

'Yes, sir. Thank you, sir.' Vincent wheeled and left the room.

The squadron leader watched the door close. 'Make sure he doesn't come back to Kingfisher, will you?'

8th August, 1940

Bluebird Squadron laboured in a steep climb due south to the coast. As they levelled out at 18,000ft, faint radio chatter drifted onto the wireless from a battle already in progress:

'…hello Sandpiper Yellow Section, 110 behind you…'

'…damn it! Close up, Peewit Red Two and watch for the 109s on your left…'

'…Magpie White Two, where the bloody hell are you…?'

'…attacking now, Sheldrake Squadron, loosen up a bit…'

'…I don't know Blue One, but there are some bastards up there at 9 o'clock…'

'…Tally-ho, Tally-ho, Sandpiper Red Leader, attacking now…'

'...*yes, I can see him, glycol leak I think, he's getting out, yes, he's bailed out, he's all right...*'

Andrew strained his eyes at the sky ahead. The backdrop of cloud looked innocuous in its white innocence until a pin-prick of orange light burst into brief effervescence, curving a slow path down towards the earth. Around the spot where the flames blossomed Andrew could distinguish black dots against the firmament, whirling like angry insects chasing one another's tails.

'Bluebird Leader to Bluebird Squadron. They're mixing it up dead ahead. Looks like fighters only, I see no bombers. Go in as sections and choose individual targets. Good luck.'

The squadron drifted apart as each flight of three planes jockeyed for their own space. The black dots grew into wheeling fighter planes and Andrew searched for the best way into the melee.

'Tally-ho, Bluebird!'

Bryan and George banked away to the right. Andrew banked left, heading towards a 109 and his wingman as they turned across his path. At full deflection he squeezed out a burst of fire that slashed the air behind the enemy as they flashed past. Andrew pulled into a climbing turn to avoid retaliation. Glancing into his mirror he glimpsed a twin-engine 110 side-slip past his tail, harried as it went by a Hurricane.

Andrew eased back and dropped in behind the Hurricane to protect his tail. Fire from the Hurricane's wings raked the German fighter's fuselage. It flopped onto its back and dived towards the ground. The Hurricane peeled away to the left; Andrew peeled away to the right.

A yellow-nosed 109 reared into view, rushing headlong towards him. Muzzle-flash sparkled from the German's wings. Andrew instinctively stabbed the firing button as he barrel-rolled under his enemy.

Banking away in a steep turn, Andrew spotted Bryan's Spitfire below him, circling above the cloud layer with a 109 on his tail.

Andrew dived towards them and pressed transmit on his wireless: 'Bluebird Yellow Leader, you have a bandit on your tail!'

'I bloody well know that!' Bryan's voice was compressed with the strain of his tight turn.

Andrew dropped into the turn behind the German, checked his mirror for danger, then concentrated on hauling the jinking black shape into the centre of his sights. Andrew thumbed the firing button sending a three-second storm of ordnance into and around the 109. The German turned violently to starboard. Andrew clawed after him, unleashing another three-second burst.

Strikes flashed along the enemy's tail and he side-slipped out of sight into the cloud. Andrew dived after him, throttling back to avoid a collision in the murk.

Moments later Andrew barrelled out of the cloud-base into empty sky, 3000ft above the water. He flew a wide circle, searching for any sign of a crash. The sea's serene surface offered no clues.

Brighton's dark mass sat like a scar on the English coast a couple of miles distant. Andrew banked north and flew for home.

****

Bluebird Squadron straggled back to Kenley in twos or threes. Andrew watched his comrades circle the field and swoop in to land. The faces of the pilots walking past him bore the brutal imprint of fear and fatigue.

Bryan appeared, flying helmet in hand, sucking hungrily on a cigarette. 'Thanks for slapping that 109 off my arse, Andrew,' he said, 'he was a tenacious little bastard.'

'I sent him home with a few holes in his tail,' Andrew smiled. 'Is George back yet?'

Bryan's face darkened and he said nothing.

'What happened?'

'Two 110s latched onto him.' Bryan flicked away his cigarette butt. 'I got some hits into one of them, but I couldn't shift them both.' He lit another cigarette. 'His kite burst into flames.'

Andrew sunk his face into his hands.

'I saw him bail out,' Bryan said.

Andrew brightened: 'That's good news.'

Bryan levelled his gaze at Andrew. 'He didn't get out for a fair while. The fire was ferocious…' he trailed off.

They walked in silence to the readiness hut for debriefing. As they entered, the telephone jarred into life on the desk. Fagan scooped it from its cradle and listened. Squadron Leader Fenton approached the desk, watching him with an intent gaze.

'Understood, thank you.' Fagan replaced the receiver and looked up. 'The army picked up Pilot Officer Anders just south of Lewes. They've taken him straight to hospital in Haywards Heath.'

Fenton raised a questioning eyebrow and Fagan answered with a subtle shake of his head.

The squadron leader walked over to Andrew and Bryan. 'You're both off the flying rota until tomorrow afternoon. I want you to visit George in the morning.'

9th August, 1940

Bryan's Humber slid into the car park outside the hospital. He and Andrew climbed out, straightening their uniforms. They entered the hospital and approached the prim receptionist.

'We've come to visit George Anders,' Andrew said. 'The army brought him in yesterday. He's a pilot.'

The girl blinked and dropped her eyes. 'Please take a seat, I'll get the doctor to come speak with you.'

After a few minutes a white-coated doctor approached. 'Hello, gentlemen,' he shook their hands in turn, 'you're in luck, George has just regained consciousness. Normally I wouldn't allow any visitors at this stage, however considering the circumstances—'

'Circumstances?' Bryan's question hung in the air.

'Follow me.' The doctor led them down a tiled corridor, stopping outside a door with obscured glass. When he spoke again, his voice was barely above a whisper: 'Pilot Officer Anders has suffered major burns to a large portion of his body, mostly his hands, arms, chest and face. The skin is largely gone from these areas. You'll see they are covered with a black substance.

'This is tannic jelly; it shrinks the tissue around the burn and reduces fluid loss. It also takes some of the heat out of the burn and makes it slightly less painful. His condition is very serious. There's little we can do except wait and see what happens over the next 48 hours.

'His mask protected his mouth to some degree so he can talk. Unfortunately he wasn't wearing his goggles.'

The doctor opened the door and ushered them in: 'Two minutes only, please, gentlemen.'

They entered a small private room where a single bed stood against the wall. A nurse sat next to the bed. On a small table she had a dampened sponge in a bowl and a bottle with a dropper. The blinds were down, making the room dim. A strong chemical smell filled their nostrils, undercut with the faintest odour of burnt toast.

George lay spread-eagled on the bed. Black jelly lathered his arms and chest. The fingers on his clawed hands looked stubbier than they should. His forehead and cheeks had a liberal covering of the jelly. The skin around his mouth and nose shone scarlet between large blisters. His eyes glimmered with a dull, unblinking milkiness. His stillness spoke to the agony of movement.

The nurse reached over with the dropper, dispensing relief into his unseeing eyes.

'Who's there?' George wilfully restrained his voice against the back-drop of his pain.

'It's me.' Andrew stepped forward to the end of the bed. 'Bryan's here too.' He bit off the natural urge to ask "how are you?".'

'I'm sorry about this chaps,' George's voice remained deliberate and careful, 'it's all a bit of a shambles. I'm beginning to think I should've stayed in the bloody crate. Might have been easier.'

The nurse picked up the damp sponge with her forceps and dabbed George's mouth. His tongue flicked greedily at the moisture left on his lips.

'Don't talk that way, old man,' Bryan murmured, 'the doctor's just explained everything they're doing to get you better. You're in the right hands.'

'It's such a shame,' George continued. 'I loved flying that plane. I've seen more beautiful things from a cockpit than I had any right to wish for. And now I can't fly.' He lifted the remains of his hands fractionally off the bed: 'And I'm blind.'

The doctor opened the door behind them. 'Gentlemen, I must ask you to leave now. My patient needs to rest.'

They turned towards the door.

'Chaps,' George's voice cracked with pain and emotion, 'don't let my mother see me this way.'

CHAPTER 17

Vastatio

11th August, 1940

'Died as a result of wounds,' Andrew murmured, 'makes it sound easier than it was.'

'You and Bryan must go to his funeral' – Fenton laid a hand on Andrew's shoulder – 'represent the squadron.'

'Thank you, sir. It would be a privilege.'

'By the way, I'm asking Gerry to join your section permanently,' Fenton smiled. 'Look after him for me.'

12th August, 1940

Andrew and Bryan surveyed the airfield through the early morning mist. Drizzle moistened their faces.

'Do you think they'll stay at home?' Andrew asked.

'It's not bad enough for that,' Bryan replied. 'The summer is slipping away and they've got a job to finish.'

Gerry walked back from checking his Spitfire. 'Hi, guys,' he said, 'I'm really sorry to hear about George.'

'It's a bloody awful numbers game, Yankee' Bryan sighed. 'God alone knows how many Germans are warming up their engines right now, how many more numbers will come up today.' Bryan placed a hand on Gerry's shoulder: 'But thank you. He was a good man.'

Andrew and Gerry watched Bryan walk back to the shelter of the readiness hut.

'I'm sorry…' Gerry began.

'Don't worry,' Andrew smiled at him, 'Bryan's right. It's as much about luck as judgement up there. Come on, let's get out of the rain.'

****

Bluebird Squadron reached 20,000ft in flight formation.

'Bluebird Leader calling Beehive Control. Any trade? Listening out.'

'Beehive calling Bluebird Leader. Much trade forming in Cherbourg area. Proceed to coast. Continue climb. Beehive out.'

The altimeter needle rose lazily to 27,000ft. Andrew noticed nascent vapour trails furling away from his wings. They grew in density, swirling like banners, as the aircraft crept higher.

'Bluebird Leader calling Beehive Control. We are now Angels three-zero. Bluebird Leader listening out.'

'Beehive calling Bluebird Leader. Orbit present position and wait for further instructions. Beehive out.'

The squadron banked into a lazy turn to port. As their noses came round to the south-west, Andrew spotted more vapour trails heading towards them from across the Channel. The squadron leader spotted them too.

'Bluebird Leader calling Beehive. Bugger orbiting, I see your trade heading our way. Bluebird out.

'Bluebird Leader to Bluebird Squadron. Fifty plus bandits to the south, probably 109s and there'll be bombers coming along after them. Those fighters have got the drop on us for altitude. Keep your eyes peeled. Tally-ho!'

The expected bombers emerged from the haze, tiny dots against the fuzzy sky. Andrew guessed they were flying at half his altitude, estimating 100 machines – Dorniers and Heinkels. He glanced down and spotted two Hurricane squadrons circling in wait for the bombers about 2000ft below him. Over to his right another Spitfire squadron at the same altitude barrelled in the same direction.

'Bluebird Leader to Bluebird Squadron. Form in sections, line astern. Tail-end Charlies, get weaving.'

Andrew dropped in behind Bryan and Gerry. He let his plane lag behind a little, then increased the throttle and banked alternately port then starboard, searching the sky above and behind for enemy fighters.

The vapour trails above him stayed stubbornly straight, drifting into the sun's glare. Andrew held his right hand over his eyes, peering through the gap between his fingers to keep track of the enemy fighters.

The wireless crackled with excited chatter as the Hurricanes joined battle with the main bomber force. Andrew resisted the urge to look down and stuck to his dazzled vigil. Sweat streamed from under his flying helmet, dripping from his chin.

The vapour trails curved into semi-circles. Squinting through his fingers Andrew sensed the Messerschmitts peeling off into a dive.

He jabbed the transmit button: 'Look out, Bluebird aircraft, 109s coming down now.'

Andrew stopped weaving and followed the rest of Yellow Section in a tight turn to port. The three aircraft formed a cartwheeling defensive circle. Seven or eight 109s flashed through the centre of their circle and more barrelled past outside it, all hammering away with machine-gun fire. Bryan hauled his Spitfire onto its back and screamed down after the Germans. Gerry and Andrew followed.

Dimly aware that fewer 109s had gone past than he'd counted in the formation above them, Andrew glanced into his rear-view mirror. As he did so, white streaks flashed past his cockpit.

'109s behind, Yellow Section. Break! Break!'

Andrew lurched his Spitfire away from the white spirals and then followed Yellow Section in a tight turn to starboard.

'I'm hit!' Gerry's voice rang with pain and panic.

Andrew scanned the sky. The lone attacker climbed away to the south, content with his hit-and-run. There was no sign of the fighters they had been chasing.

'Yellow Three to Yellow Section' – Andrew forced his voice into steadiness – 'no more bandits in our vicinity.'

'Thanks, Andrew. Keep an eye out,' Bryan answered. 'What's the situation Gerry?'

Gerry came back, breathless: 'Cannon shell hits on port wing and fuselage. There are holes in my cockpit door and my left leg hurts like hell.'

'Okay, Gerry, we'll escort you home. Course zero-five-zero.'

The section curved onto the heading and Andrew weaved along behind the others.

'Right, Gerry,' Bryan continued, 'two things: how is your engine sounding; and how much blood are you losing?'

'My engine is starting to knock a bit. And it looks like plenty of blood to me, but I think it's a lot of small wounds rather than one big one.'

'I want you to get ready to bail out. Undo your straps and unplug your oxygen. Check your parachute harness is undamaged and make sure you can reach the D-ring.'

'Check.'

'Now pull back the canopy and lock it open.'

Andrew scoured the sky to his left. The bomber formation hung over Southampton, releasing their payloads onto the port. Bomb-bursts appeared amongst the streets and buildings. High in the sky the vapour trails of remote combat swirled their silent dance.

Bognor Regis slid below them.

'Engine noise is getting worse,' Gerry called. 'I don't think it'll last much longer.'

'All right Gerry,' Bryan answered, 'throttle back a bit and we'll take it down to 3000ft. Andrew, give us top cover please.'

Gerry descended in a shallow dive alongside Bryan as the engine's racket approached a crescendo.

'There's no future here,' Gerry called. 'I'm bailing out now.'

'All right, Gerry, remember if the parachute doesn't work, you'll have the rest of your life to fix it.'

Gerry pulled out his wireless lead and unlatched the cockpit door. Wincing against the pain, he bunched his legs under him on the seat. Pushing the stick forward he dived out towards the trailing edge of the wing.

The tail flashed past his face and the roar of the other Spitfire's engine battered his ears as Bryan swooped away.

Buffeting in the wind, Gerry pulled the rip-cord and heard the fabric snap and bustle as it unfurled into the hungry air. Twisting like a big white exclamation mark in the sky, he continued his plunge towards the ground. Gerry looked up as the canopy untangled its final folds and blossomed outwards.

The straps jerked viciously at his groin and the electric pain in his leg stabbed up his back. His head jolted forward with the sudden deceleration, dislodging his flying helmet to tumble down through space between his feet.

Twisting his head, he caught a glimpse of his stricken Spitfire ploughing vertically into a meadow, scattering a herd of sheep into terrified panic.

The drone of engines persisted. Looking up he saw his comrades circling to defend his descent.

The ground rushed up to meet him. Pulling hard on the guy-ropes to miss a copse of trees, Gerry plunged into the furrowed ground. A bright flash of pain sunk him into darkness.

Andrew breathed a sigh of relief to see Gerry safely down.

'Yellow Leader to Yellow Three' – Bryan's voice broke through on the wireless – 'let's see if those bombers are still around.'

****

'You do have beautiful hair,' Molly said as she combed and snipped, 'it's so sleek and fine.'

'But will you still love me when I'm old and grey?'

Molly paused in her work, strain flickering across her face.

Andrew retrieved the situation: '...or bald?' He smiled and caught her eye in the mirror.

Molly smiled back. 'I'm sorry,' she said, 'I see you so often. I'm so much luckier than most women.'

The dusk settled into darkness over the green outside the shop.

'We just have to get through another ten weeks,' Andrew smiled, 'if we can hold on that long we'll have a whole winter to prepare. They won't have a chance at beating us next year.'

'In six weeks we'll have a baby,' Molly sighed, 'a new life for an uncertain world.'

She finished combing and took the towel off his shoulders: 'There you are, sir. You'll look your handsome best for George's funeral.'

13th August, 1940

The nurse looked in through the open door: 'I have a visitor to see you.'

Gerry winced as he hiked himself up in the bed: 'Thank you, nurse.'

Adjutant Day entered the room carrying a large box which he placed on the table under the window.

'Good morning, sir,' Gerry said.

'Ah hello, Gerry' – Day waggled his finger – 'please call me Gordon, this is no place to stand on ceremony.' He pulled off his gloves. 'I heard you got roughed up a bit, what happened exactly?'

'I got caught out in a tail-chase. Picked up a couple of cannon-shell hits and brought some shrapnel home in my leg.'

'And how is the leg?'

'They've dug out most of the bits. They plan to go in after the rest tomorrow. Then they'll keep me here for a while to make sure there's no infection amongst all that bruising. If all goes well, I'll be back in action in a week or so.'

'Excellent,' Day nodded. 'I've brought you a present from the Ministry.'

He opened the box and pulled out a brand-new typewriter and a sheaf of paper.

'Remember our chat in my office?' Day placed the typewriter carefully on the table. 'It appears this is the ideal opportunity to start writing down your experiences. Let the American people know what's happening over here.

'I understand your interview with Renton in *Collier's Weekly* has stirred some interest in America. We'd really like to keep up the momentum. Get American public opinion more on our side.'

'Is this why I've got a private room?' Gerry asked.

Day smiled and shrugged.

'I told you I didn't come here to get special treatment.'

'Gerry' – Day sat down on the chair by the bed, his voice more serious – 'we've allowed you to do what you came here to do. There are many in the Air Ministry and in Parliament who wanted you wrapped in cotton wool and placed as far away from the front-line as possible.

'I know you came here to fly and fight, Gerry. That much was obvious to me when we first met, and I have done all I can to resist pressure to move you away from the combat zone.

'But you must realise how close you came to disaster yesterday. A few inches to the right and those cannon-shells would've hit your cockpit and your fuel tank. We would've been sending the bits we could find back across the Atlantic to your parents.

'Surely you can appreciate what that would do to Winston's drive to get America more actively involved. The isolationists could just point at your grave and say 'we told you so', 'we don't want to get sucked into your foreign war'.

'So, use your hospital time to write the pamphlet. Once they have that, they will be less concerned about what happens to you. Agree to do this and I think I can persuade them to let you go back to Bluebird Squadron.'

Gerry remained silent.

'I'll leave it with you, Gerry.' Day stood to leave. 'I'm genuinely pleased you're not badly hurt,' he smiled, 'I was once a pilot. It was all rather more sedate back then. But I know how it feels.'

Day touched the peak of his cap and left the room.

14th August, 1940

The Oxfordshire countryside rolled past the Humber. Bryan took the turn off the main road for Faringdon.

'We should be spot on time,' Bryan said.

Andrew nodded, staying silent.

They drove through the town and parked on the road outside the church.

All Saints' stood in the centre of its ancient graveyard, surrounded by the lush summer foliage of the trees. The squat central tower supported a white-painted flagpole from which flew the red and white Cross of Saint George.

Bryan took a deep breath: 'We need to win this war, if only to keep the Germans out of places like this.'

They crunched up the shingled path to the church doors. Removing their caps they entered and walked down the tiled aisle between the stone columns. Choosing a pew half-way down they sat behind the already assembled congregation.

A woman seated in the front row turned to look at them. She dabbed at her eyes with a handkerchief, got up and walked towards them. Both pilots stood as she approached. She gestured them down and sat on the pew next to them.

'Are you from George's squadron?' she asked.

'Yes.' Andrew reached out to shake her hand. 'Andrew and Bryan. We've flown with George since Egypt.'

'That's right,' she said, 'he told so many stories about his friends every time he came home.' She smiled. 'I'm his mother.'

'Very pleased to meet you, Mrs Anders,' Bryan murmured, 'if only it were under different circumstances.'

She dabbed at her cheeks again. 'I understand he managed to bail out but they couldn't save him. No one told me until after...' Her voice tangled on her emotions, '...until after he had passed. I would've given anything to talk to him one last time.'

167

Bryan leaned forward and took her hand: 'The last time I saw him, Mrs Anders, he was speaking about you. You can rest assured he loved you very much.'

She fluttered her hand in front of her face, unable to contain her emotions. Nodding her mute thanks she went back to the front pew.

The organ struck up a solemn chord and the black-suited pall-bearers entered, a shining oak coffin resting on their shoulders. The slow procession moved down the aisle and the bearers placed the coffin on trestles under the pulpit. The chief pall-bearer placed a laurel wreath and lilies on top of the casket.

The organ transitioned into the first hymn. Andrew held his hymn book open but couldn't read the words through the sting of his tears.

The final chord reverberated around the stone walls and the vicar motioned everyone to be seated. He climbed the steps into the pulpit and gazed for a moment on the coffin below him before raising his face to the congregation: 'This year Britain has become our last stronghold. A fortress defended with small aircraft flown by these strange, unknown young men.' His glance flicked over Andrew and Bryan. 'But are they unknown? Look at them and you will realise you do know them. They are our sons, our nephews, friends of our sons and daughters. Each a vibrant spark of God's beloved humanity. All of them welcome in our houses and at our tables.

'Cast your mind back a few short years. We watched them in those summer days when our stronghold was nothing but their playground. They picnicked on the village greens amongst the sweet bird-chatter. They laughed and played on the beaches, kicking the water with bare toes. And later they watched and then loved the young girls dressed in coloured frocks like the most wonderful of God's flowers.

'Now the flowers have faded to khaki and the bird-chatter is stilled under the clattering machines of war. These young men have stepped forward, separated in their blue, to become the winged warriors at the end of the trails that track the vaults above our heads.

'George has gone, but he is not so far away that he cannot still see England's face. The woods he played in, the fields he crossed, the town where he grew up and the prettiest flowers that remain unpicked.

'He has flown on English air to a new world. But he can still see the world he knew just a few days past. And, in our hearts, we may yet see his frozen trail looped white across the heavens. For the air was his kingdom and he was a shield for those who lived under his wings.

'His brief life has been given up as a ransom, that we might one day be free again. He has given up the richness of days not yet lived, the chance to hear his child's voice and the solace of true love to ease his years of frailty. All this lost in a moment of willing sacrifice.

'No thanks we may give him can weigh sufficiently against what he gave. But the clouds in our English skies can entwine with our eternal remembrance and together we may bind a wreath of honour that is worthy for his grave.'

****

The pall-bearers lifted the coffin and walked in step back down the aisle. As they passed, the occupants of each pew filed out behind the procession. Andrew and Bryan stood still, the church emptying behind them.

'We should attend the burial, Bryan.' Andrew looked into Bryan's red-rimmed eyes.

'No,' Bryan whispered, 'I watched him being cremated, I can't bear to see him being buried as well.'

CHAPTER 18

Bilis

15th August, 1940

Bluebird Squadron levelled out at 30,000ft. Andrew glanced down at the flat white carpet of cloud below, gleaming in the bright sunlight. Above, the sky throbbed with an intense blue, broken only by remote wisps of cirrus. Over to the east the clouds broke up, revealing glimpses of the North Sea and the Dutch Islands. Squinting against the haze, Andrew could make out the graceful curve of the Norfolk coast. The crackling wireless broke through his thoughts.

'Hello Beehive Control, Bluebird Leader calling. We are at Angels three-zero. Many bandits in sight, heading north. Will engage.'

'Well done, Bluebird Leader. Good luck. Beehive listening out.'

Black dots advanced through the sky from the south, squadrons stepped up over squadrons. The dots resolved into three distinct groups, each containing over 100 bombers advancing across the Channel about 10,000ft below Bluebird.

High above the bombers their escort fighters threw off long white vapour trails. Each bomber group had its own umbrella of about 50 fighters, squadrons of nimble 109s and slower, twin-engine 110s.

Several miles stood between them, but Bluebird was closing fast. Andrew could make out other British fighters climbing to meet the intruders in groups of 12 or 36.

'Bluebird Leader to Bluebird Squadron. Line astern in flights.'

The squadron reassembled in two lines of six with their flight leaders flying next to each other about 50 yards apart. In this formation they entered the battle-zone.

Spitfires and Hurricanes already engaged the two furthest bomber groups. Squadrons broke up and individual fighters darted in to take snap-shots at the lumbering raiders. Two German machines slid into shallow dives towards the earth. White parachutes blossomed from one of the stricken bombers.

Bluebird approached the nearest bomber formation from its front port quarter, still 10,000ft higher than the target. Above the bombers Andrew picked out a screening squadron of German fighters.

'Bluebird Leader, going down now! Tally-ho!'

The squadron leader flipped his fighter upside down and screamed into a vertical dive, each member of the squadron followed one after the other.

Andrew pushed the joystick hard over to the left, bringing the starboard wing up at right angles to the horizon. Kicking the port rudder to prevent the nose from rising, he brought the starboard wing all the way over until his machine hung upside down. He pulled the stick and dived after the others.

Their speed mounted, creeping towards 400 miles per hour. The squadron tore through the milling fighter screen and opened up on the bombers.

Lining up his sights ahead of a Dornier, Andrew opened fire at 300 yards. His tracers spiralled past the front of the enemy. 'Too much deflection,' he told himself.

Pushing the stick further forward Andrew took his craft beyond the vertical and negative gravity dragged his head towards the perspex dome of the canopy. Blood forced its way into his temples as he fired again. Through the advancing red mist Andrew saw his fire striking the Dornier's engine and wing, fragments flying off into the slipstream.

He hauled the stick back and to the right, flashing past the German's wingtip. The gravity reversed, pushing him down into the seat. Blood flooded away from his head, darkness and quiet descended around him.

Andrew's head lolled as he blinked back to consciousness, momentarily unaware in his own world of strange silence. The noise of his engine tugged at his hearing, pervading by degrees from a painful distance.

A black shape flashed across his vision snapping him back to the moment. He swerved to follow it. A Spitfire. Checking his mirror, he banked away to his right. Another Spitfire spun past, tracing a vortex of flames and smoke to the sea, the pilots arms flailing out of the opened canopy.

Andrew snapped his head back to the front. Dead ahead a 109 curved upwards in a climbing turn. As it slowed at the top of the turn, the fuselage hung across Andrew's windscreen.

A large ace of spades decorated its bright yellow cowling. A black cross sat halfway towards the tail and forward of the cross, emblazoned in white, the number '13'. The pilot's head twisted towards him.

A sudden wave of rage crashed over Andrew. He stabbed the firing button. The Messerschmitt flew through his stream of bullets, hits splashing off the fuselage and tail. The German rolled on his back and pulled into a dive. Andrew followed.

Screaming down towards the sea, Andrew fixed his target in the gunsights and fired another long burst. Pieces broke away from the 109 and flames burst from under its cowling, streaming back along the wing-roots.

Andrew's helpless fury heightened. He pressed the firing button and held it down. The shuddering of the Spitfire's eight machine-guns vibrated tears into his eyes. A section of the 109's wingtip detached and the flaming fighter flipped into a violent spin.

The noise and vibration ceased as the guns ran out of ammunition. Andrew eased out of the dive. He checked his mirror and scanned the sky. He was alone.

He banked round and followed the smoke trail of his kill to the sea. A small oil slick marked the spot where his victim was buried, sinking quickly, strapped in, charred and nameless behind a now-extinguished engine.

A sudden chill crept over Andrew's skin; he was defenceless. Skimming over the waves, he pushed the throttle forward and headed for the Kentish cliffs.

16th August, 1940

Through the open window of the Red Cross car, the cool breeze from Southampton Water teased at Vincent's hair. The car slowed and turned up a long, tree-lined gravel drive that opened out into a vast lawned courtyard. Men walked and limped along the paths between the grass; some pushed others in wheelchairs.

'Netley Hospital,' the driver said.

Vincent ducked his head to take in the height and breadth of the building they approached. It stood like a promontory of red Victorian brick, its corners and windows clad in white stone. Atop its third floor rose brick chimney stacks, cupolas and coppered domes. It's frontage marched solemnly away to the middle distance in a column of uniformly arched windows.

The car pulled up and a nurse trotted down the steps to meet them. Vincent and the driver got out of the car. While the driver retrieved his case Vincent stared up at the building: 'Grand enough to be a palace,' he thought.

The driver handed the suitcase to the nurse: 'Sergeant Vincent Drew.'

'Thank you. Welcome to Netley, Vincent. Follow me.'

She led Vincent up the steps and into the building. 'You'll be staying in Albert House, 'E' Block.'

The dark interior closed in about them, disconnecting Vincent from the sunlit grandeur of the fascia. He lost his bearings as they twisted through the corridored edifice, climbing two flights of wooden stairs that creaked under their feet. At the top of the second flight they came to a landing with a set of double oaken doors, the letter 'E' stencilled in black on the wall. The nurse elbowed her way through the doors, beckoning Vincent to follow. They entered a corridor lined with more solid-looking doors, most closed, a few standing open.

An orderly sat on a chair halfway down the corridor watching their approach. The nurse stopped at an open door and motioned Vincent inside. Following, she placed his case on the iron-framed bed.

'Make yourself comfortable, Mr Drew,' she smiled, 'a doctor will be around to see you soon.'

The nurse left, pulling the heavy door closed behind her. Self-locking levers clonked into place. There was no handle on the inside.

Vincent sat on the bed and laid a hand on the rough striped pyjamas folded at its foot. A small chest of drawers lodged in the corner and a single window relieved the whitewashed blankness of the back wall. Through the dirty glass the bars on the outside were visible.

The light built into the ceiling was protected by a thick pane of glass. Desiccated insects littered the inside. Its flickering bulb teased the edge of Vincent's nerves. He cast around for a light-switch. There was none.

Vincent stood and walked to the window. He lifted the lower sash. It banged against restraining bolts after six inches. He pulled the top sash down to hit corresponding bolts. He stooped to look through the lower gap, the chill sea air smarting his eyes.

Outside was a courtyard surrounded by a 12ft wall topped with broken glass set in cement. Another building stood beyond the wall, all its windows barred on the outside. Isolated trees stood around the buildings and beyond them a higher wall enclosed everything.

In the corner of the courtyard rows of upright slabs stood in haphazard lines. He stared for a moment before he recognised it as a cemetery.

Vincent returned to sit on the bed. The levers in the door clacked up and the orderly entered carrying a tin plate. He handed the plate to Vincent and gave him a spoon. Cottage pie and vegetables.

Vincent looked from the food to the spoon: 'May I have a fork?'

The orderly shook his head and backed out the door. The latches dropped into place.

Vincent scooped the lukewarm food into his mouth and chewed disconsolately. It was growing dark when he placed the empty plate on the chest of drawers. He levered off his shoes and lay back on the bed.

The reverberation of a large switch being thrown somewhere in the block thrummed down the metal conduit and the light went off.

17th August, 1940

Vincent awoke as the levers clanked and the door swung open. A man in a white coat entered, followed by the orderly carrying two wooden chairs.

'Good morning, Vincent.' The white-coated man arranged himself on one of the chairs. He raised his eyebrows: 'I may call you Vincent?'

Vincent nodded. The orderly placed the other chair in front of the open door and sat down.

'Thank you,' the man grinned, 'I am Dr Robinson. I'm here to ask you a few questions.'

Vincent pulled himself up to a sitting position and waited.

'Now, Vincent, do you have any idea why you're here?'

'I had a small seizure in my cockpit that stopped me from taking off.'

The doctor nodded, leafing through a folder on his lap. 'Your record states your first patrol had a traumatic effect on you.' He gazed into Vincent's eyes: 'Are you sure your failure to take off wasn't rooted in a desire to avoid combat.'

Vincent met the doctor's gaze. 'I had a seizure,' he said quietly. 'If it had happened in my quarters I wouldn't be here, I'd still be flying with Kingfisher.'

'You've had these seizures before?'

'When I was younger.'

'What brought them on?'

Vincent broke his connection with the doctor's eyes: 'One at school, a few at home. They were random.'

'Random?'

Still looking down, Vincent nodded.

'All right, Vincent' – the doctor stood – 'I don't think you're a danger to yourself or anyone else. The orderly will take you to the shower-room and then out to the courtyard for some exercise.' He pulled a benign smile: 'And you'll be allowed to use the day-room.'

'When can I go back to my squadron?'

'We just need to observe you for a few days, Vincent,' the doctor beamed. 'It's just a routine measure.'

CHAPTER 19

Pugna

18th August, 1940

Gerry made his way up the approach road towards the officers' mess, limping on his sore left leg, but glad to be back. The heavy suitcase in his right hand forced him into a lurching gait, causing the typewriter in his back-pack to lump against his body.

At the mess door he put down his suitcase and back-pack, flexing his fingers to restore the blood flow. A faint droning thrummed in the summer air, like bees patrolling a flowerbed. Gerry left his bags and walked to the gap between the mess and the operations room, looking west across the aerodrome.

A Hurricane squadron stood dotted around at dispersal. Armourers and riggers crawled over the planes, preparing for the afternoon's patrols. The droning grew louder. The ground-crew paused, cocking their heads to listen. Something about the unbalanced throbbing caused the hairs on Gerry's neck to stand up.

'Take cover, take cover...' The shout drifted across the field, truncated by the deliberate *thud-thud-thud* of the station's Bofors guns and the winding moan of an air-raid siren. The field erupted into a melee of running men.

Three twin-engine aircraft burst over the tree-tops at the airfield's southern end. Bombs tumbled from their undersides, punching holes in the hangar roofs and detonating with clanging reverberations inside. Men ran and staggered from the open hangar doors, emerging through billows of choking black smoke.

A few bombs overshot the buildings and erupted in the grass, throwing up plumes of earth. Machine-gun fire sparkled from the bombers, stitching lines through the standing planes, scattering the ground-crews into scrambling panic.

A WAAF sergeant ran down the steps from the operations room.

'Where's Bluebird Squadron?' Gerry yelled.

The woman pointed up as she ran past, her mute face tight with tension.

Three more bombers hurtled in over the trees. They held their bombs a moment longer, curving them in amongst the assembled Hurricanes. The fighters bucked and reared amid the explosions, blossoming with bright orange plumes of burning fuel.

The report of bombs echoed to silence, giving way to the mortar-thump of cable defences firing into the sky between the blast pens on the field's west side. The steel cables snaked 700ft into the air and hung from small white parachutes unfurling at their ends.

The third trio of bombers scorched over the treetops, flying lower than the others. Their bombs dropped onto the runways, some exploding, others landing on their side, spinning and rolling across the grass without detonating.

One pilot saw the parachutes and clawed his aircraft into a vicious banking turn away from danger. The other two ploughed into the cables. One took a hit on each wing-tip and nose-dived into the ground. The other hit a cable between fuselage and engine, spun like a plate in the air and pancaked into the field beyond, breaking into pieces on impact.

Gerry ducked as engines roared overhead from behind. Six Hurricanes flashed across the airfield and banked over the descending cables in pursuit of the fleeing bombers.

The blanket of engine noise faded, replaced by shouts and curses mixed with the crackling of burning aluminium. A hangar collapsed with a long metallic creak and a billowing exhalation of smoke and flames.

Gerry looked up to see a large bomber formation higher in the sky heading in from the north-west.

****

'Beehive Control to Bluebird Squadron. Bandits directly overhead. Kenley is under attack.'

Andrew glanced upwards in confusion at the empty blue sky.

'Bluebird Leader to Bluebird Squadron. Bandits below. Individual attacks. Let's break this up or we'll have nowhere to sleep tonight. Tally-ho!'

Andrew looked down at the fat shapes of 50 Heinkels wallowing across the countryside about 10,000ft lower. The Spitfires around him rolled into dives. He flicked the safety off his firing button and followed them, slotting in behind Bryan's starboard wing.

Bryan swooped to attack a bomber on the outer edge of the formation, pouring bullets into the starboard engine until it belched black smoke.

The bomber cleaved away from the formation, losing height rapidly. Andrew circled as Bryan wheeled in to attack it twice more.

'I'm out of ammunition,' Bryan called. 'Can you finish him?'

Andrew dropped in behind the Heinkel and squeezed two bursts of fire into its fuselage. Flames licked out from the wing root and the huge aeroplane rolled over onto its back and dived into the ground.

****

Gerry watched the Spitfires nibbling at the edges of the formation; two bombers dropped away, one trailing flames. Escorting fighters fell from altitude into the battle and the Spitfires banked away to meet them. The Heinkels continued on their bomb-run. Tiny black dots tumbled from under the lead bomber. A moment later the others released their loads.

'Get under cover!' Gerry yelled across the field. He retreated to the mess building and crouched down by its wall, his fingers in his ears.

The first bombs erupted in the fields beyond the airfield, amongst the wreckage of the two attackers that lay scattered there, the thud of their explosions muffled by the heavy soil.

The bomb hits walked over the perimeter fence into the concrete blast pens, their concussive detonations accompanied by the metallic spatter of splinters against the pen walls. A direct hit threw a Spitfire spinning into the air.

Gerry gritted his teeth against the blast waves as bomb after bomb struck the base, the jarring explosions progressing across the field towards the already smoking buildings in the south corner.

The station headquarters took two direct hits in quick succession; the wreckage of the hangars clanged with detonations; and the sick-bay crumpled inwards on itself from a single hit.

The last few bombs hit the roads and houses outside the station entrance. Then silence fell.

****

Andrew climbed away, back towards the bombers. Bomb-flashes sparkled across Kenley, redoubling the smoke boiling out from the airfield.

Around the bombers, Hurricanes swirled in dogfights with twin-engine 110 fighters. A Hurricane banked past Andrew, a German fighter hanging on his tail. Andrew pulled into a tight turn, dropping in behind the 110. He fired a short burst, his tracers flashing high over the Messerschmitt's canopy.

The rear-gunner returned fire, his shots splaying wide as the alerted pilot broke away from the Hurricane. Andrew skidded round under the German's tail, out of the gunner's reach and fired several short bursts into the port wing. Flames erupted from the engine and the aircraft side-slipped away, curving into a long dive to the ground.

Andrew checked his mirror and hauled his Spitfire into a loop. At the top of the loop he sighted the bombers, rolled the right way up and dived after them. Slicing through the whirling dogfights, he singled out a Heinkel and hit the firing button. His guns chattered for four seconds until his ammunition ran out.

Andrew dived away through the bomber formation, checking his tail for any pursuit.

He pressed transmit: 'Yellow Three to Bluebird Yellow Section. Where are you?'

Bryan's voice came back: 'Hello, Yellow Three. I'm circling Redhill to land. Things looked a little too hectic at Kenley for my liking.'

****

Gerry lurched from the lee of the officers' mess and limped out onto the airfield. Ground-crew tussled with wreckage and debris, pulling them off the runway. A woman with an armful of red flags trotted around looking for unexploded bombs, planting a flag next to each one she found. Ambulances and fire-engines clattered through the main gates. Medics and stretcher-bearers tended to the wounded and dying.

Gerry moved to the end of the runway between the mess building and the smoking wreckage of the aircraft hangars, where a fountain of water gushed from a broken water main. He sighted down the runway between the craters. With an offset approach it might just be possible for a Spitfire to land without mishap. He set off to check the other runway.

Walking across the front of the hangars he came across a slit-trench. One end terminated in the ragged crater of a direct hit. At the other end, blown into a heap against the trench wall, lay the remains of four people tangled together, their clothes tattered by blast and their skin blackened by heat. Thick gouts of blood congealed in their ears and noses.

****

179

Andrew drifted down onto Redhill aerodrome and taxied across to a small group of Spitfires he recognised as Bluebird's. Shutting down his engine, he pulled back his canopy and climbed out. Bryan's anger carried his voice across the airfield.

'What do you mean?' he shouted. 'I need ammunition so I can get back in the air.'

Andrew walked towards the commotion.

'I'm sorry, sir.' An orderly grasping a clipboard withered under Bryan's glare. 'I simply don't have any armourers.'

'What's the point of having a bloody airfield if you can't make it work?' Bryan's rage notched up a level. 'I'm trying to save your baggy arse from getting bombed to Kingdom Come, and you tell me you don't have any armourers? What kind of funfair are you running?'

Andrew trotted across and put a restraining hand on Bryan's shoulder. 'We need to get away from these Spitfires, Bryan, in case this field is attacked.'

Andrew smiled at the orderly: 'Would you telephone someone, see if you can find out what we should do?'

Relief washed over the man's face and he hurried off towards a hut at the edge of the field. The pilots wandered away from the planes to sit on the grass outside the perimeter track.

'Looks like it's getting bloody serious, Bryan.' Andrew sank onto the grass. 'Did you see what they've done to Kenley?'

Bryan stared straight ahead at his Spitfire: 'Like the man once said, 'the bomber will always get through'. If every one of us shot down one bomber every time they came across, we'd still only be scratching the surface.'

'So, you think it's hopeless?'

'No,' Bryan shook his head and lit a cigarette, 'they're scared of us.'

'I don't understand.'

Bryan blew out a long stream of smoke. 'The Heinkel we just shot down carried a four-man crew. That's four empty places in their mess hall tonight. The bombers flying next to it saw what happened. They watched their own worst nightmare happen to somebody else. They're scared now, and they'll be scared tomorrow.'

'Didn't we watch that happen to Alan and George?' Andrew asked.

'There's a difference.' Bryan patted the ground next to him. 'We're fighting *for* England *over* England. Now, the Germans... everything they care about, everything they value is far away. Their homes and families are in Germany, beyond attack. How many of that bomber crew actually wanted to conquer England? How many of them dreamed of owning a nice three-bedroomed semi in Margate?'

Andrew shook his head.

'And, the poor sods that got away with it today aren't even going home. They'll be landing in France, surrounded by people who hate their guts. They'll eat what they can of their dinner amongst the empty chairs and go to bed to have nightmares about a pair of Spitfires picking out their plane tomorrow.'

'That doesn't really sound like we're winning.'

'We can't beat them, Andrew' – Bryan flicked his cigarette-butt away in a long graceful arc – 'but we can win.'

Andrew frowned: 'You're not making sense.'

'As long as we can put up at least one squadron to meet them every time they come, and that one squadron can put a hole or two in their formations, they will go back scared. As long as they go back scared, there'll be no invasion.'

****

Gerry tore himself away from the carnage in the trench. He had no help to give. A knot of ground-crew stood at the perimeter looking around, dazed at the chaos. Gerry walked towards them.

'We need to get a landing strip marked out,' he shouted. 'We need some posts and flags.'

'Equipment store is destroyed, sir. The whole thing has collapsed.'

'What about the cookhouse? Get tablecloths… knives and forks to pin them to the ground.'

Two men ran off through the rubble towards the cookhouse. Gerry took the rest onto the runway to help clear away the debris.

****

The orderly ran across the Redhill grass towards Bluebird's pilots.

'I've just spoken to Beehive Control at Kenley. They've cleared a space for you to land. You're to fly back immediately.'

The pilots climbed to their feet and started back towards the planes. Bryan brushed past the orderly. 'If I ever come back,' he glared at the man, 'and you tell me you don't have any bullets, I'll knock your bloody block off.'

One by one their engines coughed into life and Bluebird straggled into the air. Bryan and Andrew took off last, climbing to 3000ft, heading north towards the plumes of black smoke spiralling up from Kenley, eight miles distant.

Three minutes later they settled into an orbit around the aerodrome, waiting their turn to land.

Between the craters and the wreckage, a narrow grass strip stood marked out by squares of white fabric pegged to the ground along its edges.

'Beehive Control to Bluebird Squadron. One at a time please, gentlemen. Let the previous man get onto the perimeter track before you approach.'

Circling the field, Andrew looked down in dismay. Three hangars were wrecked and smoking. Half a dozen Hurricanes lay crumpled and burning. Men shovelled earth into the craters that pockmarked the grass. In the field beyond the fence an ambulance crew prised the broken bodies of men from under the wreckage of the two fallen bombers. The war had come home.

****

Gerry stood on the edge of the makeshift landing strip watching Bluebird's Spitfires land and taxi, waving to those he recognised. When Andrew taxied past, Gerry walked alongside his plane to an empty blast-pen and helped the ground-crew manhandle it into position.

Andrew climbed down from the wing and shook Gerry's hand. 'Welcome back,' Andrew said, 'you could've chosen a better day.'

'I got here just before the raid,' Gerry shook his head, 'Lord only knows what will happen if they come back. The control room wasn't hit but we've lost telephones, water and gas. Nearest phone is in the post office down the road. The controller's set up shop there.'

Bryan strolled up sucking on a cigarette. 'Hello, Yankee,' he smiled at Gerry, 'nice of the Germans to send a reception committee for you.'

An orderly strode along past the blast-pens. 'Bluebird Squadron, debrief in the officers' mess in one hour, repeat officers' mess, that includes sergeants and other non-comms.'

Bryan pulled a face, 'There goes the neighbourhood.'

****

Squadron Leader Fenton stood up and the room quietened.

'It's been a black day,' he began. 'The enemy's new tactics have worked very well. You've all seen the damage. On top of that, we've got a dozen dead and twice that many injured. Fagan estimates they hit us with well over 100 bombs. All that in a little over five minutes.

'A similar raid has hit Biggin Hill. But fighters broke up the German formations before they could concentrate over the airfield. The bombing there has been described as "inaccurate".'

Andrew tensed at the news.

'The Germans have paid a heavy price,' Fenton continued. 'Two of the low-level raiders brought down by cable, one by anti-aircraft fire and the Hurricanes are claiming two or three as well. That's a possible six out of nine gone for a Burton.

'Of the higher bomber formation, Bluebird have claimed five bombers destroyed and two damaged as well as one escorting fighter destroyed. A Hurricane squadron also engaged this formation, so I'm sure those scores will increase. Bluebird end the day with one pilot wounded and one Spitfire destroyed.

'We can hope for one of two things to happen. Either the scale of their losses will deter the Germans from mounting any more two-tier attacks. Or they'll believe they've done enough to knock Kenley out of the war and leave us alone for a while.

'Either way we're going nowhere else this evening. The army have delivered tents and sleeping bags at the main gate for those whose quarters have been destroyed. Pitch outside the perimeter track and watch out for the red UXB flags.

'Stay away from the runways, there will be heavy machinery working all night. Get off base if you can, but remember we will be on readiness from six tomorrow morning. Dismiss.'

****

On a borrowed RAF motorbike, Andrew roared through the country lanes towards Biggin Hill. Taking the dog-leg turn to Leaves Green, he slowed to look across the aerodrome. Small curls of smoke rose from a few craters. A bulldozer choked and spluttered in the fading afternoon light, rounding up the errant earth to fill the holes.

Further along, splintered twigs covered the road from bomb strikes in the roadside trees. Andrew gunned the engine and sped the last half-mile to the village.

Three craters bisected the green, half a dozen more marched east, straddling the northern end of Biggin Hill's runway. People moved around the houses lining the perimeter fence, sweeping up glass and broken roof-tiles.

Andrew turned left off the main road towards the hairdressing shop. Sitting on the bench at the edge of the green he saw Molly. Relief tingled through his clenched shoulder muscles as he pulled up and switched off the motorcycle.

'Molly!' he called, 'are you all right?'

Molly looked over her shoulder and smiled: 'Yes. Come and give me a kiss.'

Andrew hurried over to sit next to her on the bench, lingering a kiss on her lips: 'I was worried.'

She pushed a finger onto the end of his nose: 'Now you know how I feel every day.'

'What are you doing out here?'

Molly sucked in a deep breath: 'Watching. I wanted to see them.'

Andrew put an arm around her shoulders. 'It's too risky, sweetheart. Think of the baby.'

Molly looked into his eyes: 'If they win, I will have years to watch the things they plan to do to this country. Today I wanted to watch us fighting back. So if in the end they do win, I can cherish the memory of our resistance and I can tell our child we did everything in our power to stop them.

'I heard the anti-aircraft guns start up and I came to sit out here. The Germans flew in really low, across the airfield and away over the village. Two Spitfires chased one of them. He dropped his bombs late; he must have been scared. The bombs fell behind the houses over there and a couple hit the green.

'He flew directly over my head. There was a man lying down in the nose, pointing a machine-gun through a hole in the glass. He looked at me but he didn't shoot. I saw the big crosses on the wings and the bomb-doors were still open.

'The Spitfires were close behind him, firing all the time. I listened to them fly into the distance. I listened until I couldn't hear the guns anymore. He couldn't have got away. I think the man with the machine-gun must be dead now.

'It's the first time I've been really scared, Andrew' – Molly placed a hand on his cheek – 'but I was scared for you, not me.' A tear squeezed from the corner of her eye. 'The Spitfires were so fast, so close, the man with the machine-gun had no way to save himself.'

Andrew kissed the tear from her cheek. 'Will you leave now, Molly?' he pleaded, 'pack up and go somewhere safe?'

'Look at me.' She placed her hands on her distended belly. 'I'm eight months pregnant. I can hardly waddle up and down the stairs, let alone pack and move house.

'I was intending to close the shop after tomorrow, put my feet up for a while and knit some baby clothes. But if I do that after what happened today' – she gestured towards the craters 200 yards away in the green – 'it will look like I'm giving up.' She nodded towards the damaged houses: 'Those people aren't giving up, you're not giving up, so I'm not giving up.'

20th August, 1940

A voice called out over the clink of beer glasses: 'Here, Bryan, they're playing his speech. Your favourite bloke. Whassisname?'

The radio volume cranked up and the growling voice of the Prime Minister rasped out of the tattered speaker:

'…*gratitude of every home in our Island, in our Empire, and indeed throughout the world, except in the abodes of the guilty, goes out to the British airmen who, undaunted by odds, unwearied in their constant challenge and mortal danger, are turning the tide of the World War by their prowess and devotion. Never in the field of human conflict was so much owed by so many to so few. All hearts go out to the fighter pilots, whose brilliant actions we see with our own eyes, day after day…*'

'Turn that bloody man down,' Bryan shouted, 'or I'll shove the bloody radio right up *your* prowess and devotion.'

The volume faded to a gruff grumbling in the background and Bryan turned back to lean on the bar between Andrew and Gerry. Empty pint pots littered the counter in front of them.

185

'Since when did it become a World War?' Bryan shook his head. 'Half the world has left us to it.' He put his hand on Gerry's shoulder. 'No offence, Yankee,' he said, 'but the Americans *are* bastards.'

'Yes,' Gerry nodded, 'some of them are. I've met some of those.'

'Good,' Bryan drained his glass. 'Three more pints of bitter, steward.'

'But...' Gerry waggled a finger at Bryan.

'But what, Yankee?'

'But... if the shoe was on the other foot, would you go to fight a war in America?'

'No,' Andrew piped up. 'There'd be no need. America can't be defeated; it's too big and too powerful. They wouldn't need us.'

Three pints arrived in front of them.

'Russia could do it.' Bryan took a swig. 'Russia could conquer America.'

'In that case,' Andrew reasoned, 'we'd probably get involved because they'd have to go east through Canada.'

'Unless,' Gerry murmured, 'they came west across Europe.'

Contemplative silence settled over the trio.

'Hey,' Bryan called over to the steward, 'how big is my mess bill?' He turned to Gerry: 'Did you know when your mess bill reaches £100, the Air Ministry expects you to get killed in action as a patriotic gesture to cut overheads? It's harsh, but fair.'

CHAPTER 20

Grando

24th August, 1940

Vincent's shoes crunched in the shingle. He walked along the path between perfectly manicured lawns down to the water. Patients sat around in groups, talking and playing cards in the late afternoon sunshine. Their idle chatter drifted along with him. Vincent came to the railings and looked out over Southampton Water.

Barrage balloons blotted the blue sky, drifting like tethered pigs over Southampton to his right and Portsmouth, closer on his left. Three merchant ships chugged up from the Solent, seeking a night's refuge in Southampton's docks.

A low howl, faint in the distance, drifted up the channel. Portsmouth's air-raid sirens wound into their moaning dirge.

Vincent squinted into the blue dome above the port where anti-aircraft shells climbed to blossom in puffy flowers of white smoke. In between this drifting aerial garden he could make out the shapes of bombers – 50 or more stacked in layers into the sky. The AA stopped and a single intercepting squadron dived through the bomber formation.

The ghost of a black wing flashed across Vincent's memory and a phosphorus-white explosion cracked behind his forehead...

'Are you all right, mate?' The voice prised Vincent's eyelids apart. He looked up from a prone position on the spiky gravel. A patient stood over him.

'What happened?' Vincent asked, rubbing his forehead to ease the throbbing.

'Looked like you stumbled,' the man smiled with reassurance. 'Did you hit your head?'

'How long was I out?' Vincent hoisted himself off the ground.

The man helped him up. 'No more than a second or two.' He examined Vincent's forehead: 'I can't see where you knocked your head. Probably best to get a doctor to look at it anyway.'

'No…' Vincent caught himself and put a hand on the man's shoulder. 'Yes… Yes, I will. Thank you for helping me.'

A low, thunderous rumble rolled across the land. The man looked away to the east where smoke from exploding bombs curled into the air.

'Portsmouth is getting a real beating, poor sods,' the man said. A flash of flames glittered in the sky and a black smoke trail spiralled towards the sea. 'Ha, take that you bastards.'

Vincent watched, waiting for a parachute. 'That's a Hurricane.'

25th August, 1940

'They've bombed London, Yankee.' Brian flipped a copy of *The Standard* into Gerry's lap. 'Put that in your book.'

Gerry unrolled the paper, scanning the front page.

Bryan slumped into a deck chair next to him. 'They knocked seven bells out of Portsmouth in the afternoon,' he shrugged. 'Fair game I suppose – it's a military target. But the middle of London?'

'I can't write about this,' Gerry protested, 'I wasn't there.'

Bryan levelled a look at him. 'Not much of a journalist are you?' he said. 'You were on station when they bombed the aerodrome, so you know what it's like. Make up the rest.'

Gerry returned his look in silence.

'Good show,' Bryan nodded, 'I'm glad the penny's dropped.'

Andrew walked back from checking over his Spitfire.

'Ah, Andrew,' Bryan called, 'good news. Mortice has agreed to our little experiment.'

'Who's Mortice?' Gerry asked.

Andrew sat down with his friends. 'It's one of the riggers,' he said.

Gerry looked at Bryan: 'Mortice?'

Bryan grinned. 'It's not his real name,' he whispered.

Gerry's confusion mounted: 'What sort of experiment?'

'Glad you asked, Yankee, it's nice to see you're sharpening up a bit' – Bryan patted Gerry on the knee – 'you know those eight machine-guns you lug around the sky for His Majesty The King?'

Gerry nodded.

'Half of them are loaded with ball, The other half are split between armour-piercing and incendiary. Well, sometimes we put lots of bullets into bombers just to watch them fly serenely off into the distance. So I reckon the Germans are fitting a lot more armour-plating in their crates these days; the ball is just bouncing off.

'So Mortice has agreed to load four guns with armour-piercing, two each side, inboard. These hit the bandit's fuselage and cockpit. Next one out on each side has the Incendiaries. These hit the fuel tanks in the wings. The outside pair are ball. These hit the engines. Guns are harmonised for 350 yards, so if you open fire at 250 yards the spread is near-enough perfect.

'And don't write that in your book 'cos they'll only censor it and put me on a charge.'

'What's going to happen about London?' Gerry asked.

'Oh, I expect Winston will bomb Berlin,' Bryan said, 'probably very soon. I imagine he's been waiting for an excuse.'

26th August, 1940

'Come in Sergeant Drew, take a seat.'

Vincent sat down. Dr Robinson regarded him for a moment then looked down to the open file on his desk.

'We've been watching you very closely, Vincent,' he said. 'The only noteworthy observation is your persistent nightmares. But that's not necessarily so unusual in this place' – he looked at Vincent over his glasses – 'how do you *feel*?'

'I feel I'm wasting time, I need—'

'What, Vincent? What is it you need?'

'I need to protect my mother.'

'In what way?'

'By shooting down bombers. What they did to Portsmouth the other day, they could do the same anywhere. They could do it to Whitby.'

'I'm in a difficult situation, Vincent.' The doctor leant back in his chair. 'Your medical records show no history of seizures, which means you didn't mention them when you joined up. But if I believe your story that you suffered them as a child, and if I believe a seizure prevented you from taking off, it automatically makes you unfit for flying. If I don't believe your

189

story, then what you did is probably grounds for a dishonourable discharge for LMF.'

'You could say it was a one-off' – Vincent's voice stretched tight – 'that it's unlikely to happen again.'

A long silence hung between the two men.

'All right, Vincent,' the doctor nodded, 'it's highly likely we don't have enough trained pilots to win this battle as it is and, despite everything else, you are still a trained pilot. Go back to your room, I'll let you know if I can organise a posting.'

30th August, 1940

Florence Lloyd meandered along the Eastbourne sea-front in the growing warmth of the late morning sun. Soldiers lounged against the sand-bagged defences, helmets pushed back from glistening foreheads. She smiled at them and they nodded.

The undercurrent of tension in their faces reminded her. The invasion defences, the tank-traps and the sand-bags were almost invisible to her now, fading to grey in her daily scenery. But the weight of mortality in a soldier's eyes as he waits for war was not so easy to assimilate into routine.

The whisper of the sea-breeze took on a faint rasping edge. The intruding noise deepened in tenor and acquired an uneven undulation. She looked up and stumbled to a halt. Strewn across the blue sky, black lines of bombers, layer above layer, advanced on Eastbourne from the south. Above and around them flocked the smaller silhouettes of their escorting fighters.

'Oh, dear.'

From the town behind her the first sonorous thumps of anti-aircraft fire buffeted through the air. Clusters of mushroom-coloured smoke erupted in the sky amongst the raiders. A shell burst close under one of the black shapes and a finger of fire belched from its wing. Dropping away from the formation in a lazy side-slip, the fat black fuselage disgorged three fluttering objects. Two snapped open into white canopies, slowing and swaying on the wind. The third twisted and writhed like a wind-sock, plunging towards the sea.

'Poor man,' she thought and closed her eyes as the body hit the water.

Teeth gritted against the impending maelstrom, she waited. But above her the invading swarm disarticulated, tearing itself into four groups, splaying out over the town and grinding inland, each gaggle to a different target.

****

The orderly dashed out of the hut: 'Bluebird Squadron, scramble!'

Chairs clattered to the ground and newspapers skittered away in the breeze as the pilots dashed for their aircraft. Andrew skidded around his Spitfire's tail and jumped onto the wing. He caught the flash of Bryan's manic grin as he shoe-horned himself into the cockpit.

Bluebird Squadron roared across the field and lifted into the late summer sky.

'Bluebird Leader to Control. We are airborne. Listening out.'

'Beehive Control to Bluebird Leader, make Angels fifteen, vector one-six-zero towards Eastbourne. Many bandits heading your way.'

The squadron wheeled onto course in a steep climbing turn.

'Bluebird Leader to Bluebird Squadron. Try to avoid the fighters, chaps. I know they're more fun to play with, but we need to keep the bombers away from the airfields. Loosen up and attack in sections.'

The squadron drifted apart into groups of three. Andrew swayed back and forth behind Gerry and Bryan, scanning the sky for danger.

'Fifty-plus bombers at 12 o'clock. Tally-ho!'

Andrew saw the Heinkel bombers flying in close formation at the same level, heading in a shallow diagonal across their path.

'Yellow Section, let's hit the top row,' Bryan called, 'break left after attack.'

Andrew eased back on the stick to follow the other two up, then nudged it forward to bring the onrushing bombers into his gunsight. Stabbing the fire button he lurched his Spitfire over the Germans as they flashed past below. Banking hard left he latched onto Gerry's tail.

The enemy formation wavered as the rest of Bluebird wheeled into their ranks; some damaged aircraft dropped away, heading for home.

'Yellow Section stick with me,' Bryan called, 'we've got some cold meat to clear up.'

Andrew glanced upwards: 'Escort coming down now, watch your tails.'

Bryan chose a fleeing Heinkel, diving south towards the coast. Black objects fell from its underside as it traded its bomb-load for speed.

'Yellow Leader calling, remember, 250 yards from dead astern.'

191

Bryan dropped in behind the bomber as the rear-gunner sprayed bullets into the sky around him. Bryan opened fire; a long burst raked the fuselage and hits flashed off the wings and engine cowlings. Bryan peeled off and zoomed away.

'Fairly certain the gunner has bought it' – Bryan's voice held a flat calmness – 'your turn, Yankee. Try 200 yards.'

Gerry swooped down and closed on the bomber's tail. A body fell from the open bomb doors; a parachute plumed behind it. The Heinkel wallowed to and fro, attempting to evade the attack. Gerry opened fire, matching the bomber's zig-zagging banks. Pieces of aircraft skin fluttered out behind the bomber's tail and a thin ribbon of black smoke streamed from the starboard engine.

Andrew scanned the sky behind: 'Yellow Three calling. Looks like the escort has stayed with the main formation. I am attacking now.'

Either the German pilot had given up evasion, or his controls had been damaged. He flew straight and level. Andrew crept closer. Coming within 100 yards he pressed and held the fire button.

A cascade of destruction danced around the bomber. Orange flashes spattered the wings between engines and fuselage, releasing tongues of flame to leap from the wing-roots and lick the length of the fuselage. The Heinkel shuddered under the onslaught and rolled over into a steep dive. Twisting a spiral column of smoke in its wake, it crashed in a fountain of fire amidst a patch of woodland.

'Well done, Yellow Section,' Bryan called. 'That'll teach him to crack walnuts in church. Let's go home.'

The three Spitfires reformed and headed north-west. Bryan led them in a shallow dive, losing height on the approach to base.

'Beehive Control to Bluebird Squadron' – the wireless rang with a copper hollowness – 'bandits approaching Kenley and Biggin Hill, low- and high-level. Divert Redhill for refuelling.'

'Ha!' Bryan barked, 'Yellow Leader to Yellow Section. I don't want to go back to Redhill as long as I live. Do you two have any ammunition left?'

'Yellow Two. I sure do.'

'Yellow Three. Plenty to play with.'

'All right, gentlemen. Let's look for this low-level raid. Buster, buster!'

Andrew knocked the throttle through the boost-gate and leapt after the other two Spitfires. The altimeter ticked down until Bryan levelled them off at 300ft and throttled back. Sevenoaks spread a grey smudge amongst the green countryside. Shadows flitted across its streets.

Gerry's voice crackled over the air: 'Yellow Two calling. Nine bandits at 2 o'clock. Low and fast. Heading towards Biggin Hill.'

'Thanks, Yankee,' Bryan called, 'Junkers 88s, and they're burning it. Buster, Yellow Section. Buster, buster!'

Andrew curved down at the back of the section into a tail-chase with the bombers. His engine whined and rattled in protest as he continued full-boost.

The bomber formation ahead loosened up, spreading out for their bombing run. The rear-gunners fired speculative bursts at their pursuers. Ahead of them a flight of Hurricanes clawed into the sky from the end of the Biggin Hill runway.

'Individual attacks, Yellow Section. Tally-ho!'

Andrew splayed out to his right to attack the starboard section of bombers. At 400 yards he punched a one-second burst of fire at the formation. The outermost bomber banked away to the right. A lucky hit on a control cable or the pilot losing his nerve? Andrew let him go, fixing his attention on the section's leader.

The gap closed to 300 yards as Biggin Hill's perimeter flashed by below. Black shapes fell away from the bombers. Andrew squeezed another burst and then gasped as his Spitfire bucked in the shock wave of explosions.

A moment of hell flashed across Andrew's vision: monolithic plumes of earth thrown up by high explosives; figures running and falling; smoking trails of Bofors shells traversing the sky; a building fell in on itself; a truck cartwheeled in the air. He eased back on the stick, fighting to trade speed for altitude and avoid a stall. Shapes flashed over his canopy, the Hurricanes hammering north-west after the fleeing raiders.

Andrew pulled into a shallow climb and banked north to avoid trouble. He pulled a few gentle manoeuvres to check for damage. The controls were tight and responsive.

As the adrenalin of action dissolved, a memory invaded his mind: silver bi-planes at an air-pageant, streaking through this same sky, playing at fighters and bombers in a game where the bombers always lost. He banked left around the smoking bomb-craters speckling the airfield below and remembered his first sight of Molly in the crowd.

'Yellow Leader to Yellow Section.' Bryan's voice deflated his daydream. 'Let's go home and re-arm.'

Breathing a sigh of heavy sorrow he held his turn and set course for Kenley. Leaves Green wheeled around below him. His life and his love, no more than a speck on someone else's invasion map.

Andrew headed west, catching up with Bryan and Gerry a couple of miles from base. They put down between the white flags and taxied over to dispersal, a rigger on each wingtip, guiding them past the rough earth of recently filled bomb-craters.

Andrew climbed out of his cockpit to find a rigger examining the fuselage.

Gerry approached: 'What happened to you?'

Andrew grimaced: 'I flew straight through a bomb-blast. Knocked all the wind out of my sails. I was lucky not to stall.'

'Shrapnel damage, sir,' the rigger called up from under the plane, 'right the way along the fuselage and tail. Starts just behind the cockpit' – he craned his neck and grinned at Andrew – 'which was a spot of luck.'

Andrew lit a cigarette. 'Will she fly again?'

'Certainly not today, sir. I'll need to check all the control lines are sound and patch the holes. I'll get the chief to assign one of the reserves in case you need to go again.'

'Thanks.' He turned back to Gerry: 'Did you and Bryan have any luck?'

'We emptied our guns into one. He looked pretty beat up, then two Hurricanes barged in and put him into the ground about five miles north of here.'

Bryan strode up to join them. 'I've just given Mortice a slap on the back for his loading job,' he beamed, 'that'll be par for the course from now on.'

They walked together back to the readiness hut where a knot of pilots stood conversing in low voices and smoking cigarettes. The tension hanging over them was palpable. From the wireless inside a disembodied voice repeated a morose litany: 'Beehive Control to Bluebird Leader. Are you receiving me? Beehive Control to Bluebird Leader...'

'What's wrong?' Andrew asked.

Fagan looked up with a drawn expression: 'Squadron Leader Fenton isn't back yet.' He chewed the end of his pencil. 'No one has seen him since the escort waded in... I don't suppose you—?'

Andrew shook his head: 'Yellow Section went south after a Heinkel running for home.'

Fagan raised his eyebrows.

'We shot him down in flames,' Andrew said, 'crashed just south of Tunbridge.'

'Good show,' Fagan nodded absently.

The wireless crackled again: 'Beehive Control to Bluebird Leader. Are you receiving me...?' Silence whined against the static. 'Beehive Control to Bluebird Leader. Are you receiving me...?'

The telephone jangled. Fagan grabbed it from its cradle. 'Bluebird.' He listened in tight concentration and gave a short nod. 'Thank you.'

Silence fell over the assembled pilots.

Fagan looked up with a wan grimace: 'A Spitfire dived vertically into the ground just outside Lingfield at about the same time Bluebird Squadron engaged the bomber formation. Observer Corps report the pilot was in combat with three 109s shortly before he crashed. They saw no parachute.

'The Army will get some engineers onto it, dig out the wreckage. Until I know what they find I will be posting Squadron Leader Fenton as 'missing'. I'll suggest to the station commander that Pilot Officer Hale is made acting squadron leader until we know something definite.

'I'm sorry, gentlemen. Another bad day at the office.'

CHAPTER 21

Agnus

31st August, 1940

Bryan walked into the office and let the door swing closed behind him. He sat down at the desk, careful not to disturb anything. Lighting a cigarette, he looked around for somewhere to flick the ash. Half a dozen cold cigarette butts lay crumpled in a metal 'Burton Ale' ashtray on the edge of the squadron leader's desk. He froze for a moment, staring at the logo.

A knock sounded at the door and the adjutant walked in.

'Hello, Bryan.' He pursed his lips. 'Bad news I'm afraid. The army have dug the Spitfire out of that ruddy great hole and found Squadron Leader Fenton in the cockpit. Well, what was left of him, the poor sod.

'So it looks like you're in the hot seat for at least the next few days. I know it's a bind, but I'll try to keep some of the bullshit off your desk. Most of it's routine, easy enough for me to deal with.'

'Thanks, Madge,' Bryan smiled, 'I appreciate your help.'

'I'll get someone to collect Malcolm's things. The station commander and myself are off to visit his wife later on this afternoon. Sad times.' He turned to leave. 'Oh, one thing, though,' he said on his way to the door, 'we've got a new intake arriving tomorrow afternoon. Two new bods fresh in from flight training and one hospital discharge. You'll have to give them their induction, if that's all right?'

Bryan nodded.

The adjutant opened the door and left. As the latch clicked behind him Bryan picked up the ashtray and emptied it into the wastepaper basket.

****

Bryan stood at the bar between Andrew and Gerry: 'Right, let's get this started.' He turned to face the room.

'Gentleman. May I have your attention, please.' Bryan's voice quelled the murmuring in the room.

'You know why we're gathered here this evening. Yesterday we lost our squadron leader. Today they recovered his body from the seat of the

Spitfire in which he spent so many hours playing merry hell amongst our enemies.

'Bluebird Squadron has lost many pilots this year. Some have left ragged holes in our lives, some we barely noticed, gone as quickly as they arrived. But yesterday the Germans got one of the irreplaceables. This man was a leader in a sense of the word that politicians and kings struggle to fulfil.

'I can't remember an interception where we haven't been outnumbered by at least five-to-one. Yet never have I been daunted by those odds, not as long as I'm flying with Bluebird. Squadron Leader Fenton made me feel safe while he led us into unspeakable dangers.

'Let's not forget, it took three of them to knock him down. And those three will be back tomorrow, and the next day. So every time you have a 109 in your sights, think of Malcolm Fenton and show no mercy. Shoot to kill.'

A voice called out from the back of the room: 'Three cheers for Squadron Leader Fenton! Hip-hip…'

The mess erupted into cheers. Bryan turned back to the bar and took a long draft from his glass.

Andrew leaned across: 'What a wonderful speech, Bryan. Didn't know you had it in you.'

Bryan shrugged: 'My father is a vicar. I was forced to sit and listen to his sermons every week' – he grimaced – 'the theme is the same really, your miserable life is blighted by an acquired fear of God, and then you die, usually quite horribly.'

Gerry frowned: 'Your father is a man of the cloth and you don't believe in God?'

Bryan snorted: 'I don't believe in anything, least of all my father and his God.' He turned to shout over his shoulder: 'Drinks all round, lads!'

The steward lined up more pints in front of them.

Bryan caught him by the wrist: 'Put the round on Fenton's mess bill.'

'But, sir—' the steward protested.

'Has anyone told you to close his mess bill?' Bryan hissed.

'Well, no, sir—'

'In that case it's still open,' Bryan smiled and released the steward, 'and it will stay open for the rest of the night.'

1st September, 1940

Vincent snapped to attention as the door opened behind him.

Bryan strode round the desk and regarded the three pilots lined up before him.

'At ease, gentlemen.' Bryan sat down. 'I'm Acting Squadron Leader Hale. I acquired this position after our real squadron leader became one with his Merlin engine at the bottom of a 12ft hole.

'He was a well-liked man. In that regard I do not expect to follow in his footsteps. I have a job do. I have to prevent the Germans from beating us. One small part of that is to keep them from killing the three of you. If I can get you through your first three combat sorties, there's a small chance you'll be around to celebrate Christmas.

'Over the next few days you'll be going up as wingman to an experienced pilot. They'll put you through your paces and report to me. These 'familiarisation' flights will take place well north of here, outside the usual stamping grounds of the 109s. You will only go on combat missions once I am reasonably certain you have at least a small hope in hell of coming back. Do I make myself clear?'

One of the pilot's piped up: 'I'd rather get straight on with some Hun-bashing, sir.'

Bryan blinked at the man. 'Would you, now? Well, I'd rather not have to write a letter to your mummy telling her how brave you were, and that we'll send your body back as soon as it washes up at Pevensey Bay.'

The pilot looked down, blushing.

'Right. Drew, you stay here. Otherwise dismissed.'

The other two pilots left the office. Vincent tensed, not sure whether to stand to attention again.

Bryan cleared his throat: 'Sergeant Drew, it says on your posting papers you've just been discharged from hospital.'

'Yes, sir.'

'It also says you were "under observation".'

'Yes, sir.'

'Why were they observing you, sergeant?'

'I had a c-close call, sir,' Vincent said. 'It shook me up a b-bit.'

'Are you telling me you've just been released from a loony bin?'

Vincent focused on the wall over Bryan's shoulder: 'I'm not mad, sir.'

'Don't get me wrong, Drew.' Bryan lit a cigarette and blew a stream of smoke into the air. 'I do sympathise. Having a 109 up your arse is not a pleasant experience. But I can't carry a pilot who's going to get windy every time we—'

'I'm not a c-coward, sir.' Vincent took in a deep breath to steady himself. 'I want to do my bit. It's what I've been trained for.'

Bryan inspected the nicotine stains on his fingers as he thought. He stubbed out his cigarette and leaned forward: 'All right, Drew, you'll be put on the training flights with the others. But you're bottom of the reserve rota, understand? No combat flying until I'm sure you're not a liability. Dismissed.'

'Yes, sir. Thank you, sir.'

Vincent left the office and walked out onto the airfield. He sucked the air into his lungs and willed his shoulder muscles to relax. The faint tang of aviation fuel sizzled in his sinuses. Across the grass, armourers worked on a Spitfire. He ambled off in their direction.

The men glanced up as he arrived, nodding by way of salute, not pausing in their work.

Vincent looked over the Spitfire. The paint around the cockpit door was chipped and peeling, the wing root below it worn to the metal by the passage of flying boots. Behind the cockpit, forward of the yellow-bordered roundel, the fighter's skin bore a cluster of repair patches, unevenly riveted and painted over in a mismatched green. Long streaks of oily soot fingered back from the exhausts, soiling the edges of several small swastikas painted under the canopy. Black stains intersected the wings, unfurling like funereal banners from each of the eight gun-ports.

Vincent glanced at the colour-coded ammo boxes spread out on the grass. 'That's unusual,' he said.

The armourer glanced at him from below the wing.

'I'm sorry,' Vincent smiled, 'I was an armourer before I took pilot training.'

The man nodded: 'Twice as much armour-piercing as normal, sir. We call it the Hale-storm.'

'Hailstorm?'

'This is Pilot Officer Hale's aircraft. The munitions mix is his idea.' The armourer replaced a panel and shimmied out from under the wing, wiping his hands on a rag. 'He says the Germans are installing more armour plate around their aircrew. Makes 'em more difficult to kill,' the man grimaced, 'and he does like to kill his Germans, our Mr Hale.'

'Does it work?'

The armourer shrugged. 'His section took out a Heinkel the other day. He says the AP stitched it up really nicely before it went down' – he gave a short bark of laughter – 'but he was a bit miffed because one of the Krauts managed to bail out.'

Vincent nodded: 'He does seem a bit of a firebrand.'

The armourer dropped the rag into his toolbox. 'You have to understand, sir, Mister Hale is a professional. He's flown with this Squadron since '35, back when they had bi-planes. There were five originals when we moved to Kenley. Now there's only two; Mr Hale and Mr Francis. They take it seriously.

'Some of the pilots that come through here, they think it's a bit of a lark. Trouble is, the lark doesn't last very long for that sort. We had one last week, straight out of training, didn't even stay long enough to unpack. Took off in a brand-new Spitfire and never came back. We still don't know what happened to him.'

'No one saw?' Vincent asked.

'It's a fast moving game up there, sir. All we can do is count them out and count them in again.' He picked up his toolbox. 'It's down to numbers and time now, I'm afraid. Whether we have enough planes and pilots to make it through to November' – he glanced up at the blue sky – 'it seems a long way off on a day like today, doesn't it.'

The distant jangle of a telephone was followed by shouts of 'Bluebird Squadron, Scramble!'

The crew-chief trotted up: 'Is she ready to go?'

The armourer nodded: 'All set.'

'Mortice!' Bryan's shout rasped across the field, 'get me a starter battery, damn it!'

The rigger whirled away: 'Yes, sir.'

'Hurry up man, they're plastering Biggin Hill again!'

Bryan ran to the plane and jumped onto the wing in one fluid motion. Cramming himself into the cockpit he looked out past his cowling.

'Starter battery!' he yelled, 'where's my bloody starter battery?'

Two ground-crew bustled up, pushing the starter on a sack barrow. As they busied themselves attaching the cables, Bryan looked across at Vincent. His eyes glittered with unspeakable intent, a brutal and inescapable purpose. Vincent retreated, shaking his head against the sudden pressure of unbidden memories. The Spitfire barked into life and howled to a diabolical crescendo that buffeted his back like rampant mockery as he hurried away.

****

Molly heard Andrew's motorbike choke to a halt outside and waited for the sound of his key in the door. She stirred soup on the hob as his footsteps creaked up the stairs. A moment later his arms entwined her from behind, squeezing between her pregnant belly and her breasts.

'I love you,' he whispered into her ear.

'You haven't tasted the soup yet,' she smiled. Turning in his embrace she placed a finger over his lips: 'Please don't nag me about moving. I heard the bombs today, I heard the guns, I know it's dangerous. But this is my home, our home. If it all comes to an end tomorrow, wouldn't you rather I be here with you tonight?'

Andrew kissed her forehead. 'Biggin Hill is out of action. If they hit Kenley again we'll likely be the same. The other airfields can't be much better. I think we're close to the end, Molly. Soon there'll be no safety to run to.'

Sudden tears sprung to Andrew's eyes. 'I'm so tired' – he swallowed back a sob – 'there are so many of them, every day, so many…'

'Shush.' Molly kissed the tears from his cheek. 'Let's just forget all about the war and eat supper. Then you can get some rest,' she smiled, 'fresh sheets on the bed tonight, what a treat.'

They ate their soup in near-silent denial of the world outside their walls, holding hands across the table. When they'd finished, Molly cleared and rinsed the dishes while Andrew peeled off his clothes and slid into bed. He was already drifting into sleep as Molly snuggled in beside him. He grunted with pleasure at the warm touch of her skin against his.

'It's always darkest before the dawn, my sweetheart,' she whispered. 'Everything will be all right.'

2nd September, 1940

Bluebird Squadron swooped in to land and taxied to dispersal. Bryan swung out of his cockpit and trudged towards the readiness hut for debriefing. Andrew and Gerry caught up with him.

'Hell of a morning,' Andrew said.

Bryan glanced at him and smiled: 'No thanks, I've just had one.'

They entered the hut and slumped into the chairs around Fagan's desk. He looked up and smiled.

'What's the story, gentlemen?'

'Repetitive.' Bryan lit a cigarette.

Fagan switched his gaze: 'Andrew?'

Andrew leant forward: 'Control vectored us to a raid coming in over north Kent,' he said, 'two-hundred plus, mixed Dorniers and 110s.'

'How many of each?'

Gerry piped up: 'Impossible to tell, it got very hectic, very quickly.'

'Any victories?'

'Yes,' Bryan blew out a stream of smoke, 'we all came back alive.'

Fagan's gaze returned to Bryan. He cocked an eyebrow but said no more.

Gerry interjected: 'We must've been over…'

'Margate,' Andrew offered.

'…yes, Margate… for about 20 minutes. There were maybe three other squadrons involved. The whole thing was pretty crazy.'

'And then' – Bryan crushed his cigarette in Fagan's ashtray – 'about fifty 109s showed up so we decided to hoof it.'

Fagan scribbled a few notes on his pad. 'Thank you, gentlemen. There's fresh tea on the trellis table.'

The trio walked over to the tea urn. The adjutant stood there, stirring a steaming tin mug.

'Hello Bryan,' he said, 'may I have a word?'

'Yes, certainly.' Bryan poured a mug of tea.

The adjutant glanced at the other two pilots.

'It's all right.' Bryan sipped his tea. 'I don't mind if they listen. One of them will be taking over if I get my head blown off this afternoon anyway.'

The adjutant nodded: 'Well, I've had a complaint from the armoury stores. Apparently Bluebird's armourers are taking far more armour-piercing bullets than they should.'

'I've changed the mix,' Bryan said. 'It works better.'

Andrew and Gerry nodded in mute agreement.

'Yes, but,' the adjutant looked from one to the other, 'it's far more expensive to make AP. Someone will notice the discrepancy.'

Bryan frowned: 'And just who are we saving the money for, Madge? Hitler?'

'And what about the tracer rounds?' the adjutant persevered.

'I took them out,' Bryan said.

'But, why? They're essential to help correct your aim.'

'Not so,' Bryan countered, 'we have gunsights for that. New pilots should be trained to use the gunsight, not follow the fireworks. On top of that, tracer tells your target you're shooting at him.'

'And from which direction you're shooting,' Gerry added.

'So I took them out,' Bryan repeated. 'Anything else?'

'Yes,' the adjutant sighed, 'I noticed you took off with only nine aircraft. You left the new intake behind.'

Bryan's face hardened. He put his tea down on the table, reached into his flying suit and pulled out his service revolver.

The adjutant lurched backwards. 'What the hell are you doing, man?'

Bryan leaned forward with a menacing snarl: 'I'm off to shoot the new boys.'

'What are you talking about,' stammered the adjutant, 'are you mad?'

'If I'd taken them up this morning against 250 bandits they would all be dead by now. So, if I go and shoot them, we'll have the same conclusion, except I wouldn't have wasted three Spitfires getting there.'

An orderly stuck his head round the door: 'Bluebird Squadron to readiness, please.'

Bryan holstered his revolver. 'Excuse us, Madge,' he said, 'we've got a war not to lose.'

203

CHAPTER 22

Hostia

6th September, 1940

'What time is it?' Andrew's deckchair raked back at full recline.

Gerry looked at his watch: 'Nearly 1 o'clock.'

'Why is it so quiet?' Andrew leaned forward and struggled out of the deckchair, slapping his legs to restore circulation.

'Maybe we beat them?' Gerry said.

'Ha!' Bryan barked, 'we can never beat them. We can only make them believe they haven't beaten us.'

'Why would they think that?' Andrew said. 'You've seen the state of Biggin Hill, our own field is hardly any better. How long can we carry on feeding the meat-grinder?'

Bryan lifted his head. 'The airfields don't matter.'

'How so?' Gerry asked.

'As I've said before, as long as we can put up a couple of squadrons to meet the bombers every time they come,' Bryan explained, 'they'll postpone the invasion.'

Andrew sat down. 'But surely those squadrons need airfields.'

'We need *fields*,' Bryan conceded, 'fairly flat with decent grass. England is infested with those. Everything else can be shunted around in trucks. Hell, I reckon we could operate two or three squadrons from The Mall if we had to.

'In fact, we're only in this mess because London is so close to the Channel. If Newcastle was the capital of England, we'd hold them off for years.'

'Where's Newcastle?' Gerry asked.

'Exactly, Yankee. Exactly.'

'I'm sorry to interrupt gentlemen.' The adjutant walked towards them. 'I need to steal Gerry for an hour or so, official business. There's an officer from the Air Ministry here to see you, Gerry.'

Bryan and Andrew watched the two men walking away.

'As long as control has nothing building on radar,' Bryan said, 'I suggest we take the two new boys for a spin.'

****

The four men stood in a loose circle in front of the Spitfires.

Bryan cleared his throat: 'The Germans seem to be taking an afternoon off. So we're going to take you two on a survival course. You…' he pointed at one of the new pilots.

'Sergeant Townley, sir.'

'…Townley. You'll fly as my wingman. And you…' he pointed at the other pilot.

'Sergeant Huggins, sir.'

'…will fly as wingman to Pilot Officer Francis.

'We'll be flying two sections of two in a finger-four formation' – he held out his hand, tucking his thumb underneath his palm – 'the middle two fingertips represent the section leaders, the outer two fingertips are their wingmen.'

'Excuse me, sir,' Townley interjected, 'we didn't learn this in flight training.'

'No, Townley,' Bryan said, 'I don't expect you did. This is the formation the Germans have been flying all summer. They've used it to shoot down countless Spitfires and Hurricanes whose pilots were engrossed in flying line-astern or line-abreast… like they taught you in flight training.'

Townley nodded silently.

'Right, let's go.'

****

The four Spitfires climbed away from Kenley, the new pilots jostling into the unfamiliar flying formation.

'Bluebird Leader to Beehive Control,' Bryan called, 'four Spitfires airborne on familiarisation flight, heading north-west. Not, repeat, not available for interception. Listening out.'

****

The adjutant opened the door to his office, ushering Gerry inside.

'Hello, Gerry. It's very good to see you again. How is your leg?'

Gerry recognised Gordon Day. 'Hello, sir. The leg's doing fine, thank you.'

Day smiled: 'Take the weight off it, son.' He indicated the seat across from him. 'I've come to find out how the writing is coming along.'

Gerry eased himself into the chair: 'I have a couple more chapters to go, I'll be finished soon.'

'Chapters?'

Gerry smiled: 'There's too much for a pamphlet, it's kind of grown into a book.'

Day leaned forward:- 'And what do you expect to put into the last couple of chapters?'

'Well,' Gerry began, 'we were just discussing this outside. We figure as long as fighters are showing up to intercept the raids, the Germans will hold off risking an invasion. So we just need to string it out until the end of October. It will be seen as a great victory,' he smiled, 'and the American public love a winner.'

Day pushed his glasses up and pinched his nose between thumb and forefinger. 'What if the Germans send across *all* their bombers escorted by fighters? And while you're up there flying the flag, they send across a couple of hundred transport planes, protected by more fighters. The transports are loaded with paratroopers who drop onto our airfields and capture them while you're still in the air. What happens then?'

'Paratroopers?' Gerry sat stunned.

'We have agents who tell us such plans are being discussed at the highest level in the Wehrmacht.'

Gerry blinked: 'So it's over?'

Day reached into his pocket and pulled out a square of paper, handing it to Gerry. 'The Home Forces HQ at the War Ministry has issued a Preliminary Alert No.3,' Day sighed. 'They believe invasion is probable within the next three days.'

Gerry stared at the paper in silence.

'I've been instructed to retrieve the materials you've written so far, so they're safe and can be of some use to the War Office. Just in case—'

'I understand,' Gerry nodded.

'I've also been authorised to offer you a transfer to a staff position, away from combat duties. If you accept the offer, you'll leave with me today. I understand they have a speaking tour of the US in mind.'

Gerry looked down at his feet. 'You're welcome to take the manuscript as it stands, sir. Given the circumstances, it makes perfect sense. But I'll be staying here to finish the final chapters.'

****

'All right, Townley,' Bryan called, 'imagine I'm the nasty German who wants to shoot you down. Give me up to the count of three, then come and get me.'

Townley watched Bryan's Spitfire side-slip and bank away to the left.

'One… two… three…' he pulled into a left turn to follow, craning his neck in desperation to find his adversary in the empty blue dome.

'Look in your mirror, Townley.'

Townley jerked his head up to see Bryan's propeller boss just 20 yards behind his tail.

'How much throttle have you got on?'

Townley looked down and cursed, pushing the throttle forward. He raised his eyes to an empty mirror.

'Count to three, then come and get me.'

'Damn! One… two… three…' Townley pulled into the hardest turn he could manage. A fuzzy mist crept over his vision as the g-force pushed down on his eyeballs. Still nothing in the sky apart from the other two Spitfires circling above, witnessing his humiliation. He kicked his plane into a roll, reversing the turn to the opposite bank, pulling hard to minimise the circle, eyes straining at the empty sky.

'That's better, Townley,' Bryan's voice snapped into his earphones, 'look in your mirror.'

Townley's eyes flicked up. Bryan's Spitfire crept into view from under his tail to sit 20 yards behind him in the arc of the turn.

'All right, lad. Straighten up and reform on me. Andrew, let's see what your man Huggins can do.'

****

'They're useless, Madge' – Bryan took a swig of his pint – 'complete stiffs without a bloody clue about dog-fighting.'

'They're all we've got,' the adjutant said, 'it must be getting the same way for the Germans, mustn't it?'

'Doubt it,' Andrew said, 'they've been putting their show together since '33. I've never come across a bad German pilot.'

Bryan nodded his agreement.

'You can't leave them on the ground indefinitely,' the adjutant said. 'It makes no sense. The Air Ministry will go loopy if this gets out.'

'Don't I have some sort of duty to protect the men under my command from needless danger?' Bryan asked. 'It's not the charge of the bloody Light Brigade, you know.'

'It's not far off,' the adjutant said. 'I reckon you need to shoot them down at a rate of three-to-one to turn this thing around. You can't do that with pilots on the ground.'

Andrew leant forward: 'Put Townley and Huggins in a section under me. I can look after them.'

'No, Andrew,' Bryan shook his head, 'you can't play Bo-Peep to these idiots. You'll end up getting killed as well.'

'I don't know,' the adjutant sighed, 'something has to be done.'

'All right,' Bryan snapped, 'Drew's had some combat experience with Kingfisher Squadron. Put Townley and Huggins in a section under him.'

'That's the ticket,' the adjutant smiled.

'It's a sorry waste of Spitfires,' Bryan muttered.

7th September, 1940

'This is either very good news or very bad news,' Gerry said.

'Shush,' Bryan opened his eyes and darted a look at Gerry, 'you'll jinx it.'

'It must be nearly 4 o'clock,' Andrew yawned, 'the light will be fading soon. They're not coming today.'

Bryan flashed his look at Andrew.

'I don't know.' Gerry sucked his teeth. 'I've got a funny feeling about this.'

'Will you two please shut up?' Bryan hissed, 'you'll bloody well jinx it.'

Behind them a telephone jangled in the hut. Bryan buried his face in his hands.

A head poked through the window; 'Bluebird Squadron, scramble. Patrol base at Angels twenty.'

'Bugger!'

****

Vincent glanced at his altimeter. The squadron levelled out at a little over 20,000ft and fell into a wide turn to port, circling the airfield in four vics of three.

Vincent glanced over his right shoulder; Townley sat snug behind his wing. Over his left, Huggins meandered back and forth, watching for trouble.

'Beehive Control to Bluebird Leader. Two-hundred plus bandits with escort heading towards Biggin Hill and Kenley. Maintain orbit.'

Vincent closed his eyes for a second and took a deep breath. 'Two-hundred,' he thought. Fear danced over his skin and tickled at his entrails. He opened his eyes and checked over his instruments.

****

The adjutant strode across the grass to the dispersal hut as the air-raid siren wound into action, its desultory wail rolling across the airfield. He walked through the open door to see Fagan seated behind his typewriter, hands clasped in front of him as if deep in prayer.

'Come on, old man,' the adjutant chided, 'we need to get to the slit-trench, sharpish.'

Fagan opened his eyes and regarded the adjutant from beneath his creased brow. 'That won't do us any good this time.'

'What on earth do you mean?'

'I've just come off the phone to control.' Fagan polished his spectacles absently. 'The observers have called in a raid of over 300 bombers crossing the Kent coast between Folkestone and Dymchurch. Two-thirds of them are heading this way.'

'Strewth...' The adjutant removed his steel helmet and sat down.

'They're out to destroy the fighter bases once and for all, Harold. We're about to get well and truly clobbered.'

'Is this it, then,' the adjutant asked, 'has the invasion started?'

Fagan nodded: 'But it's unlikely to be any further concern of ours, my friend.' He opened a drawer in his desk, pulling out a bottle of Johnny Walker whisky and two glasses: 'I was saving this for something else, as it happens.' He poured two generous measures. 'Never mind...'

The adjutant accepted his glass and took a sip. 'It's a shame, really. The boys were putting up such a fight. They deserved to win it.'

'I don't know if they ever had a chance,' Fagan swirled his whisky, 'we're losing over a hundred every week.' He picked up a report from his desk: 'As of today we have 700 pilots to fly 600 planes. They're making fighters quicker than they're training pilots. Soon we'll have spare planes with no one to fly them.' He drained his glass and poured a refill. 'It's difficult to argue with the mathematics.'

The adjutant leant forward to accept more whisky: 'Well I hope the Germans are decent to them when they get here. None of those lads wanted a shooting war.'

Fagan smiled: 'None of them except Pilot Officer Hale.'

****

'Bluebird Leader to Beehive Control. We cannot see your bandits. What's going on?'

'Beehive Control calling, stand-by please, Bluebird Leader, continue orbit.'

'Shiny-arsed bastards,' Bryan muttered, scanning the airspace below him with suspicion. Minutes ticked by.

'Beehive Control to Bluebird Leader. Raid is heading north. Vector zero-one-five, maintain Angels twenty. Buster, buster.'

Bryan shook his head in dismay and relief: 'Bluebird Leader to Bluebird Squadron. The bastards are heading towards London. Let's get after them.'

Vincent pushed his throttle through the gate and his seat vibrated in sympathy with the straining engine. One minute... two...

'Christ Almighty...' Bryan's voice crackled through. 'Bandits at 2 o'clock. Loosen up and attack their port beam in sections. Let's get in amongst the bombers before the escorts see us. You're spoilt for choice, Bluebird. Tally-ho!'

Vincent's mouth dried out. Ahead of him the sky filled with black shapes, stacked up row upon row through a full mile of airspace.

Drawing level with the raiders, the first section of Spitfires banked right and rushed at the bomber stream's flank.

Vincent pressed transmit: 'Red Leader to Red Section, attacking now.' He pulled into a starboard turn and levelled out, the section moved to line-abreast. The lumbering black shapes loomed larger in their gunsights.

An unknown voice cut through: 'Look out, Bluebird! 109s coming down now!'

An orange flash to his right caught the corner of Vincent's eye. Townley's Spitfire burst into flames, the roaring fire engulfing the cockpit as it fell away. Two grey-painted fighters dived past and curved away over their kill.

Vincent stabbed the firing button and held it, spraying un-aimed bullets into the mass of enemy bombers in his path. To his left Huggins opened fire and his plane wallowed around with the recoil. His port wing struck the rear of a Heinkel, dislocating the bomber's tail and sending his Spitfire cartwheeling into the cockpit of the next plane in the formation.

Bombers flashed by, above and below. Vincent's gritted teeth vibrated in harmony with his chattering machine-guns. Then white lights stabbed him in his eyes and the explosion behind his forehead swaddled him in blessed silence…

…a distant rattle teased at Vincent's senses. It broke through the whistling in his ears and blossomed into the roar of his engine.

Vincent hauled back the throttle and the engine coughed into idleness. He eased back on the stick and the suburban rooftops swung down from his windscreen, giving way to blue sky and clouds as he pulled into a gentle climb. He glanced at his altimeter, it read 13,000ft.

Gripped by a sudden lurch of panic he threw his fighter into a twisting turn, screwing his neck around in a febrile search for danger. He was alone.

Out to the north the grey smudge of massed bombers advanced across the clouds towards the London docks, their path marked with the smoking pyres of downed planes. Vincent stared wide-eyed. One of those columns of smoke was Townley; one of them was Huggins.

Vincent swung round and headed south-west, away from the battle, away from the hornet's nest of German fighters buzzing around the bombers, away from the terrifying proximity of imminent, fiery annihilation. He dived for home.

****

Vincent dropped in to land, the first from Bluebird Squadron to return. He taxied in and climbed from his cockpit, an orchestra of hammers pounding in his forehead.

The armourers pounced on the plane, unlatching panels and hauling out the empty ammunition belts. 'Any luck, sir?'

'I'm not sure.' Vincent became aware of the slick of sweat on his face and the nausea squirming in his belly. 'There were so many. It was impossible to miss them' – he paused and bit his lip – 'I lost my section.'

Vincent turned away to hide the sudden sting of tears in his eyes. He hurried towards the dispersal hut, urgent with the need to file a report and end the day so he could close his eyes and leave it all behind. He wiped his cheeks and entered the hut.

'Good Lord!' The adjutant stood up, wobbled and sat down again. 'What are you doing here?'

'Back to re-arm and refuel, sir,' Vincent replied.

Fagan squinted at him over his glasses,: 'Where are the bombers?'

'They're over London, sir.'

'London?' the adjutant's voice croaked with disbelief, '300 bombers are attacking London?'

Vincent nodded.

Fagan cleared his throat and pushed his whisky glass away across the desk: 'I'd better take your report.'

'Yes, sir.' Vincent's cheeks twitched. 'I lost my section…'

This time he couldn't hide the tears.

****

Andrew and Molly lay in silence in the darkened bedroom. The window faced north towards the capital and the open curtains admitted the soft red glow throbbing from the horizon like a demonic sunset. Molly rested her hands across her distended belly.

'How can anyone decide to do something like that?' Molly asked. 'London is full of good people, people who never asked for war, and now they're being killed in their own homes.'

'We were told they were coming for us,' Andrew murmured. 'We were circling around Kenley waiting for them and they just sailed by, heading for the East End.' He hugged her closer. 'Why did Winston have to attack Berlin? Why can't he stick with bombing their invasion barges? Maybe this is just a revenge attack. Maybe tomorrow they'll come and finish us.

'We lost four pilots today, Molly, three killed and one bailed out badly wounded. Only two-thirds of the men who took off at 4 o'clock this afternoon came back at five. We'd spent the morning sun-bathing.

'Fagan and Madge were drunk when we landed. They'd cracked a bottle of whisky and sat there drinking, waiting for the bombs to blow them to pieces. It's all becoming a complete shambles.'

'In four weeks' time you become a father' – Molly snuggled into his side – 'that's all we've got now; just you, me and our baby. We've just got to carry on.'

10th September, 1940

'How is Molly?' the adjutant asked as the two men strolled between the Spitfires at dispersal. 'She's a remarkable woman, Andrew, she does you proud.'

'She's looking forward to having the baby, sir,' Andrew said, 'just under a month, now.' He cast a wistful eye across the sky. 'Who knows what the poor child will find when it gets here.'

'It's a terrible thing they're doing over London,' the adjutant said, 'but it does mean they've left us alone for a few days.' He gestured at the teams working on runway repairs. 'Fagan tells me most fighter aerodromes are back in action, landing strips patched up and squadrons on standby.'

'What about the invasion?'

The adjutant pursed his lips. 'I've been trying to work this out,' he said. 'Attacking oil storage tanks and docks looks like a useful strategy on the face of it. But refineries and docks don't oppose invasions. If I was in charge I'd split my bomber force in two, send one to attack our airfields and the other to pound the defences around the Channel ports.'

'So, they've given up the idea of a landing?'

The adjutant shook his head: 'No, I don't think they've completely given up on invasion.' He regarded Andrew squarely. 'But I suspect someone in charge has given up the prospect of beating fighter command any time soon.' He took off his cap and scratched his forehead. 'Maybe they believe we'll sue for peace to protect our cities from their bombs.'

'Could that happen?'

'Ha,' the adjutant barked a laugh, 'Winston has already told them we'll never surrender. I'm sure he'd carry on shouting his defiance from underneath the very ruins of Westminster Palace.

'Look, Andrew, I don't want to give you false hopes, especially a man in your situation. You must realise the bombers will keep coming over, every day they're able, right through the winter. Your job won't get any easier for a long time yet. But you should have some faith that your wife and child will be safer than you think, at least until the spring.'

'I dream of holding my baby sometimes,' Andrew said, 'but I know I have no right to expect...' he trailed off, reaching for his cigarette packet.

The adjutant let the silence hang for a moment; rolling out platitudes to combat pilots had worn thin weeks ago. Instead he changed the subject.

'Bryan's promotion came through this morning, he's officially squadron leader.'

'That's good news.' Andrew lit his cigarette.

'Is it?' the adjutant asked. 'I'm not really so sure.'

****

Vincent sat outside his tent as a gaggle of pilots spilled from the officers' mess and converged on the big, black Humber parked outside. A rigger walked along the line of tents towards him, carrying a bucket of steaming water. He paused by Vincent, following his gaze to the source of the shouts and laughter drifting through the failing light.

'Looks like the posh lads are off on the piss,' he said.

Vincent remained silent, chewing his bottom lip.

The rigger set down his bucket and squatted on the grass. 'My name's Maurice,' he nodded across the field, 'the posh lads call me "Mortice".'

Vincent looked up: 'I've heard the squadron leader talk about you. He seems to like you.'

'He's not a bad sort, as his sort go,' Maurice said. 'He's a top pilot and he knows his stuff when it comes to shooting down Germans.'

Vincent's eyes followed the Humber as it lurched towards the station gates: 'He reminds me of my father.'

'Isn't that a good thing?'

'No. We weren't' – Vincent paused – 'c-close.'

Maurice looked away across the field: 'You had a rough time the other day.'

Vincent nodded: 'I lost my section in three seconds flat.'

'Can I give you some advice?' the rigger smiled, 'don't dwell on it. Worrying only queers your own pitch.'

Vincent nodded in silence.

'Right!' the rigger stood, picking up his bucket. 'I've got three smelly armourers who are gagging for a wash.'

The grumble of the Humber's engine faded in the distance.

****

'My eyes are dim I cannot see, I have not brought my specs with me…'

The raucous singing reverberated inside the Humber as it wound its way down the lanes to Leaves Green. Gerry and Andrew squeezed in the front passenger seat next to Bryan, the adjutant and four other pilot officers crammed together in the back.

'Ow!' Gerry squealed, 'be careful with the stick-shift, Bryan.'

'I've no idea what you mean, old man,' Bryan shouted above the cacophony, 'you'll have to learn English.'

Another verse rolled around: *There was Yank, Yank, having a cheeky wank in the stores, in the stores…'*

The car barrelled past Biggin Hill's gates and snaked into the village. Bryan leant on the horn as they passed Molly's hairdressers. They shuddered to a halt outside The Crown and the singing reached a big finish: *'In the Quar-ter Mas-ter stooores…'* and the revellers bailed out into the car park.

'Wait, wait, wait everybody,' Andrew called out, 'let the squadron leader spearhead the attack.'

Bryan led them through the doors into the smoky beer-laced fug: 'Eight pints of bitter, please.' Bryan squeezed his way to the bar.

A group of pilots grudgingly shifted along to make room.

'Cheers, lads.' Bryan squinted at their insignia. 'Who are you?'

'Sandpiper Squadron, flying Hurricanes out of Biggin.'

'Ah,' Bryan waved to the barman, 'and get a round in for these fine young tractor-drivers will you?'

Andrew reached over, handing pints back across the crowded heads. 'Let's raise a glass to Squadron Leader Bryan Hale,' he shouted. 'Long may he reign over us.'

Molly pushed her way through the door and paused, smiling at the scene. Wary of jostling elbows she shimmied her way through the crowd to Andrew's side.

'Hello, darling,' she smiled up into his face.

'Molly, sweetheart,' he bent to kiss her forehead, 'I was hoping you'd hear us.'

'Hear you? You made more noise than the German air force,' she smiled. 'Would you get me an elderflower cordial, please?'

She watched Andrew squirm his way to the bar and tugged Bryan's sleeve. 'Congratulations, Bryan.'

Bryan turned. 'Thank you, my dear.' He looked her up and down: 'My, you're… blossoming.'

Molly blushed: 'I need your help, Bryan. It's our wedding anniversary on the 30th. I'm putting on a little surprise party here at the pub. Will you make up some excuse to get him down here?'

215

Bryan nodded: 'Certainly. Leave it to me.'

'It's secret, don't forget.'

Andrew arrived at the bar and ordered Molly's cordial.

'Who's the loudmouth?' a pilot next to him asked.

Andrew looked around: 'Oh, you mean Bryan? He's just been promoted to squadron leader so he's a bit cockier than usual tonight.'

'He doesn't have a very high opinion of Hurricane pilots, called us "tractor-drivers".'

'That's just a joke he's fond of, he doesn't mean it really. We all see the work you do down in the bomber stream. It's hairy stuff. We lost a pilot to a collision only the other day.'

'Beam attack?'

'Yes, it was actually.'

The Hurricane pilot hunkered down on the bar. 'Very dangerous way to approach it,' he said. 'Think about it. Flying across the middle of a bomber formation? Like a cat running across a busy road.' He tutted. 'Suicide.'

'So, better to attack from astern?'

'No,' the pilot shook his head, 'you're travelling too slowly in relation to the rear-gunners, they can easily get a bead on you with their pea-shooters.' He swilled the rest of his beer. 'Frontal attack is the only way to go,' he grinned, 'straight at them and straight through them. Breaks 'em up a treat.'

'Another pint for this gentleman, please barman.' Andrew turned back to the Hurricane pilot: 'Isn't that even more dangerous?'

'It's about confidence,' the man said, 'just rely on the fact that the German will get out of *your* way and you're through scot-free. Cheers.' He took a swig from his fresh pint. 'But you need to practise it. Take a couple of sections up and fly directly at each other for a while. You'll soon get used to it.'

CHAPTER 23

Consummatio

15th September, 1940

'Feel that?' Andrew asked. 'There's a distinct chill in the air.'

'Mmm,' Bryan mused, 'it'll soon be Christmas.'

'Thanksgiving first,' Gerry said.

Bryan cocked a quizzical eyebrow: 'What the hell is Thanksgiving?'

The telephone in the hut jarred the moment. The three pilots strained to decipher the mumbled conversation, quickly terminated by the *ding* of the receiver clattering back into its cradle. The orderly walked out of the hut, making straight for Bryan.

'Beehive Control want to take Bluebird to 'standby', sir.'

Bryan blinked at him. 'They want us to sit in our Spitfires?'

'Yes, sir,' the man nodded, 'something big is brewing and they're having trouble working out what's happening.'

'Right.' Bryan glared at the orderly: 'You'd better tell everyone then. Sitting in Spitfires it is.'

The pilots straggled off across the grass and climbed into their fighters. They tightened straps and plugged in headsets. Ground-crews lounged on the grass or leant against wings. From the trees at the edge of the field a crow cawed once and fell silent.

Bryan's patience was mercurial. He switched to transmit: 'Bluebird Leader to Beehive Control. I have 12 Spitfires at standby. When can I expect to scramble?'

'Hello, Bluebird Leader. We're deciphering plots. Maintain standby.'

'Plots usually do two things, Beehive,' Bryan's tone dripped acid, 'they drop bombs and they shoot at us. We generally prefer to be in a position where we can shoot back.'

Beehive remained silent and empty static whirred in the squadron's headsets as the minutes ticked by.

Inactivity and expectation chafed at the edges of nerves. Sweat trickled down temples and seeped into underclothes. Prickly itches sprang up between the toes of booted feet. And all the time, the ghastly weight of the leaden moments grew with the accretion of each trivial thought that danced, dodged and delayed the final apocalyptic notion: 'Will it be me today?'

'Beehive Control to Bluebird Squadron. Scramble. Two-hundred plus bombers with many escorts crossing the coast, Dungeness to Ramsgate. Vector one-zero-zero, Angels twenty-five.'

Engines coughed into life, belching out blue smoke that writhed across the airfield in the breeze. The fighters rolled out to the landing strip, formed into sections and raced into the air, banking onto the vector.

'Bluebird Leader to Bluebird Squadron. It looks like Adolf might be on his way after all. Increase rate of climb, let's get high enough to bounce the bastards.'

Noses tilted skywards and airspeed indicators ebbed. The hollow groan of labouring engines reverberated in cockpits and ears popped in protest as the squadron clawed upwards into space, through the haze to the placid alien blue of the upper troposphere.

In the south the flashing glints of sunlight on perspex sparkled in the sky as another Spitfire squadron climbed on a converging course, condensation trails swirling behind their wings like the sleeves of ball-gowns.

With no discernible transition, the sky ahead filled with dark specks, dropping away in a curtain of aircraft that seemingly draped all the way to the ground.

'Bluebird Leader to Bluebird Squadron. Bandits dead ahead, coming right at us. Engage top cover fighters. Red and Yellow section break right. Green and White section break left. Let's mix it up. Tally-ho!'

From the corner of his eye Andrew sensed the other Spitfire squadron roll onto their backs, diving to attack the bombers below. He drifted out of formation to give himself firing space and then the 109s were upon them. Yellow noses reared large and gunfire sparked at him from thin grey wings. Andrew thumbed the firing button and the leading Messerschmitt lanced through his bullet-stream; it flashed past underneath him, hits dancing along its fuselage.

'Hold it,' he told himself. He flew straight and level until the last two 109s bolted past by his starboard wing, dragging empty sky behind them.

Then Andrew hauled the Spitfire into a vicious right turn, his propeller slashing through the Germans' slipstream.

The two enemy fighters banked left, seeking to re-engage. Andrew's tighter turn scissored them into his gunsights and he stabbed out a snapshot. Pieces flew from the first German's wing and he flipped onto his back, diving away from danger. Andrew kicked into a roll, reversing his turn, and latched onto the tail of the second fighter. The pilot jinked in desperation, pulling up into a climbing loop. Once more flying inside his opponent's turn, Andrew loosed a five-second burst. Black smoke unfurled from the 109 and tongues of flame licked from its exhausts. The angular canopy flew off and the pilot stood up, his slipstream clawing him out and away into the void.

Andrew glanced in his mirror for danger and pulled up into a climbing turn, searching for another target. The sky around him was interlaced with woven con-trails and Andrew pointed his aircraft towards the thickest cluster. A flash in the sky scratched a fiery curve across the blue as a Spitfire dropped away from the battle, looping lazily into its long descent to destruction. German machines also dropped away from the melee, diving south, heading for home.

'Bluebird Leader to Bluebird Squadron,' Bryan's voice rattled in Andrew's earphones. 'They are breaking off. Let them go. Reform in sections, let's bully some bombers on the way home.'

The Spitfires coalesced amongst the vapour trails. Andrew picked out Bryan and Gerry, falling into formation behind them.

Bryan dropped them into a long, lazy dive to the north, banking gently to westward. The Essex suburbs stretched out below them as they cruised across the bomber route out of London.

'Yellow Two here,' Gerry called. 'Bandit at 2 o'clock below, heading south. Appears to be in a hurry.'

'Thanks, Yankee.' Bryan led them into a slow turn to port, calculated to converge with the fleeing bomber. 'Looks like a Dornier. Follow me in.'

The bomber flew at top speed, but the momentum of the diving Spitfires gave its pursuers the advantage. Bryan's fire peppered the fuselage and tailplane. Then Gerry attacked the port engine, knocking chunks off the cowling and dragging black smoke from the crippled motor.

Andrew dropped into position behind the raider and paused, thumb hovering over the firing button. An orange glow filled the rear-gunner's position. It took a moment before Andrew recognised it as fire. The inside of the bomber's fuselage rippled with flames.

Andrew throttled back, falling away from the crippled enemy but compelled to witness its end. The tail section wobbled in the air-flow; its oscillation grew in wildness until it disengaged from its melting mountings. It dropped away from the aircraft, tracing a curve of thin black smoke. Losing stability, the bomber flipped onto its back and nosed into a dive. Trailing a blowtorch of fire from its rear, the Dornier lanced its incinerated crew into oblivion on the ground.

'Job well done, Yellow Section,' Bryan chirped, 'let's go home for some lunch.'

****

Bluebird Squadron straggled down to the airfield. They dropped into a hum of activity, immediately immersed by a wave of riggers and armourers, scrambling over their planes with ammunition boxes and fuelling hoses.

Andrew pulled back the canopy to be greeted by his rigger's grimy, grinning face inches away from his own: 'Any luck, sir?'

Andrew pulled himself upright, 'A 109 destroyed, two damaged. The other two got themselves a Dornier.'

'Magic, sir.' The man's grin broadened: 'I reckon we've got 'em on the run.'

The memory of the falling Spitfire invaded Andrew's mind. He looked around at the dismounting pilots, wondering who was missing.

'Is it just me,' Bryan stood behind his wing, 'or did those 109s seem a bit windy to you?'

Andrew jumped down and the pair walked towards the dispersal hut.

'They looked keen to get home,' Andrew answered, 'but we're all keen to do that.' He paused. 'Who did we lose?'

Bryan grimaced: 'Another new boy from Drew's section. I have his name written down somewhere.'

As they reached the hut, Vincent emerged, bumping into Bryan.

'I'm sorry, sir.' Vincent's pale, drawn face blinked in recoil from the collision. 'I b-beg your pardon.' He hurried away.

Andrew and Bryan entered the hut and Fagan regarded them from behind his typewriter. 'Sergeant Drew takes the losses in his section very seriously, almost personally.' He took off his glasses and rubbed at his eye. 'It's none of my business I know, but do you think he's suitable to be a section leader?'

Bryan sat down heavily. 'I don't think he's suitable to be a fighter pilot in the first place,' he said, 'but somebody else made that decision, so we're stuck with him.'

'It's the shortage of pi—'

'Shortage of pilots?' Bryan exploded. 'We train men half-way in the basics of flying and then send them into battle against the most dangerous air force the world has ever seen?' Bryan's spittle flecked the air. 'Some poor mother's son just roasted to death in his cockpit because he didn't have the faintest clue about air combat. How does that solve a shortage of pilots?'

Bryan subsided into the chair, defeated by his own rage. 'Every time we go up against these kind of numbers, at least one of us isn't coming back,' he said quietly, 'and we have to carry on as if we don't care.'

The phone chimed into the silence and Fagan picked it up. 'Yes. Thank you.'

Bryan looked up with a resigned smile: 'What does the nice telephone say?'

'Bluebird Squadron is back on standby.'

****

Vincent sat outside his tent watching the twilight steepen towards darkness. A figure crunched across the gravel to the officers' mess, paused, hand on the door handle, and then turned to walk towards him. Vincent made to stand up, but the figure waved him back down, shaking his head.

'Relax, sergeant,' Andrew smiled, 'it's been a long day.'

'Yes, sir. Thank you, sir.'

'It's been a rough day, too.' Andrew lit a cigarette and sat down on the grass. 'I've never seen so many planes in the air at the same time. It's a miracle we didn't lose more people.'

Vincent nodded; a wretched pallor masked his face.

'Let me tell you about my friend Alan.' Andrew blew out a stream of smoke. 'Alan was one of the nicest blokes you could hope to meet. Even when he was snoozing at dispersal he had a smile on his face. He was a concise and methodical fighter pilot. He knew all there was to know about flying, a complete wizard at aerobatics.'

Vincent remained silent.

'Alan collided with a Stuka over Dunkirk.'

A tremor ran over Vincent's body. He clenched his teeth to stop it.

'And my friend George,' Andrew continued, 'he was a bit younger than me, a rowdy bastard after a few pints, always up for a laugh. Vain as a peacock; he'd check his reflection in every window he passed. He was determined to become an 'ace' as soon as possible.'

Vincent squeezed his eyes shut and waited.

'George was shot down in flames by a 109. He didn't bail out quickly enough.'

'Why are you telling me this?' Vincent's voice quaked with fragility.

'They were both flying in my section on the day they copped it.' Andrew stood and put his hand on Vincent's shoulder. 'Get some rest, son. Tomorrow's another day that we both need to get through.'

29th September, 1940

'Settle down, gentlemen, please.' Fagan's shout quelled the murmur of conversation in the crowded dispersal hut.

'Good morning to you all.' Fagan's glossy smile flashed around the room. 'You are all aware that things have quietened down over the last two weeks. I would like to be able to tell you that this is because you've won what Winston likes to call 'The Battle of Britain'. Sadly I don't believe that battle is yet over.

'Until France is retaken, German bombers will remain within easy range of London, and indeed, within easy range of our fighter bases. So we are a long way from being out of the woods. However, the Air Ministry has received some interesting intelligence that has come to us via the American Ambassador to Switzerland. Although this information is classified, Squadron Leader Hale and myself feel you have a right to be told.

'It appears the German high command are preparing domestic press releases stating that Britain will be defeated by the effects of bombing and blockade alone. It seems they are distancing themselves from their previous commitment to invasion.'

A murmur of hushed voices rippled around the room.

Fagan held up a hand and the talking ebbed away: 'This is by no means certain. But you should allow it to give you some heart. If we spend the next six months building fighters, training pilots and honing flying skills, by next summer we might be in a position to stop the bombers getting through.

'Thank you, gentlemen. You should be very pleased with yourselves. Dismiss.'

A ragged cheer rose from the pilots and they filed out under a buzz of chatter.

'Great news, Andrew,' Gerry slapped him on the back as they left, 'I wouldn't have missed this day for the world.'

'Yes.' Andrew looked down, his eyes glistening.

'What's up, buddy?'

Andrew shook his head: 'I wish they could've been here to hear that.'

'Who?'

'Alan… George… all the hundreds of others. I wish they could've believed this was possible. That their homes and their families might survive.'

Gerry put a hand on Andrew's shoulder: 'God willing, they know it now.'

CHAPTER 24

Astrum

30th September, 1940

Bluebird Squadron sat at readiness, waiting for daylight raids that didn't come.

Andrew stood and sniffed the air: 'It's a decent enough day for flying, perhaps we should take a flight up for some training.'

Gerry nodded: 'It would be better than sitting around here.'

Bryan pulled a face while he considered the proposition. 'All right, take two sections up for a bit. I'll stay here with the others in case there's a flap.'

Andrew winked his thanks and called out: 'Green Section, follow me. We're going to stretch our legs.' He spotted Vincent sitting apart from the others: 'Sergeant Drew!'

Vincent looked up.

'I need you fly third man in Yellow Section.'

The six pilots congregated, walking towards the Spitfires in dispersal. Ground-crew, spotting their movement, bustled to ready their starting batteries.

'From what Fagan said yesterday' – Andrew raised his voice so the group could hear him – 'we can expect to face more bomber formations in the future, if not this year, then certainly next spring.'

The group reached Andrew's Spitfire and stood next to the plane in a loose circle.

'Many times we end up chasing a bomber formation. In some ways this is the least effective way to attack. Your closing speed will be a little more than 100 miles an hour, less than that with a Junkers or Dornier, less still if the enemy has already dropped his bombs. This means you'll present an almost stationary target to the rear-gunner. In a reasonably large formation you may get five or six rear-gunners take an interest in you.'

Wry laughter rippled from the men.

'A beam attack is better. Their return fire is always less accurate. Your approach speed is 300 miles an hour, but your target is moving past you at

200 miles an hour. For this reason, always attack the leading planes in the formation. The others have to fly through your bullet-stream. Break away above or below the formation, never try flying through.'

Vincent looked down at his feet.

'But,' Andrew continued, 'the most effective way to disrupt a bomber formation has been championed by the squadron leader's beloved tractor-drivers.'

Another round of quiet laughter traversed the group.

'The Hurricane boys from Biggin have perfected the head-on attack. It's by far the hairiest way to approach the enemy for two reasons: everything happens far more quickly – the combined approach speed is at least 500 miles an hour; and flying head-on at another plane goes against everything you were taught when you learned to fly.

'But,' Andrew wagged his finger, 'that's why it's so effective. The German pilot will *want* to get out of your way. He'll pull up, he'll turn, he'll do anything to get out of *your* way. This breaks up the formation. Once you've split them up they make individual decisions. At the very least the concentration of bombs hitting their target is disrupted. At best, a large proportion will dump their bombs and head for home.'

Andrew smiled from one face to the next: 'Right, Yellow Section – that's me, Yankee and Drew – will fly as bombers. Moderate speed, straight and level in vic formation. Green Section, you'll be the interceptors. I'll talk you through all the approaches I've just mentioned.'

The men nodded.

'Good. Let's get up there.'

****

The landlord surveyed the decorations and beamed a smile: 'I never imagined the back-room could look this pretty, Molly. Well done.'

Molly blushed. 'It's only paper-chains and bunting, Geoff,' she smiled, 'it's really nothing special.'

'It looks lovely,' Geoff said. 'Here, hold on a minute.' He ducked out the door.

Molly straightened the tablecloth on the side-table and put a cake-tin in the centre.

Geoff reappeared and thrust a bottle into her hands: 'Happy anniversary to you both.'

225

Molly cradled the bottle. 'Port?' she gasped, 'I can't take this, it looks really expensive.'

Geoff shook his head: 'You deserve it, love. He deserves it. Him and his friends, for what they do. I wish I had a decent bottle for every one of them.'

****

Gerry checked his airspeed and glanced across to his right. Ahead of him Andrew spearheaded the vic. To the leader's right, Drew bobbled up and down in the margins of Andrew's slipstream. 'He should edge out.' he thought, 'Loosen up.'

'Bluebird Yellow Leader to Green Section.' Andrew's voice cut into his reverie. 'You're doing really well. Let's try the head-on attack before we go home. Make sure you get far enough ahead to give yourselves time to straighten up and line up your target. Don't forget that closing speed will be very fast.'

Green Section accelerated away and vanished into the blue, a faint glimmer of sun on perspex the only clue to their position.

'Green Leader to Yellow Section, turning onto attack run now.'

Vincent checked his instruments and fidgeted in his seat. The sun through the perspex made him uncomfortable with sweat. He pulled back the canopy a bit to get some airflow around the cockpit.

Gerry squinted against the flat blue sky. He murmured: 'There' – three black dots barrelling through the heavens towards them.

Vincent looked across at the section leader's plane. He had edged too close. 'Ease out a bit,' he intoned.

A black shape flashed by above him, a concussive blast of air punched into the cockpit with a roaring rasp of deafening noise. Vincent's instinctive spasm rammed the stick to his left.

Gerry ducked his head as Green Section's three Spitfires slashed past only feet above him. Then he hauled back hard on the stick as the huge, flat shape of Drew's fighter lurched across his vision.

Vincent felt a shuddering impact on his starboard wing and a shape careened away in his peripheral vision. The world jolted into a vicious spin.

Gerry levelled out, banked left and looked down. Andrew's Spitfire tumbled towards the ground, end over end, while its tail section spiralled away on a different trajectory.

Gerry pressed transmit: 'Andrew! Bail out! You've lost your tail!' He sucked in great gulps of air to quell the visceral panic rising in his throat: 'Andrew…'

The somersaulting Spitfire hit the centre of a ploughed field with a pluming splash of burning fuel. The fuselage bounced once into the air, scattering debris, before it crumpled to rest, thick black smoke belching from the fire that engulfed it.

'Andrew?'

Vincent wrestled with the stick and kicked at the rudder, fighting with all his might against the flat spin gripping his Spitfire. The whirling slowed and stopped; Vincent pushed the nose down to prevent a stall, then straightened up. Panting with terror and exertion he looked out at his wing. The leading edge crumpled into a huge dent and a dislocated machine-gun breech bulged the top surface.

Looking around in desperation for a safe place to set down, he pumped down the undercarriage, gasping with relief at the *clunk* as the legs locked into place. Throwing a nervous glance at the damaged wing, he hauled back his canopy, locking it in place. Circling, he picked a large meadow bounded by a low fence.

The horses in the meadow galloped in circles of blind terror as Vincent's Spitfire set down amongst them. Rumbling and jolting to a halt, Vincent turned off the engine and shut the fuel cocks.

Behind his eyes the pressure mounted, then vented as the sudden white-hot explosions in his head blinded him to the world. Vincent jerked and spasmed against his harness.

****

Bryan stirred from his doze, the ringing of the dispersal telephone tearing away his peace. The murmuring voice inside the hut went on for longer than usual. He sat up and waited.

The rattle of receiver into cradle begat a silent pause. Bryan peered into the gloom of the hut. The orderly's measured steps sounded on the wooden floor and the man emerged into the sunlight with a drawn look of concern weighing down his features.

'There's been an accident, a collision,' he said. 'Two of Yellow Section's planes have gone in. The army have sent ambulances and fire-trucks to the scene.'

Silence fell like a shroud over the pilots. Bryan sagged back into his deckchair and closed his eyes under the weight of pain and exhaustion. He sat immobile, refusing to hope or believe, until the growl of Merlin engines broached the silence above his head. His eyes flicked open and he hauled himself onto his feet, walking away towards the landing strip.

The pilots watched him go in silence.

****

Molly pulled on her patterned dress, wriggling and squirming to reach the zip and clasps on its back. She walked to the mirror and looked herself up and down. The pleats of the dress stretched themselves almost flat across her pregnant belly, but she had nothing prettier that she could still squeeze into.

She nodded in satisfaction and went to the dressing table. Opening a small drawer, she smiled with affection at the contents: foundation, powder, lipstick, eye-liner and eyeshadow, all bought for her wedding day before war-time scarcities bore down on such simple pleasures. She picked them out one by one, arranging them in a semi-circle on the dresser. Looking in the mirror she pulled and stretched her skin experimentally, searching for lines or wrinkles. She leant forward and crinkled her brow into a frown, then burst into laughter at the stern face she'd made. Still smiling to herself, she reached for the foundation.

****

Bryan stood with arms folded as the four returning Spitfires circled the field. He squinted at the descending planes until he could make out the white identification letters on the leader's fuselage. It was Gerry bringing them home. His head sagged and his stomach writhed with conflicting emotions.

Gerry taxied to a standstill and cut his engine. Climbing out, he spotted Bryan and walked slowly towards him.

'What happened, Yankee?' Bryan asked.

Gerry reached him and they walked together towards the dispersal hut.

'Yellow Section were flying as bombers and Andrew was talking Green Section through all the quarters of attack. He started them with an attack from astern and took them right around the clock' – he paused – 'the last one was a head-on attack. They cut it very fine, close enough to spook me.'

'And?'

Gerry blew out a deep breath: 'Sergeant Drew over-reacted, pulled a sharp left bank. He and Andrew collided.'

'Parachutes?'

'Andrew's tail was chopped off. The plane somersaulted in. He didn't have a chance to get out.'

'What about Sergeant Drew?'

Gerry shook his head: 'I didn't see what happened to him. I couldn't raise him on the wireless. I think we've lost him too.'

Bryan stopped, covering his eyes with one hand: 'Practising bomber attacks. What a waste.'

'He took Fagan's lecture to heart,' Gerry said, 'you can understand why, after all his wife does live next to an airfield and...' he faltered into silence.

Bryan dropped his hand from eyes that glistened with tears: 'It's their bloody wedding anniversary, Yankee. She's organised a party.'

They walked the few dozen yards to the dispersal hut under the silence of their grief.

The orderly stood waiting: 'Sir?'

Bryan nodded for him to speak.

'They've recovered Pilot Officer Francis from the wreckage, sir. He's been taken to Croydon morgue.'

'Thank you,' Bryan breathed.

'And they've found Sergeant Drew, sitting in his Spitfire in a field of horses. Force-landed. They've taken him to hospital for a check-up.'

Bryan fixed the orderly with a gaze that nailed several seconds of silence to the man's forehead: 'Tell Beehive Control that Bluebird Squadron are standing down.'

****

Molly took the carrot-cake from the tin and wiped a bread-knife with a napkin. She pondered cutting the cake, but no, the squadron might be held up, it would be a shame for it to go dry. She uncorked the port and sniffed its deep-fruited aroma. Pouring a small measure for herself she walked through to the bar.

Geoff paused in his glass polishing: 'Just waiting for the other half?'

Molly patted her belly. 'The other third,' she smiled broadly. 'Cheers.'

****

Bryan fastened cufflinks into his sky-blue shirt, turned up the collar and reached for his dark blue tie. He avoided his own gaze in the mirror, focusing instead on tying his knot and centring his tie-pin.

He stepped away from the mirror and shrugged on his jacket, fastening the buttons and securing the belt. Reaching for his cap, he returned to the mirror. At last he looked into the reflection of his own eyes. He settled the cap onto his head, checking the peak sat dead straight across his forehead. On impulse he reached up and undid his top jacket button.

****

Molly sat at the bar, nursing her port and chatting with Geoff. A group of pilots from Biggin Hill sat around a table in the window murmuring in wearied conversation, and an elderly gentleman perched at the other end of the bar like a sack of discarded clothes at a jumble sale.

The familiar growl of the Humber's engine and the crunch of wheels on the gravel turned Molly's head.

Sliding off the barstool, she clasped her hands over her breast to contain her excitement.

Bryan walked in and stopped. He looked into Molly's eyes.

'Oh,' Molly said, 'are they not allowed to come?'

The pilots by the window fell silent, first to sense the portent. Bryan took off his cap and held Molly's gaze.

'Oh my God,' she gasped. 'Andrew's been hurt!'

Bryan shook his head.

Realisation flowed over Molly. Her head drooped and her shoulders sagged as she crumpled into herself. She swayed like a wraith in the breeze and Bryan stepped forward to catch her in his arms.

'It was very quick, Molly,' Bryan whispered into her hair, 'he didn't suffer.'

The pilots finished their drinks and filed out quietly, each nodding respect to Bryan as they passed. The elderly man retired to the toilet. Geoff stood staring down into the middle distance.

Molly heaved a rasping, ragged breath that shuddered through her body. 'It hurts.' Her voice keened with the serrated edge of raw grief. 'It hurts so badly.'

Bryan tightened his embrace, trying to stem the haemorrhage of her distress. Molly wracked with visceral sobs against his chest, each convulsion subsiding into the next until she trembled to stillness. She pushed gently against Bryan and he released her. She walked to the window and sat down.

'I've often imagined this moment.' Her voice was quiet but steady through her tears. 'Not when I said goodbye to him.' She shook her head. 'Not while I waited for him to come back.' Fresh tears welled into her lashes. 'But when he came back' – a grim smile creased her wet cheeks – 'I knew he only came back because somewhere a woman like me had lost a man like him.

'Thank you, Bryan, I'm glad I heard it from you.' She stood and straightened her dress. 'I think I'll be off home.'

'I can stay with you a while if you want,' Bryan said, 'I don't want you to be alone.'

'No.' she smiled again. 'I won't be alone' – she rested a hand on her belly – 'I have a piece of Andrew right here.'

CHAPTER 25

Luctus

1st October, 1940

The army truck growled to a halt outside Kenley's gate. Vincent jumped from the rear and waved his thanks to the driver as the engine gunned and the truck rolled away.

The guard nodded as Vincent walked past towards the airfield, carrying his parachute over his shoulder. Passing between the officers' mess and the control room, he walked out to the dispersal hut. The squadron sat reading papers and smoking in the limpid sunlight.

Vincent walked up to Bryan: 'Sergeant Pilot Vincent Drew reporting for d-duty, sir.'

Bryan rocked slightly in his chair at the sound but didn't look up. 'You're not on the rota today, Drew. Report for readiness at first light.'

'Yes, sir.' He paused. 'They told me Pilot Officer Francis c-crashed, sir. I'm s-sorry.'

Bryan sprang from his chair: 'Yes!' he leant into Vincent's face, 'it's bloody difficult to stay in the air when you've got no tail.'

Gerry placed a restraining hand on Bryan's shoulder: 'It was an accident, Bryan.'

'An accident?' Bryan whirled on Gerry. 'Was it?' He spun back to confront Vincent: 'Or have we got a jinx on the squadron?'

Gerry stepped between the two men: 'Come on, Bryan. The kid feels bad enough as it is.'

Bryan fired a glare at Vincent and stormed away across the field.

Gerry took Vincent by the arm: 'Come on, sergeant. Let's get you away from here.'

They walked towards the line of tents at the edge of the field, 'You were there, sir,' Vincent said, 'what happened?'

'Green Section cut it too close, is all,' Gerry said. 'I'm pleased you made it down in one piece.'

'Maybe I am a jinx,' Vincent said. 'I should've stayed on the ground. Should've stuck with being a powder monkey.'

'Why did you volunteer for flying?'

'I was told the Germans were coming, sir. I mean, really coming, on the doorstep so to speak.' Vincent blushed. 'I just wanted to do the best I could to protect my mother.'

Gerry smiled: 'That's the exact same reason I'm here.'

3rd October, 1940

The orderly leaned out the window: 'Control needs a section to patrol off the coast at Hastings, they think there may be a weather reconnaissance stooging around.'

Bryan hauled himself out of his chair. 'Yankee,' he shouted, 'find me another pilot – we've got a weatherman to hunt.'

Bryan strode to his Spitfire and jumped onto the wing. As he climbed into the cockpit Gerry jogged past with Vincent behind him.

'Sergeant Drew's flying Number Three,' Gerry called as he passed.

****

Molly stared at the hospital ceiling. A tear crept from the corner of her eye and trickled into her ear. A throb grew in her lower back and climbed up her abdomen leaving her muscles rigid in its wake. She tensed her jaw against the sensation, a visceral grunt escaped from her throat. The pain peaked and passed.

The nurse checked the watch pinned on her apron: 'It won't be long now, Mrs Francis.'

'Call me Molly.'

****

'Bluebird Yellow Leader to Yellow Section, we'll take one more run along the coast and call it a day. It's getting too cloudy for this game.'

Stacked cumulus clouds drifted across the coast west of Folkestone. Yellow Section plunged into their ethereal embrace and the mist smothered their canopies like white muslin.

Gerry peered across the space at the other two planes. Bryan's Yellow One was indistinct but still visible as a murky shape in the swirling mire. Vincent's Yellow Three, out on Bryan's starboard side, flickered in and out of vision like a spectre in a dream.

'Yellow Leader to Yellow Section,' Bryan called, 'keep a careful eye on your instruments. Maintain current heading and keep feet off rudders. Stay smooth and straight until we get out of the murk.'

Gerry eased out further to port, putting an extra 20 yards between himself and the other planes. He glanced from the artificial horizon on his instrument panel to the ghostly form of Bryan's Spitfire and back again.

Vincent stared at the crowded control panel. The familiar instruments took on an alien remoteness. The wobbling wheel of the compass looked primitive. The vibrating needles wavered with uncertainty. He stared for a moment through the windscreen. A translucent cotton wool cloak pressed against it.

Swallowing his panic, Vincent searched for the section leader. Ahead and to his left, he could make out the silhouette of Bryan's Spitfire flitting in and out of sight. Fixing his eyes on this oasis of security, he edged closer.

Bryan held his control column in his right hand and locked his right elbow against the cockpit wall. He scanned out over his left shoulder and saw the dim profile of Gerry's aircraft drifting further out to port. He turned back to check his heading and looked out over his right shoulder. He could see nothing. Bryan checked his heading again and craned his head hard back over his right shoulder. Something moved in the mist at the edge of his vision. Bryan snapped his eyes up to the rear-view mirror. Yellow Three loomed tight on his starboard side.

'You're not having me too, you bastard,' Bryan murmured and hauled his stick to the right.

Vincent yelped in surprise as Bryan's aircraft flipped onto its starboard wingtip, lurching across his path. He yanked the stick back into his belly, hurling his Spitfire into a sudden, steep climb to avoid the collision, clenching his teeth against an impact that didn't come. Panting with rising panic, Vincent pushed the stick forward and centred it. He looked around wildly into the dense, blinding whiteness then back at the spinning compass. The engine choked and sputtered into a stall. Vincent's stomach lurched as his Spitfire slid away into a flat spin.

Gerry glanced back to his instruments, checking his heading and artificial horizon. He looked out to his right and stared at the white blankness for long moments. Bryan had vanished.

Bryan held his steep right bank for a few seconds and then slewed into a diving turn to port. He watched his altimeter tick down and his compass settle. He came around to the correct heading and levelled out 1000ft lower.

Gerry, unnerved at losing contact with the formation, allowed his plane to drift more to the left and eased the throttle back a notch.

****

Molly's scream tore the air. She sucked a breath in through clenched teeth and roared again into the anguish of her pain.

'Almost there, Molly,' the nurse murmured, 'I can see the head.'

Molly's muscles quivered and clenched into iron spasm. A wave of blinding pain crashed up through her abdomen and burst in her temples, grinding her teeth in her clenched jaws.

'Make it stop…' she whimpered.

A white-hot crescendo transfixed her spine. She lay impaled on its impossible agony for one searing moment, then a whirlpool of ecstasy and relief dragged her down and away from the suffering.

'It's a girl, Molly. It's a lovely, healthy little girl.'

****

The return to light dazzled Gerry. He squinted against it and recognised the blue dome of the sky about his head and the grey, white-flecked sea stretched out below him. The dense cloud bank receded in his wake.

'Yellow Leader to Yellow Section,' Bryan's voice came over the wireless, 're-form on me, please, it's about time we went home.'

Gerry quartered the sky above and around him searching for the others. Glancing down, he spotted Bryan's Spitfire much lower on his starboard side. Banking his machine into a shallow dive, he switched to transmit: 'Yellow Two to Yellow Leader. I am above you on your port side. Coming down now. How did you get all the way down there?'

'How did you get all the way up there?'

Gerry pulled into station next to his leader and looked across into the canopy.

'Yellow Leader calling Yellow Three, Yellow Leader calling Yellow Three' – Bryan's gaze held Gerry's – 'Are you receiving me, Yellow Three?' Bryan finally unlocked their eyes and looked away into space: 'Where are you, Vincent, old boy?'

Dungeness flashed by underneath as Gerry followed Bryan's banking turn onto a north-west heading to base.

'Bluebird Yellow Leader calling Beehive Control. Yellow Section returning to base. Listening out.'

****

Gerry landed in formation on Bryan's port side. The two Spitfires slowed to taxiing speed and bumped away across the grass to their dispersal bays.

Gerry shut down his engine and hauled the canopy back. His mechanic jumped onto the wing and helped undo the harness.

'Any luck today, sir?'

'No, nothing doing.' Gerry pulled himself out of the seat. 'Has Yellow Three landed yet?'

'Just the two of you so far, sir.'

Gerry jumped to the ground and strode towards the other Spitfire. Bryan climbed down onto the grass as he arrived, chatting with his mechanic.

'What happened up there, Bryan?' Gerry's voice held an edge.

Bryan glanced at him from under a frown and turned back to his mechanic.

'Just top her up with fuel and that should do it; everything else is working spotlessly.'

The man nodded and moved away.

Bryan glared at Gerry: 'Don't ever use that tone to me in front of my ground-crew, do you understand?' He stalked away past Gerry's shoulder.

Following, Gerry persisted: 'What happened, Bryan? One second you were there on my starboard side, next second you were gone – and Vincent has disappeared.'

Bryan pulled up short, rounding on Gerry. 'We flew into clouds,' he hissed. 'People vanish in clouds.'

Gerry studied the other man's face.

Abruptly the menace dropped from Bryan's features. 'You'd better flight-test your altimeter, Yankee,' he said. 'I think it might be broken.'

Bryan strode to the dispersal hut with Gerry trailing in his wake. They entered the hut just as Fagan replaced the receiver on his telephone.

'Good afternoon, gentlemen,' he said, 'that was Beehive on the phone. The Observer Corps report seeing a Spitfire diving vertically into the sea just off Camber Sands about 15 minutes ago. Yours was the only section airborne' – he looked at them over his glasses – 'I'm posting Sergeant Drew as missing.'

Bryan tutted and shook his head: 'Bloody cloud. Ten-tenths. Like bloody soup, it was.'

****

'You do know what you're suggesting, don't you?' the adjutant frowned.

'I'm just telling you what I saw,' Gerry replied.

'Well, you're not are you' – the adjutant leaned back in his chair – 'because you didn't actually see anything.'

Gerry remained silent.

The adjutant pursed his lips: 'Three Spitfires fly into ten-tenths cloud and become separated. It's hardly an Agatha Christie.'

'Squadron Leader Hale has had it in for Sergeant Drew for a long time.'

'That's not surprising now, is it? He and Andrew had been flying together since '35; they were best friends.'

'That isn't an excuse for what happened.'

'But you don't *know* what happened, Gerry. That's the whole point.' The adjutant passed a hand over his face. 'Look, I can't take any action on this. And I suggest you forget about it. Hale is a solid leader, Bluebird could do a lot worse.'

Gerry stood to leave: 'Thank you, sir.'

The adjutant waited for the door to close and reached for the telephone.

6th October, 1940

A teasing breeze cut through the wrought iron gates in the brick arch, agitating the first of the autumn's leaf-fall around Bryan's shoes. The funeral attendees drifted away in groups and he maintained a respectful distance while they departed. Molly remained alone at the graveside.

As Bryan approached she looked up with red-rimmed eyes: 'Thank you for coming, Bryan. It's a long trip for you.'

Bryan put his arm around Molly's shoulders. 'He was my best friend,' he said quietly, 'he was the best of men.'

Molly leant her head against Bryan's chest, gentle sobs rose and subsided in her throat.

'Would you like to go for a walk, maybe get some tea?' Bryan asked.

Molly straightened herself, wiping the tears from her cheeks. 'I have to go and feed my baby,' she smiled through her tears. 'I have responsibilities, you know.'

'Of course.' Bryan took her hand and kissed it: 'I'll always be there.'

Molly nodded and turned for the gate.

The blue of Bryan's uniform drained into the grey of the early autumn sky. He bowed his head and surrendered himself to tears.

10th October, 1940

Gerry paused at the door of the officers' mess. Down the driveway he could hear a female voice rising in distress. He strode down to the guard-hut where a woman was in heated conversation with the guard.

'I'm sorry, Madam,' the guard said, 'we're an operational airfield on war footing. I can't let you in without express permission.'

'Hello,' Gerry said.

The guard snapped to attention.

'You're the American,' the woman said. 'Vincent wrote about you in one of his letters.'

'Mrs Drew?' Gerry shook her hand. He nodded to the guard: 'It's all right, I'll look after this.'

'Thank you, young man. Please call me Eileen.'

They walked up the drive together.

'I wanted to see where he worked,' Eileen said. 'It's so difficult when there are no...' The word caught in her throat. 'When you can't have a proper funeral.'

They crested the rise and Eileen stopped. She gazed out at the aeroplanes dotted around the airfield.

'Did he really fly one of those?'

Gerry nodded.

Eileen looked into Gerry's eyes through the beginnings of soft tears: 'My son was murdered.'

Gerry returned her gaze: 'Murdered?'

'How can anybody teach a young man like my Vincent to fly a machine like that in six weeks?' She searched his face as she spoke. 'The RAF needed numbers, that's all. They made my son into cannon fodder.'

'I wish I could tell you it wasn't true, Eileen.'

17th October, 1940

Gerry entered the office. Day stood up and smiled broadly: 'Sit down, Gerry.'

Gerry sat and placed a brown envelope on the desk between them. 'The rest of my manuscript.'

Adjutant Day picked up the envelope, stuffing it into his briefcase. 'Thank you.'

'Is that all that's required of me?'

Day smiled and laced his fingers together: 'Your compatriots have caught up with you at flying school. We now have enough trained Americans to form a squadron. The adjutant at Bluebird suggested you might make a suitable leader. Winston is very keen to call it Eagle Squadron.'

31st October, 1940

Samuel Drew climbed the two steps and leant over into the narrow metal pen. The bullock snuffed in alarm. Samuel pressed the bolt-gun against the beast's forehead and the shot echoed around the room.

The creature dropped to its knees on the sloping floor, lolling against the side of the pen. Samuel climbed down and pulled a lever. The pen swung open and the bullock rolled out onto the floor.

Samuel stepped over to the rack on the wall, selecting a long, thin, flexible rod. Crouching next to the stunned animal he inserted the rod into the bolt-hole, thrusting it through the brain. Jabbing and twisting, he found the end of the spinal column and pushed the rod down its length. The body quivered and quaked. He removed the rod and the animal shuddered into stillness.

Samuel attached a chain to a back leg and pressed a green button mounted on the wall. An electric motor whirred into action, hoisting the creature into the air; its tongue lolled from its mouth.

The hoist clicked off and Samuel selected a long, straight knife from the rack. In one easy motion he slashed the bullock's throat.

Dark red blood splashed onto the ground. Samuel stood back as the flow spurted to the beat of the failing heart, slowly diminishing to a trickle. Another man appeared with a large wheelbarrow. Samuel plunged the knife into the bullock's navel, drawing it down in a straight line to the bottom of the neck.

The creature's intestines and viscera sloshed out into the wheelbarrow. Samuel leant into the carcass to cut loose the connections and the man pushed the steaming barrow-load away.

The electric motor whirred into motion again and the bullock moved along the overhead rails to the cutting room to be skinned and butchered. Samuel hosed down the floor and lifted the side of the pen, clicking it back into place.

'Next!'

The door at the end of the pen opened into the holding room and another bullock was corralled into the narrow space.

Samuel leant into the pen and held the bolt-gun in place. Another cartridge crack echoed off the walls. Samuel pulled the lever and turned to the rack. Behind him he heard hooves scrabbling on concrete, turning in time to see the bullock lurch to its feet.

The huge black bulk fell into Samuel, crushing him against the wall. The tools on the rack transfixed his back and the sickening grind of broken ribs sent electric shards of pain through his chest.

The stunned bullock fought to stay on its feet, bouncing and jostling its weight against the trapped man. With no air in his lungs, unable to draw breath, Samuel could only stare, slack-jawed as the light faded from his eyes.

The flat slap of cleavers in flesh drifted through from the next room where the men butchered the recently killed carcasses.

****

I hope you have enjoyed Bluebirds and will consider leaving an honest review on Amazon.

Visit my website at **www.melvynfickling.com** and sign up for the Bluebirds Newsletter for updates on the next books in the series.

Like my page at **Facebook.com/MelvynFicklingAuthor** for day-to-day news about my writing.

Follow me on Twitter **@MelvynFickling**

Glossary of Terms

Abyssinia – Historical nation in the north of present day Ethiopia

Abyssinia Crisis – Incident resulting from the ongoing conflict between the Kingdom of Italy and the Empire of Ethiopia

Adjutant – Administrative assistant to a senior officer

Airframe – Structural skeleton of an aircraft

Aileron – Movable surface usually near the trailing edge of a wing; controls the roll of the aircraft

Angels – Code word for altitude; Angels ten means 10,000 feet

Anson Trainer – Double-engine aircrew trainer

Anthony Eden – British Secretary for Foreign Affairs during Abyssinia Crisis

AOC – Air officer commanding

Armour-Piercing (AP) – Ammunition designed to penetrate plate metal

Avro Tutor – Bi-plane used by the RAF to train pilots

Axis Powers – Germany, Italy and Japan

Ball – Standard machine-gun ammunition

Bandits – RAF slang for enemy aircraft

Beehive – Fictional codename for the sector control room at Kenley

BEF – British Expeditionary Force

Bf 109 – Messerschmitt 109; German single-seat fighter

Bf 110 – Messerschmitt 110; German double-seat fighter

Biplane – Aircraft with two sets of wings, one above the other

Blenheim – British twin-engine light bomber aircraft

Bounced – RAF slang for being attacked from above

Brass – RAF slang for officers

Buster – Running a fighter engine on full boost; not recommended for long periods due to likelihood of damage and/or fire

Cable defence – Heavy cables fired into the air in the path of approaching low-level attackers

Chocks – Triangular lumps of wood used to wedge against aircraft wheels to prevent movement on the ground

Cowling – Curved panel covering the engine of an aircraft

Crate – RAF slang for aeroplane

Deck – RAF slang for the ground

Demon – Two-seater bi-plane fighter used by RAF between the wars

DH-5 – Bi-plane in service during The Great War

Dispersal – Area where planes are scattered widely to reduce potential damage if attacked

Do 17 – Dornier 17; German twin-engine bomber

Dogfight – RAF slang for fighter versus fighter combat

Dorsal – Machine-gun position on upper side or back of a bomber

Elevator – Movable surface on the tail, controls pitch of the aircraft

Flagmen – Men who mark the flightpath across a field for a crop-duster

Flaps – Movable surface on an aircraft, usually near the trailing edge of a wing; increases lift and decreases speed

Flap – RAF slang for emergency

Flight – A fighting unit usually consisting of six aircraft

Fuselage – Main body of an aeroplane

Gen – RAF slang for intelligence, information

G-force – Force acting on a body as a result of acceleration or gravity

Gilly – Shore crab

Gone for a Burton – RAF slang for getting killed

He 111 – Heinkel 111; German twin-engine bomber

Heliopolis – A suburb outside Cairo, Egypt

Homebrew – Fictional codename for a sector control room

Hurricane – Single-seat British fighter; slightly poorer performance than the Spitfire

Incendiary – Ammunition designed to encourage fire

Jink – To fly erratically to put off an attacker's aim

Ju 88 – Junkers 88; German twin-engine bomber

Kite – RAF slang for aeroplane

League of Nations – Intergovernmental organisation founded in 1920 after the Paris Peace Conference at the end of the First World War

LMF – Lack of Moral Fibre

Mandrake – Codename for one of the sector control rooms

Me 109 – Messerschmitt 109; German single-seat fighter

Me 110 – Messerschmitt 110; German double-seat fighter

Monoplane – Fixed-wing aircraft with a single main wing plane

Orbit – To fly in a circle

O'clock – Used to locate the enemy in relation to line of flight; 12 o'clock is straight ahead, 6 o'clock is directly behind

Orderly – Officer in charge of administration of a unit or establishment for a day at a time

Panzer – Heavy German battle tank

Plots – Radar contacts translated to markers on a map

Port – Left-hand side of an aircraft; a port turn is to the left

Prop-wash – Blast of air caused by a propeller

Radial engine – Engine configuration in which the cylinders 'radiate' outward from a central crankcase

Rotary engine – An early type of internal combustion engine

Roundel – Concentric red white and blue circles used as identification for British planes

Rudder – Movable surface on an aircraft, usually on the tail; controls yaw of the aircraft

Section – Fighting unit of aircraft usually consisting of two or three aircraft, normally codenamed with a colour

Side-slip – Where an aircraft moves somewhat sideways as well as forward relative to the oncoming airflow

Slipstream – Flow of air around an airborne aircraft

Somaliland – Self-declared state internationally recognised as an autonomous region of Somalia

Sopwith Camel – Bi-plane in service during The Great War

Spitfire – Single-seat British fighter; slightly better performance than the Hurricane

Squadron – Fighting unit of aircraft usually consisting of 12 aircraft with six in reserve and 24 pilots

Starboard – Right-hand side of an aircraft; a starboard turn is to the right

Stick – Control column

Stooge – To fly around without an apparent aim

Stuka – Junkers 87; German dive-bomber

Swastika – Ancient crooked cross symbol adopted by the Nazis

Tail-plane – Also known as a horizontal stabiliser; a small lifting surface located on the tail

Tally-ho – Huntsman's cry to the hounds on sighting a fox; adopted by fighter pilots and used on sighting enemy aeroplanes

Top Brass – RAF slang for commanding officers

Tracer – Ordnance that glows in flight to show path of bullet-stream

Undercarriage – Wheels of an aircraft; can be fixed or retractable

UXB – Unexploded bomb

Vector – Code word for heading

Vic – An arrowhead formation of aircraft

Wellington – British twin-engine, long range medium bomber

Windy – RAF slang for cowardly

Yaw – Twist or oscillate about a vertical axis

Author's notes

This is a historical novel based on real events. It is not a history of those events or of the people who found themselves entangled in those events.

Andrew Francis and Gerry Donaldson are based on the true-life trajectories of real people. Their characters and personalities are fictionalised as I have never spoken to anyone who actually met the men on whom they are based. I have taken care to mould them as people to whom their families would find no objection.

Vincent Drew is a fictional character. He is involved in two incidents that actually occurred. There is no intent or implication that he reflects in any way the person who was actually involved in those incidents. Any similarity Vincent may bear to persons living or dead is coincidental.

Bryan Hale is a fictional concoction in his entirety. Any similarity Bryan may bear to persons living or dead is coincidental.

A.W. Fagan was the name of the intelligence officer at Kenley during the Battle of Britain. It is used here as tribute to all the supporting players who never featured in combat reports or citations. The Fagan who serves Bluebird Squadron is wholly fictionalised and any similarity to persons living or dead is coincidental.

All other characters including the families of the men represented in this novel are wholly fictionalised, although some locations and occupations reflect historical reality to a certain degree.

Locations are real, although the details of real locations have been fictionalised in a sympathetic manner.

The backdrop of events against which the novel is set is well documented elsewhere, particularly the Dunkirk evacuation and the Battle of Britain. I have kept as close as possible to the actual timeline, but some events may have been shifted slightly to accommodate plot requirements. No disrespect is implied or intended to the people who were involved in those events.

Sources

Yankee in a Spitfire – Arthur Gerald Donahue

Clouds of Fear – Roger Hall, D.F.C.

Battle over Britain – Francis Mason

Narrow Margin – Derek Wood and Derek Dempster

Eagle Day – Richard Collier

Dunkirk – Robert Jackson

1940: The World in Flames – Richard Collier

Action Stations: Military Airfields of East Anglia – Michael Bowyer

Fighter Aircraft of the 1914-18 War – Lamberton and Cheesman

Aircraft of The Battle of Britain – William Green

Pilots' Notes Spitfire IIA and IIB (Facsimile) – Sapphire Productions

Me 109 – Martin Caidin

Luftwaffe – Alfred Price

The Few – A poem by Edward Shanks

The speeches of Sir Winston Churchill

Personal correspondence and conversation with Su Baccino

Personal correspondence with Kenneth L. Weber (Arthur Donahue's official biographer)

Original combat reports of 64 Squadron

The Bluebirds Trilogy continues with Blackbirds. Bryan Hale leaves Bluebird Squadron to fly night-fighters as Britain struggles to find an effective opposition to the Luftwaffe's night-time bomber raids that are devastating English cities. His task takes on added pathos as his relationship with Jenny, a friend from his school-days, develops amidst the bohemian streets of a Blitzed capital.

Join the Bluebirds Newsletter at **www.melvynfickling.com** to be in the front of the queue on publication day.

BLACKBIRDS

CHAPTER 1

6th October 1940

A teasing breeze cut through the wrought iron gates, agitating the early autumn leaf-fall around Bryan's shoes. The funeral attendees drifted away in groups and he maintained a respectful distance while they departed. Molly remained alone at the graveside. As Bryan approached, she looked up with red-rimmed eyes.

'Thank you for coming, Bryan. It's a long trip for you.'

Bryan put his arm around Molly's shoulders, 'Andrew was my best friend,' he said, 'he was the best of men.'

Molly's chin dropped and she crumpled against Bryan's chest, sobbing gently.

Bryan clenched his jaw against his own emotion, holding her as much for his own comfort as her need for support. She took a deep breath and the sobbing subsided.

'Would you like to go for a walk, maybe get some tea?' Bryan asked.

Molly straightened herself, wiping the tears from her cheeks. 'I have to go and feed my baby,' she smiled through her tears, 'I have responsibilities, you know.'

'Of course,' Bryan took her hand and kissed it. 'I'll always be there.'

Molly squeezed his arm and turned for the gate.

She climbed into a car and Andrew's father closed the passenger door after her. He glanced over at Bryan, loss and empathy in his gaze. Bryan nodded once and looked away. The car coughed into life and moved down the lane. Bryan bowed his head and surrendered to his own quiet tears.

Someone nearby cleared their throat, awkward and self-conscious. Bryan raised his head, blinking the moisture from his eyes to focus on a man dressed in rough, mud-streaked clothes. A flat-cap dangled from one hand, the other clasped a spade. The man glanced at the soil heaped on boards next to the oblong hole in the turf and raised an eyebrow.

'Yes, sorry,' Bryan muttered. He squared his shoulders to the grave and drew himself a touch straighter, but he did not salute. Andrew wasn't in the RAF anymore. Swivelling on his heel Bryan strode back through the arch.

The man jammed the flat-cap onto his head and plunged his spade into the heavy, clodded earth. The rhythmic, boxy echo of soil striking oak receded as Bryan walked away from the cemetery gates along the road towards The Railway Hotel.

People slowed their pace as they passed him on the pavement, offering wan smiles of condolence. None of them knew who he was, but in the small town of Wells-On-Sea they had all known about Andrew, and Bryan's uniform broadcast the obvious connection on this funeral day. Face after face looked into his eyes, searching for something to take away, something to talk about, something that might place them closer to events they had no hope of understanding.

Bryan's breathing constricted around the bubbling anger in his throat as he fought the urge to shout in their faces about the fear, the bullets and the fire, how much he hated and loved it at the same time, how better men, indeed the better man now inside that wooden box, had gone to an early grave to save them their lazy, gossiping hours of freedom. He struggled to bite his tongue and they mistook his anger for grief, gifting him the mantle of disguise he needed to make it back to the hotel porch.

The clunk of the closing door brought the manageress into the hall.

'Will you be dining with us tonight, Mr Hale?'

'No.' The word rang harsh; he cleared his throat and continued in a softer tone; 'I'm leaving today. I won't be staying another night.'

'Oh,' the woman dithered, thrown by the change. 'Would you like me to prepare your bill?'

Bryan started up the stairs, 'Yes, please.'

He fished the key from his pocket and pushed his way into the room. Scooping his shaving gear into a toilet bag, he glanced into the mirror and paused. A haggard edge pulled at his features, his tear-reddened eyes added an aged weariness beyond his twenty-eight years. Behind it, he discerned a faint shadow of fear, the unspoken, uncertain count of days separating him from his own hole in the ground.

Bryan slung his duffel-bag over his shoulder and descended to the hall. The manageress stood waiting, twiddling with a hand-written bill. Bryan took the bill and scanned the scrawled writing. The total included the room charge for the second night. Bryan glanced up, but the woman had busied herself straightening a picture on the wall. Bryan folded a ten-shilling note into the bill and handed it back.

'Keep the change.'

Bryan pushed through the door, back into the crisp, early autumn day. The brisk breeze was bedecked with the salt and seaweed smells of a North Sea fishing harbour. He wrinkled his nose against the onslaught, set his back to the water and walked down the hill towards the railway station.

Steam billowed above the station's slate roof. An engine had just arrived and would be ready to leave the terminus within the hour. He'd make it back to London in time to catch a bus to Kenley.

***

The train clonked and lolled as it slowed into its approach to Liverpool Street station. The unlit urban landscape echoed the darkness in the carriage, the city's life made anonymous under its thick curtain of black-out, its packed acres of buildings skulking behind a delusion of safety, hoping that a simple absence of light might deflect the German night raiders.

The carriage lurched over points, rousing Bryan from a fitful snooze. Squinting through the carriage window he could make out the looming silhouettes of tenements lining the track, here and there a leaking glimmer of light outlined an ill-fitting curtain. His eyes were drawn up to the black dome of the night-sky and a spasm of anxiety crawled over his skin.

A conductor sidled through the carriage, 'No alerts yet tonight, ladies and gentlemen. Have a safe onward journey.' He passed to the next carriage and his litany drifted back, 'No alerts in London yet tonight...'

The train jolted to a halt and Bryan pulled his duffel-bag from the overhead rack. He champed against the dryness in his mouth; he needed a drink. Shuffling off the train he skirted around the throng of travellers and strode towards the station entrance. Once outside he paused to make out his surroundings in the dark. Cars and buses trundled past and people tripped and stumbled on their way. Across the road a door opened, a brief slant of light escaped with the hubbub of voices and the clink of a bottle against glass. Moving with exaggerated care across the road, Bryan headed for the now-closed pub door. On the far pavement, he bumped into an older man who cursed under his breath as he disappeared into the gloom. Bryan scrabbled for the handle and pushed through the heavy curtain inside the door.

The immediate warmth in the smoke-filled room relieved the press of hovering menace suspended in the blank, black skies outside. Bryan lit a cigarette. Drawing deeply on the smoke, he moved to the bar.

'Pint of bitter, please.'

As he waited for his drink he glanced about. A few uniforms dotted the room, mostly soldiers. Other men wore civilian clothes, standing at the bar in drinking groups or sitting apart, at tables with their wives.

Bryan's eyes came to rest on a table directly across the room. Four people sat there. Two sailors in uniform accompanied two young women. One woman chatted with some animation to the sailor at her shoulder who leant forward, watching her lips as she talked and laughed. The other woman stared straight back at Bryan.

'One pint of bitter, sir.'

The barman set the dimpled mug down and Bryan turned to pay him. He waited for the barman to retrieve his change from the till, thanked him again and took a long draft of the ale. He could still feel the woman's eyes penetrating his back. Taking another long draw on his cigarette he surveyed the room again, avoiding a direct glance at the group's table. From the corner of his eye he caught the smile spreading across the woman's face as she continued to stare at him. He abandoned his ruse of nonchalance and returned her gaze.

The woman sat with her legs crossed. Her skirt and blouse looked smart, but not flashy, and her shoes had moderate heels. Her long dark hair was pinned high and a slight thrill fluttered in Bryan's stomach as he imagined it falling free. Her eyes shone deep chestnut, their shape emphasised with black liner. Her nose was straight and thin, and her lips celebrated in vibrant red lipstick. These features were infused with beguiling magic by the widening smile that beamed from her face.

Bryan glanced at the woman's female companion, a blonde with a slightly blocky figure. She continued to talk and gesture, her sailor raptly entangled in her words. The other matelot glanced from one woman to the other, laughing half-heartedly at the blonde girl's stories, sipping nervously at his beer.

Bryan's attention returned to the dark-haired woman. Her gaze remained unbowed for long moments, then she dropped her eyelids and came to a resolve. Standing, she walked across the bar towards Bryan, leaving her handbag and coat draped on her chair. The blonde stopped her flow of words and frowned. The nervous matelot's face dropped in confusion. Bryan maintained eye-contact as the woman stopped before him. She chewed her lower lip for a moment and squinted into his face.

'You have no idea who I am, do you?' she said.

'I'm afraid you have me at a disadvantage,' Bryan answered.

'Jenny Freeman,' she raised her chin to look him square in the face. 'I was in your year at school, Bryan.'

'Good Lord, yes,' Bryan's shoulders relaxed, 'the name does ring a bell.'

'I was quite skinny and very shy,' she smiled, 'and you were rather tall and quite loud. Anyway, now you're here, I have a use for you.'

'A use?'

'I need saving from the Navy,' she grimaced, inclining her head towards the sailors. 'My flat-mate Alice got herself a date. He had a friend. I got talked into it, but...'

'Oh, I see, yes.' Bryan gulped down the rest of his beer and slung his duffel-bag across his shoulder. 'I'll follow your lead.'

Bryan walked with Jenny back to the table, picked up her coat and held it for her to put on.

'I have to be away, everybody,' she held up a hand. 'This is Bryan, an old friend. He's offered to walk me to the tube station.'

'Gentleman,' Bryan nodded to each sailor in turn. 'Miss,' he raised his cap to Alice. Placing his hand on the small of Jenny's back, he guided her between the tables to the door.

Once outside they lurched to a halt, their sight momentarily disabled by the dazzle of the bright lights they'd just left.

Jenny tutted, 'I will never get used to groping about in the dark.' She gripped Bryan's arm. 'Can you see anything yet?'

People-sized shapes loomed around them as their eyes adjusted.

'It's starting to come together.' Bryan placed his hand over hers, 'Where are we heading?'

'Northern Line. Bank Station is probably the easiest. This way.'

They set off along the pavement.

'Thank you for getting me out of that, it really wasn't any fun at all.'

'Your friend… Alice? Will she be alright?'

'I wouldn't worry about Alice.' She smiled up at Bryan, 'So, you're wearing RAF uniform. Which branch are you in?'

'Fighter command,' Bryan said. 'Bluebird Squadron. Spitfires.'

'You're a fighter pilot?'

'Yes.'

'Crikey, what's it like?'

'Very fast and not a little dangerous.'

Jenny laughed, 'Sounds a bit like Alice.'

Bryan joined her laughter, 'And what do you do?'

'Ministry work. Archiving and records mostly. Can't say too much about it. They made me sign a bit of paper.'

They came to a crossroads and Jenny squinted into the darkness.

'Straight across here.' They hurried across the road and stepped up onto the curb. 'So, what brings you to London with your duffel-bag?'

'I'm on the way back to my squadron at Kenley.'

'Have you been on leave?' Jenny asked. 'Visiting your girlfriend?'

'I was attending a funeral,' Bryan said, 'a friend from the squadron.'

Jenny stopped and looked into his face, 'I'm sorry, Bryan. I didn't mean to be so clumsy.'

'Think nothing of it,' Bryan said. 'And I don't have one.'

'Excuse me?'

'A girlfriend,' Bryan started walking again, 'I don't have a girlfriend.'

They continued together for a short distance before Bryan broke the awkward silence, 'Which means I can buy you a drink sometime if you'd like.'

Jenny said nothing for a few steps, her eyes fixed on the ground. Then she nodded, 'I think that might be nice.'

The pavement became more crowded and many of those that thronged about them carried suitcases and rolled blankets. Caught up in this implacable human flow they swept around a corner to the sandbagged Tube station, a dull glow emanated from its depths.

Jenny pulled Bryan to one side. 'Here.' She took a small notebook from her handbag and wrote down a number. She tore off the page and pressed it into his hand. 'This is my home number. I do a fair bit of overtime these days, so you'll have to trust to luck to find me there. Thanks again.'

She stood on tip-toes, planting a kiss on his cheek. As she turned to leave, a low wailing penetrated the middle distance, rising to peak at a flat, mournful moan. The shelterers quickened their rush for the stairs and Bryan gazed upwards as searchlights pricked and probed at the clouds. A policeman stood nearby, ushering the crowd off the pavement. Bryan tapped his shoulder.

'What's the best way to get to Victoria?'

'Down the steps, sir. Look for the Circle Line eastbound.'

Bryan smiled his thanks and started down the steps. Some way ahead he spotted Jenny amongst the crowd streaming through the open barriers, his eyes drawn to the sway in her walk. In a moment she vanished, swallowed into the throng flowing down the tunnel towards the Northern Line. Bryan slowed to read the signs overhead, jostled by the river of people moving around him. He found the eastbound tunnel and squeezed down the steps to the platform. He picked his way through the groups of shelterers, each marking their territory for the night with blankets.

Bryan found a clear spot mid-way down the platform and lit a cigarette. Minutes later the next train arrived and he stepped onto the near-empty carriage. Already flushed from exertion and his chance meeting with Jenny, the stuffy warmth in the tube carriage pricked sweat onto his eyebrows. He removed his overcoat, folded it carefully and sat down, tucking his duffel-bag between his calves. A man opposite studied Bryan's uniform with a mixture of interest and disdain.

'You a pilot?' a slur dulled the man's voice.

Bryan nodded, 'Yes.'

'So why don't you get up there and fight the bastards?'

Murmurs of approval drifted down the carriage from a group of women. An elderly man made no noise, but peered over his glasses at Bryan, waiting for his answer.

Bryan looked around the group and back to his questioner.

'That's what I have been doing. Almost every bloody day.'

The man barked a laugh, 'What good is that if they're coming back every bloody night?'

The tunnel's darkness flashed to the bright lights of the next station, Aldgate. The man's eyes remained steady and hostile. Bryan stood up and stepped from the carriage. Better to wait a few minutes for the next train than to continue in an argument he had no interest in winning.

Prostrate Londoners filled most of the space around him, bedding down on the smooth, hard platform, trading comfort for safety. Bryan kept his back to the carriage while the train drew away. Directly in front of him a small girl in grimy clothes slept with only a thin woollen blanket between her and the warmth-sapping concrete. Three inches from her face a large gob of snot and spittle glistened in the lights.

Swallowing hard, Bryan fixed his attention on the white tiles that covered the curved tunnel wall and waited until a train whined in behind him. He boarded, avoiding eye-contact as he sat down. The tube train whisked him away through the tunnel, alternating darkness and harsh illumination. The lights at each station revealed a different human tableau; people hunkered on the indurate platforms, grasping to them the things they treasured the most. Mothers clasped their children; the children clasped their dolls. Above ground, their homes, temporarily abandoned for the sake of subterranean safety, stood at ransom to the random interplay of gravity and high explosives, of switches thrown and buttons pressed thousands of feet above them in the cold, dark sky.

Victoria Station rolled around. Bryan bundled off the train and up the stairs. The chill night air dried the sweat on his face. Shivering, he pulled on his overcoat while booming explosions reverberated from the station walls in a demonic rhythm set by a nearby anti-aircraft emplacement. In the distance, the soft crump of bomb-blasts drifted on the air. Bryan hefted his duffel-bag and walked out to the lines of buses. A ticket-collector strolled past.

'Excuse me,' Bryan caught him by the arm, 'I need to get to Kenley Airfield.'

The man pointed at a double-decker parked in the row.

'That one there,' he smiled at Bryan. 'You're a lucky man. It looks like you've caught the last bus.'

Made in the USA
Monee, IL
30 March 2021